# The Legend of
# Satan's Hound

### Joseph C. Ellers

**Land of the Sky Books**
Alexander, North Carolina

Publisher: Ralph Roberts

Editor: Pat Roberts

Cover Design: Ralph Roberts
Interior Design & Electronic Page Assembly: **WorldComm®**

Copyright ©2002 Joseph C. Ellers

Reproduction and translation of any part of this work beyond that permitted by Sections 107 and 108 of the United States Copyright Act without the permission of the copyright owners is unlawful. Printed in the United States of America.

10  9  8  7  6  5  4  3  2  1


Trade paper ISBN 1-56664-235-3
Hardback ISBN 1-56664-237-X


The author and publisher have made every effort in the preparation of this book to ensure the accuracy of the information. However, the information in this book is sold without warranty, either express or implied. Neither the author nor Land of the Sky Books will be liable for any damages caused or alleged to be caused directly, indirectly, incidentally, or consequentially by the information in this book.

The opinions expressed in this book are solely those of the author and are not necessarily those of Land of the Sky Books.

**Trademarks:** Names of products mentioned in this book known to be a, or suspected of being trademarks or service marks are capitalized. The usage of a trademark or service mark in this book should not be regarded as affecting the validity of any trademark or service mark.

Land of the Sky Books—a division of Creativity, Inc.—is a full-service publisher located at 65 Macedonia Road, Alexander NC 28701. Phone (828) 252–9515, Fax (828) 255–8719. For orders only: 1-800-472-0438. Visa and MasterCard accepted.

Land of the Sky Books is distributed to the trade by aBOOKS Distributing, 65 Macedonia Road, Alexander NC 28701. Phone (828) 252–9515, Fax (828) 255–8719. For orders only: 1-800-472-0438. Visa and MasterCard accepted.

This book is also available on the internet in the **Publishers CyberMall**. Set your browser to http://abooks.com and enjoy the many fine values available there.

*Dedicated to my loved ones*

## Acknowledgements

A work of this nature is the culmination of a lot of effort by a lot of people. Special thanks go to Ralph Roberts for taking a chance on me and to Pat Roberts for her thoughtful editing. Many other people contributed along the way, as well, including Katie Spurlock, who helped me with some authentic mountain stories and Brian Clipp who helps the areas come alive with the maps he contributed.

I especially want to thank my Dad, John Ellers, who not only contributed some insight into hunting and woodcraft but also read every word as it came to him—even the revisions—and provided a great sounding board.

My gratitude goes back even further to all of those people who have encouraged me along the way from my grandmother to a few teachers and professors who kindled the interest. I am especially grateful for all of the authors who have inspired me and the places they have taken all readers who will spend the time to go there with them. I hope that this place I have depicted is a place you want to return to, as well.

—*Joseph C. Ellers*

# 1

**Monday, November 3, 1904
Near Hagood's Mill, Tennessee**

About forty years before, Billy Sherman had led his blue-coated locusts through this area on his way to capturing Atlanta. His scorched earth policy had not bothered the folks much because they had very little before he came. The people of the Appalachian Mountains were different in a lot of ways from the flat-landers who settled most of the South. The mountain people were primarily Irish and Scottish while the others were primarily English. They disliked each other on the eastern side of the Atlantic and carried their dislikes with them to this side.

Before the War of Northern Aggression, the mountain people had kept pretty much to themselves, scratching out a subsistence living with small farms while huge fortunes were made in the low country plantations. In fact, when the war came, the mountain people did not support it like their flatland brothers and Tennessee provided a few Billy Yanks to go along with the patriotic Johnny Rebs. After the war, because of their lack of enthusiasm for the war effort, the state governments pretty much forgot about them. They built few new roads, railroads or schools and because of this, the area became even more isolated.

The area for this particular story is the little community of Hagood's Mill, tucked away in the mountains of eastern Tennessee. It was east of Chattanooga and west of Murphy, North Carolina and generally if it wasn't the end of the world, most folks thought you could see it from there.

You called it a community because you couldn't quite call it a town. It had a general store, run by Sam Butler, who everyone called Mr. Mayor but it was an honorary title (if some honor could be squeezed out of it). It had a Baptist church, presided over by Preacher Jeremy Elrod (whose palm was perpetually calloused from thumping his Bible). It had a school and a school marm, Sarah McGee, who most folks agreed was the prettiest girl in the area—if not the smartest. It also had a blacksmith named John Smith (nicknamed "Black" because of his generally sooty appearance) and what community didn't? And of course, it had a mill. Hagood's Mill. And a genuine Hagood (Bobby, in this case) who ran it. There was also ol' Doc Ammons who was neither old nor a doctor, but more about him later.

There was also a little cluster of houses surrounded by a little cluster of agricultural enterprises that were generously called farms. "Generous" because a small patch of red clay that runs more vertical than horizontal is really not much of a farm. Ray Potter allowed that on part of his farm the mule had to walk upside down to plow a furrow but Ray was a notorious storyteller and almost no one believed him.

For the most part, the people of Hagood's Mill kept to themselves. They didn't spend much time outside of their little area and some of them proudly said that they had never been more than fifteen miles from home in their entire life. Fifteen miles over a winding track called the Chattanooga Road would put you at the county seat of Boonesville where you could find a courthouse, a really big Baptist Church, a train station, a telegraph and the County Fair, at the right time of year. You could also find most of the county's elected officials there when they weren't off hunting or fishing (which was often) or actually working (which was a rarity).

The people were also mostly related. There was not much inbreeding, you understand. They were always careful to move out to at least second cousins for serious romances although for minor dalliances a few more people became eligible.

These people had always been clannish and superstitious and this was a tradition they were proud of and intended to keep. They were also good story-tellers. Old country ghosts, witches and banshees dominated but there was room for a few new ones if they scared the hide off you. The stories were told and retold–around winter fires on cold evenings or anytime folks gathered. Over the years they added new stories of their own, pulled from local events.

A scratching on the door of a lonely cabin was probably a branch blown by the wind but it might be the long nails of an old witch. The mournful hoot of an owl could still send shivers up the spine of an otherwise brave man as he walked through the dark woods at night and a far-off howl of a dog could raise the hairs on the back of your neck.

The baying of a hound had special significance to the people of Hagood's Mill because a Satanic Hound was part of the very foundation of their community and every once in a while it seemed to reappear with a vengeance.

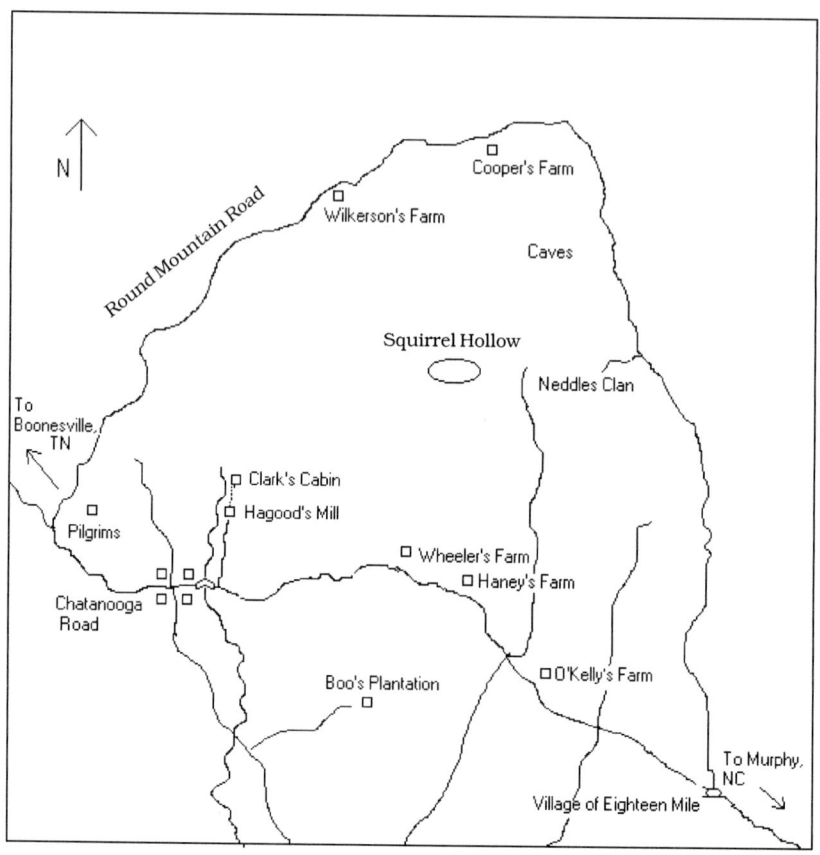

## Monday Afternoon

The Wheeler boys, fourteen-year-old Ben and his twelve-year-old brother Zeke, had set out from home after school to hunt squirrels. Pap had given them each one shell and they aimed to come back with a squirrel apiece. It had been a lazy late fall day with the sun shining warm though the bare branches and rustling brown leaves. Lugging their heavy shotguns, the boys had set out in the direction of a particular hollow where they knew they would find several nests of gray squirrels all fattened up and ready for the lean winter months to come.

They walked across their cornfield until they reached an old deer trail that took them through a creek bottom filled with waist high rustling sedge and along a ridge where they could see other mountains afar off through the forest of pines. It took an hour of meandering to reach the hollow that the locals called Squirrel Hollow. About halfway there, the boys detoured off the path to see if there were any apples left on the trees over on the back side of Old Man Haney's place. He had chased them away before but they figured the old man wouldn't be worried much about his apples as he should have picked most of them by now. They had to be dried or put up soon, the boys knew.

They came to the tumble down split rail fence that used to mark the back of the pasture when the old man had a few cows. They clambered over the fence and ambled leisurely, but cautiously, through the pasture. Sure enough the trees still had a few gleaming red apples hanging on the higher branches. Casting a wary eye for Mr. Haney, the boys each climbed a tree.

When they reached the higher limbs, they started pulling apples and filling the empty bags that hung loosely at their sides. When they each had about a dozen, they quickly climbed down the trees and headed back across the pasture to the ridge track.

Back on the trail, they pounded each other on the back and had a cackle about putting one over on their neighbor.

They didn't have anything against him but it just didn't seem right that he had all those apples and wouldn't share.

"Zeke," said Ben, "let's head on down to the spring. I'm thirsty and a cold drink'd go good with these apples." The younger boy nodded his agreement and they left the trail and headed north. About two hundred paces away, there was a little clearing where a spring broke the surface and made a small pool before it trickled down the hill to join up with a creek. The afternoon sun lit a patch of browned grass that had been flattened out by the boys before. They leaned their guns against a tree and went to the pool and dipped out handfuls of the cold spring water, slurping each drink noisily. They went back to the grass, sat down and opened their sacks and munched away until they had their fill, throwing the cores around them.

"I reckon I'll stretch out here a while," said Ben. "We got an hour or two of daylight left and I just don't feel like movin."

"All right," said Zeke, who was a lot more interested in shooting his gun than taking a nap. The boys pulled their hats over their faces while the breeze stirred the treetops.

The pine trees were casting long shadows when Zeke woke up. His back was stiff and he knew that he had been asleep awhile. He poked Ben, "Come on, we got to get goin or them squirrels'll be back afore we get there."

Ben immediately sat up and rubbed his eyes. "We gotta hurry, Zeke," he mumbled sleepily. "Gotta pick out a nestin tree an be waitin on 'em."

"I know it," said Zeke, impatiently. "I done this afore." They stood up, picked up their guns and loped back to the trail.

"We just gotta get us a squirrel. If we don't get nothin Pap won't let us come no more."

"We'll get us a squirrel all right."

The path was completely in shadows with the setting sun just visible over the top of the western mountains as the boys reached the narrow cleft that was the opening to "Squirrel Hollow." The boys stopped running and each loaded their sole shell into their shotguns. Each boy dropped his sack to the ground at the base of a big scrubby oak tree just outside the hollow and they entered as quietly as possible.

The hollow was in shadows for most of the day. Nothing except moss grew on the ground. With dusk, the spot was dark and gloomy. Ben's red bandana looked gray in the dim light. Ben circled to his left to the base of a tree where he thought there was a squirrel nest. Peering up through the branches, he saw what he was looking for and leaned against the tree to wait. He heard his brother still walking—still looking for a spot of his own. The squirrels would be returning to their nests very soon. Ben could hear the sounds of the animals. For some, this was the end of the day. Others, like owls, raccoons and possums would just be stirring. The hollow was sheltered from the wind so it was easy to spot the sounds the squirrels made as they headed back to their nests. Branches shook and rattled, bark fell and occasionally an angry call came from one of the squirrels. Ben stood very still—hoping his brother would find a spot and stop moving so he could get his shot off. He was peering intently through the gloom up through the branches. The last of the sun's rays were striking a cloud way up—putting a reddish haze overhead. Ben saw the flash of a bushy tail in the reddish light. He held his breath and raised his shotgun as he moved slightly away from the tree. He closed his left eye and looked along the barrel—sighting the squirrel. He braced his legs and squeezed the trigger.

The gun banged loudly and slammed back into his right shoulder and he could not see whether he hit the squirrel or not but through his partial momentary deafness, he heard the satisfying thump of the squirrel hitting the ground. He stood motionless. All sounds in the hollow had stopped-even the insects. Ben kept still for several seconds, not even breathing, until the natural sounds began again. It was almost completely dark in the hollow.

Ben leaned up against the tree and waited. He was about to call to his brother to give up when a second bang shattered the silence and Zeke gave a whoop, "I got one! I got one!"

"Grab 'im up and let's go then," Ben shouted. The boys met under the oak outside the hollow.

"We'd better hot-foot it home, Zeke." The boys put their squirrels in their sacks and slung them over their shoulders and began trotting down the path. The sun was gone but there was still some light outside the hollow and the boys had no trouble picking out the trail. "Ma'll be glad to get these. Said she'd make us a stew," Zeke panted.

"I love Ma's stew," agreed Ben.

The last of daylight was almost gone when the boys reached the turnoff to the Haney place. The breeze had died down and the woods were quiet. The only sounds were those of the boys' footsteps on the dead leaves and their panting breaths as they hurried home.

"Let's rest a second, Ben." They stopped and Ben noticed that the heavy shotgun Zeke carried was about as tall as he was. "Here, give me your gun and you take the sacks," he said. The boys were about to start trotting again when they heard the sound of crashing brush then pounding steps coming from behind them. Without really wanting to, the boys turned to see what it was—half expecting a deer.

When they saw it, they both screamed in terror. Zeke dropped his sacks and ran quickly along the path. Gripping the guns tightly, Ben followed his fleet-footed brother down the path. For a few minutes, they could hear it gaining on them as they ran—its guttural growls seemed to be right behind them. Their hearts were hammering in their chests and their lungs burned as they ran. Ben had regained some of his senses, however, and after a couple of minutes; he could no longer hear anything behind him. He risked a quick glance over his shoulder while continuing to run as hard as he could. There was no longer anything there. He stopped running and called to Zeke to stop.

At the sound of his brother's voice, Zeke stopped and looked back. Ben kept running until he reached Zeke and then they both stared up the path behind them—doubled over, gasping for breath. Not really believing what they had seen, they continued to stare but nothing was there. Satisfied that they were alone they walked quickly toward their farm constantly casting quick, darting glances over their shoulders.

When they reached their place, Pap was out on the porch waiting for them. He was leaning against a porch post, his arms crossed—a sure sign of trouble. "Where you boys been? Your Mama's waited dinner on you."

"Pap, we seen it!" blurted out Zeke.

"Seen what?"

"The hound. Satan's Hound. We seen it!" said Ben.

"What you boys talkin bout?"

"The hound, Pap. We was up at Squirrel Hollow and we both got us a squirrel." Ben stopped and looked at Zeke but since he had dropped the sacks, their proof was gone along with the stew. Ben went on, "We was comin home and we was runnin cause we knowed we was late. We'd stopped to catch a breath and we heard it acomin."

"A hound? Sure it wasn't a bear."

"No, Pap. It was a hound. Biggest hound I ever saw and its face was on fire. It was so fierce 'n evil. Me 'n Zeke was real scared cause we had taken some of old man Haney's apples so we was sure it was comin' to get us and take us to Hell." Ben stopped—out of breath.

"Well, we're goin up to that ridge at daybreak to see what it was. If you're lyin, you're gonna get a hidin!" He paused, "You say you was stealin?'"

The boys looked at the ground. "Yes, Pap."

"Well, you got one hidin comin anyway! Get washed up and go on in the house. We'll see to the hidin later."

"Yes, Pap." The boys hung their heads.

"O'course if you're not tellin tales, we might have us somethin diffrent. Might want to go see ol' Doc Ammons. He'll know a thing or two."

The boys washed up while Ezra Wheeler thoughtfully went into the house.

# 2
**Tuesday Morning**

Since arriving in the isolated mountain community of Hagood's Mill about five years ago, Clarkson (Clark) Ammons had learned a lot about the place and the people. And they knew a lot about him—but not everything. They knew he was good at doctoring animals and people, too, when the need arose. They knew he could play a fiddle well and that he liked to read. They knew he lived in a small cabin at the end of the old logging road way up past the Hagood's Mill. They knew that he raised ginseng and that he was knowledgeable in the healing power of plants. They knew that he was sweet on Sarah McGee, the school marm. They knew he liked privacy but that he was a friendly sort that helped his neighbors. They also knew that he didn't like gossip, rumors or superstition. Beyond these things, they didn't know much and it bothered them in a way.

In that part of the world, they were fond of saying, "Most of us is cousins." But Clark wasn't. He said he came from "further down south." Atlanta, New Orleans? He wouldn't be more specific. Had he ever been married? An enigmatic smile was his only answer. He admitted to some schooling, not medical, he said, but he had to learn his skills somewhere. What kind of education, then? "School of hard knocks," he would say with a friendly smile that took the sting out of not answering the question.

Because of his good looks, he had caused quite a stir when he first came to town. He was a rugged six feet with brown hair and pale blue eyes that could look into your soul. At least that's what one lady said when she first saw him. He had aroused the interest of several young girls and one or two of the married women had sized him up—for unmarried relatives, of course.

His first visit had been on Sam Butler (who owned the general store). Clark had liked him immediately. His next call was on Preacher Jeremy Elrod who he didn't like (but he almost kept that to himself). From Sam, he learned where there might be some land for sale (a tract owned by Bobby Hagood). From the preacher, he learned when church services were at the Hagood's Mill Baptist Church: Sunday morning, Sunday evening, and Wednesday evening.

He had sought out Bobby Hagood that day and arranged to buy a few rocky acres perched on the side of the bluff with an old cabin on it. Hagood had chuckled at the price he got, then began to feel bad when he got to know Clark better. His relief was palpable when Clark not only seemed to love the place but regularly joined Bobby on his front porch to pick a tune or two, obviously not holding the sale price against him.

Over the next few months, Clark put up a small barn, fixed up the cabin, went to church regularly and started doctoring the local animals. He also made the polite acquaintance of everyone in the community.

He charged reasonable rates for his services and took food (or nothing) from neighbors that were a little short. He paid respectful attention to the ladies in the community without any indication of improper interest.

After a while, the community gave an almost audible sigh and relaxed but there was still the nagging question of who he really was and folks with nothing much else to do spent a lot of idle time making up stories that accounted for him. A stranger without kin moving there was simply unheard of. People left but no one ever came except by birth. The situation was so unusual that the chief law enforcement officer of Jackson County (which nominally contained the Hagood's Mill community), Sheriff Tom Mosley, paid him a call.

It had been a wonderful fall day with bright, warm sunshine and Clark had been sawing some wood to repair one of his cabin walls when the Sheriff had come riding up the trail. Clark had few visitors in those days so the sound of hooves startled him.

"Mr. Ammons," said the sheriff, swinging off his horse. "I'm Tom Mosley, the duly elected sheriff in these parts, and I wanted to introduce myself on the chance that you'll be staying and doing your duty in the Democratic primary this fall."

Clark smiled at the introduction, wiped his hands off on his wool shirt and shook hands. Mosley had a jovial smile on his moon face and mopped at his brow with a huge red handkerchief.

"Sheriff, I've always done my civic duty."

"Well, that's good. We still need men here to help out from time to time. It's not like over in Chattanooga where I used to work before I retired over here. They have a real police force over there. But here," he gestured, "It's just me and my deputy, Charley Pell. The people of this county don't want me to be tempted by too much money so they don't give me any." He paused and looked speculatively at Clark. "Much as I'd like your vote, we both know that I'm here to kind of check you out. I can't find any warrants on you, at least not under your name. And your description doesn't match any wanted posters I've got hanging up at the stockade. I mean no disrespect, but are you hiding from something?"

Clark grinned and looked around. "This is a good place for it." He paused. "I don't have a problem with your asking. I'm not hiding from anything. I'm seeking. A place to think in peace. To do some work. Play a little music. Maybe write."

The Sheriff thought about his answer for a minute. "Well, generally it's a peaceful place. Matter of fact, about the only thing that has happened around here lately is you." He paused. "You probably already know how it is. The people around here—they know everything—maybe too much, in fact, about each other. You come along, you don't answer questions, people are curious."

"Well, I'll behave Sheriff. And if you care enough about this part of the county to come all the way up here to check me out, I'll probably even vote for you."

The Sheriff grinned at that. "Well, that puts one vicious rumor to rest. Some folks speculated that you might be a Republican. Of course, in that case, you couldn't vote for me. Not that a Republican vote is likely to be counted around here anyway." He brightened, "With your vote, I might just carry this precinct this time."

"With one vote."

"Yep, you see, a few years ago I got one of the Owens clan mad at me about a land dispute. The Owenses have been voting against me ever since. Of course, since the other half of the folks don't like the Owenses, I get all their votes by default. The problem is, they're about half and half around here."

"Looks like I just need to pick a fight with one or the other faction to be popular with at least half of them," said Clark.

"It's not that bad," said Tom. "You're not burdened by public service, but I'd be careful, if I were you. They still shoot each other up here occasionally—and I'm pretty certain that everyone has forgotten what they're mad about. Say the wrong thing to the wrong person and you can make yourself a whole passel of enemies for life."

"Good advice, Sheriff. I'll try to keep a low profile."

"Not all that low, apparently. They tell me in town that you're a good hand with animals?"

"I've picked up a thing or two over the years."

"Well, when you come to Boonesville to register to vote, drop by the prison farm. Maybe you can help us with our animals."

"I'll do that," said Clark.

The Sheriff looked around. "The place is lookin pretty good." He stuck out his hand. "Welcome to Jackson County, Mr. Ammons."

Clark shook the offered hand. "It's a real pleasure to be here."

The sheriff pulled himself up into his saddle (which required a little effort) and with a final wave headed back down the track.

A few days later, Clark had gone to the county seat to register and while he was there he had gone out of town to the prison. The Sheriff had started using him for some veterinary work but it was their mutual interest in puzzles that cemented their friendship.

One beautiful spring evening, not too long after arriving in the community, Clark sat on the porch of Butler's General Merchandise, playing checkers with Bobby Hagood. Night was just beginning to settle in when a local man rushed up to the store with a story about the spook he had just heard up the road apiece. "What's it all about, Mac?" one of the men had asked.

"Well, I was cuttin through the old O'Grady place an I heard some strange noises comin from in there. You know all them O'Gradys died of the fever a few years ago and ain't no one gone near there since. Well, it even sounded like the old man callin out from inside. I've never heard the like of it so I ran all the way here. Plumb forgot why I was comin. I'll be in trouble with the missus, for sure."

Clark's eyes gleamed in the dim light of the solitary lantern on the porch. "Did you have a look inside?"

"No, I didn't. Just high-tailed it here. I tell ya, it's them O'Gradys—theys a hauntin the place."

Clark spoke up. "Would you mind if I went up there and looked into it myself?"

"I don't have no objection. You plan on runnin up there in the morning?"

"No, I thought I'd go now."

"But it's gonna be pitch dark up there," someone said.

"That's OK. Anyone want to come with me?"

A few of the men said they would—if for no other reason than to see Clark scared out of his gourd. Clark had led the men back to the old O'Grady house. When they approached the house, he heard low moaning sounds and some pawing coming from inside the house. He thought he recognized the sounds and took one of the lanterns and approached what was left of the O'Grady place. The house had turned into a lean-to because about half of it had collapsed. He found a place where he could enter and found what he expected to find—a deer that had poked its head inside and gotten stuck.

He crawled back out. "It's a stuck deer. I'm afraid that there's no safe way to get it out. We'll have to shoot it."

One of the men shot the deer and two of them carried it back down the hill, presumably to eat. But by going up there at night, Clark had shown something to the community.

The Sheriff got quite a chuckle out of it when he heard the story a few days later. "So Mac's ghost family was a deer. I bet they all got quite a kick out of that."

"They did. Ray Potter asked Mac what he thought of the 'deerly departed.'" Clark went on, "Its just the natural inclination of folks around here, you know, to attribute anything they can't easily explain to something supernatural."

"You weren't afraid?"

"Not of ghosts, Tom. And besides, I like a good puzzle."

The Sheriff looked at him shrewdly. "You know, you just might be able to help me out from time to time. I get a puzzle or two around the county and it might be good for both of us if I got you involved."

"There's nothing I enjoy more." From that time on, folks came to Clark for him to look into anything unusual.

A scant few years later, Clark, now known as "Doc" had become a regular, if still somewhat mysterious, member of the community. This cool, fall morning he was elbow deep in one of Milt Pilgrim's cows trying to help a new calf into the world. He'd been raised out of his warm bed before daybreak by one of the Pilgrim boys to come help. The calf just wasn't behaving. First of all, it was coming at the wrong time of year. Second, it wasn't coming at all. So, he had come back with the boy and now had the calf positioned about right to come on out.

The Pilgrim children were concerned, standing just outside the barn in a tight knot peering anxiously into the gloom. Now, with birth proceeding as nature planned, Clark had reclaimed his arm and gone over to a bucket hanging next to the lantern to wash up. "Mrs. Pilgrim's got you a hot breakfast inside, Doc," said Milt. "I'll stay out here if you want to eat."

"Then I think I'll let Bessie finish up without me. I'm hungry." Clark stopped to tell the children that he thought everything would be all right before going inside the warm Pilgrim kitchen. Mrs. Pilgrim had just set a hot plate of ham, eggs, and grits in front of him when he heard voices outside.

He took a sip of steaming hot coffee and smiled as he recognized the voice. As the visitor mounted the steps, Clark called out, "You got it all wrong, Tom. It's a calf not a child. No hope of a vote out of this one."

Sheriff Mosley walked inside, "Don't be too sure. Last election about half my opponent's votes came from the churchyard. Reckon I can counter that with a few votes from the barnyard."

"Will you have some breakfast, Sheriff?" asked Mrs. Pilgrim.

"No, thank you ma'am," he said with a smile in her direction, "but a cup of coffee would be greatly appreciated." She set out a second mug of coffee as Tom sat down at the table across from Clark.

"Doc, I got a little puzzle for you."

Clark leaned forward expectantly. After swallowing a bite of salty ham, he prompted, "What's going on?"

"Well, I just happened to be at the general store and I ran into Ezra Wheeler. You know 'im, don't you?" Clark nodded. "He was on his way to see you. It seems that his boys, Ben and Zeke, were huntin up at Squirrel Hollow last evening and got the scare of their life. Said they were chased by Satan's Hound."

"Satan's Hound?"

"Yep, they've got some sort of story around here about a hound that lives in one of the caves, and supposedly the cave leads straight to hell. Occasionally smoke comes out of it or something. Anyway, the hound is supposed to have come out on several occasions and taken sinners to the devil."

"You don't believe that."

"Of course not. But a lot of folks do. Anyway, Ezra took the boys up there at daybreak and he could see that they took off running, scared by something." He paused. "Funny thing, though, he couldn't find any tracks. Ezra speaks for his boys. They've been roaming around these hills since they were knee high and Ezra says they've never acted like this before. When I heard his tale, I knew that it would appeal to you. Another chance to put one of these things to rest. Me and my deputy are tied down trying to deal with a bunch of rowdies right now so I just can't spare the time. But I told Ezra I'd ask you to look into it. Can you lend a hand?"

"Of course. You're right. I would love to get to the bottom of it. Tell you what I'll do. I'll finish up here and go talk to the boys. Maybe go up there and look at the place myself. Ezra's a good tracker, but I'll see if maybe he missed something."

The Sheriff drained his cup and stood to leave. "Thanks, Doc. Let me know what you find, if anything."

After thanking Mrs. Pilgrim and checking on the new calf, Clark swung up onto his horse and headed in a southwesterly direction along the track that led from the Pilgrim's to the cluster of buildings that constituted the village of Hagood's Mill. His horse, Traveler, knew the way so Clark could devote his thoughts to the little problem Sheriff Mosley had given him. Clark knew there was no such thing as Satan's Hound. But he thought the boys had probably seen something. Could have been a wild dog or even a bear. The absence of tracks... that was the interesting point. Maybe the boys had misjudged how close the animal was or maybe there was another reason.

On his left, as he came down the road to the village, was the schoolhouse. It had been rebuilt a few years ago when the area's only other "outsider" had arrived. Her name was Sarah McGee and Sarah (or Miss Sarah) as most folks knew her was more than just the schoolmarm to Clark.

She had arrived in the area only a few months before Clark. The men (and boys) liked her because she was pretty. The women liked her because she never looked at any of their men. The girls liked her because she had helped them to realize that there was more to life than just having babies. She had a passion for teaching and her enthusiasm had caught on with even some of the rowdiest boys in the group like Old Tom. They called him Old Tom because he was a little old (fifteen) for his grade (third). His parents had doggedly continued to send him to school and he had doggedly refused to learn much of anything until Miss Sarah got hold of him. After only a few months, he had learned enough to move up three levels and was dangerously close to enjoying reading—but he thought he could stave it off.

Clark fell into the category of men that thought she was pretty and their mutual love of books and their outsider status had been the foundation of a relationship that had quickly passed from politeness to friendship to real warmth. For reasons not exactly known by anyone, including the two people involved, they had not quite committed to matrimony—although the community was all for it.

So when Clark had volunteered to go by the school that morning, he had more than one motive. When Clark peered around the coat rack into the room, Sarah had her charges bent over their desks practicing Palmer Method. She was prepared to be annoyed at the interruption but she smiled when she recognized him, then immediately adopted a stern face and tone to match, "You're late for class, Mr. Ammons. You'll have to stay after school." The children chuckled and used the excuse to stop writing and look at their visitor. "Hey, Doc," several called and he grinned at them and waved a greeting. "Miss Sarah, I will certainly return after class to face my punishment but I wonder if I can borrow the Wheeler boys for a minute."

"Only on two conditions. One, you have to return them. And two, if you promise to come by for supper this evening."

"Yes, ma'am."

"All right, Benjamin and Ezekiel. You're excused but you

are to return to class the instant Mr. Ammons is through with you."

"Yes'm." The boys got up from their bench and followed Clark outside.

"Boys, Sheriff Mosley asked me to talk to you about what you saw up there on the ridge last evening."

"It was Satan's Hound!" blurted Zeke. Ben nodded his head vigorously.

"Tell me what you saw."

"Well," began Ben, "it was just after sundown. There was still some light but not much."

"We was just passin ole man Haney's apple orchard," said Zeke.

"We'd been huntin in Squirrel Hollow," said Ben.

"We each got one," said Zeke.

"Me an' Zeke was hurrying home cause we was late. We stopped at the cutoff to Ole Man Haney's to rest. I had handed my poke to Zeke and I took his gun so's we could maybe go a little quicker. Well we was just getting ready to set off when we both heard somethin runnin down the path towards us."

"It was six feet tall an black as night," said Zeke. "An its face was on fire."

"On fire?"

"Yessir. It was fearsome an' horrible ugly."

"What happened then?"

"Well," Ben began, then paused. "Zeke threw the sacks down an ran as fast as he could down the path. I had both them big guns an' I lit out after him but I couldn't catch him. I could hear it growlin, a kind of rumblin, an I felt its hot breathin on my back. We run as hard as we could for a mile or more then I couldn't hear it no more so I looked back an' I couldn't see it so I called out to Zeke to stop runnin." He finished.

"You went straight home after that?"

"Yessir, we did."

"Sheriff Mosley told me that you and your Pa went up there this morning and couldn't find any paw prints."

"That's right, Doc. Pap didn't believe us so we went up there and he could see where we walked and when we commenced to runnin but we couldn't find no sacks."

"Couldn't find no paw prints, neither," said Zeke. "That kind of proves it was Satan's Hound, don't it?"

"Your pa's a pretty good tracker and if he couldn't find any prints, there probably weren't any but that doesn't prove that it was Satan's Hound. There may be another answer and that's what I want to find out."

Ben looked around to make sure that no one was near, then added, "It was real scary, Doc. I'm tellin you that it wasn't no bear or no deer or nothin. It was the Hound."

"I'm sure you saw something unusual boys. I'll look into it and see what I can find. Thank you for your help. I'll stop by and let you know what I find out. Now you boys better get back in there to your lessons." Clark followed the boys inside. "Miss Sarah, I returned your pupils. What time should I call?"

"About six or so."

"I might be a little later, I have to run up to Squirrel Hollow this evening. Will that be all right?"

"As long as you get there." Sarah smiled.

Clark smiled, too, and tipped his hat to her and waved goodbye to the children and went outside. He took his horse by the halter and led him down the street to Sam Butler's store. Sam was hauling sacks off of a wagon behind his place when Clark walked up with his horse. "Here, Sam, let me give you a hand."

Sam looked over the top of one of the sacks he was carrying, his spectacles and balding pate gleaming in the slanting rays of the fall morning light. "Howdy, Clark. Thanks. You know an old man like me is likely to get apoplexy workin like this."

"I like to do a nice turn for the elderly," Clark grinned as he picked up one of the heavy sacks of sugar. "Where's your help?"

"Who knows? You know them Haskell boys. Reckon they worked just long enough to get their Ma off their backs. Ain't seen 'em in days." Sam dropped his heavy sack just outside the back door of his store. Clark did the same and they headed back to the wagon for more sacks. "Jimmy Haskell fell back here–was horsin around probably and he laid out a day or two then his brother Mark stopped comin, too."

"The boys aren't very dependable," said Clark. "Mark worked on my place for a spell and helped me with the animals. He was good with them or I thought so until I saw him hit Traveler with a stick. I let him go."

Sam nodded. "They've worked for just about everyone around at one time or another. Course, what could you expect comin from a home like that?"

Clark nodded. Few of his neighbors had read Washington Irving or knew who Rip Van Winkle was but the Haskell family was a southern version of it. Their pa was a ne'er do well who spent most of his life avoiding work. His wife continually took him to task for failing to work on the rocky patch of ground that her Pa had given them as a wedding present. He responded to his wife's outbursts by spending as much time as possible roaming the hills–hunting or fishing or maybe making moonshine. Everyone suspected but nobody really knew. His absences became longer and longer until one day he just never came home. His boys had the same aversion to hard work and their Ma's sharp tongue so they worked odd jobs when they had to and escaped to the hills when they could.

"Anyway," Sam was saying, "I might've had to ask them to leave any way." He pointed to the wagon full of sacks. "You see all this?" he asked rhetorically. "This is the third load of sugar I've bought this fall. I sell a lot of it but I can't remember sellin this much. Some of my sacks must've got legs and walked off."

"About now, I'm wishing they used their legs to walk in," said Clark as he dropped another sack.

"Of course," Sam went on, "Maybe I sold it and just can't remember." Clark and Sam hauled the last sacks off of the wagon and dumped them unceremoniously on the floor.

"Thanks," said Sam, wiping his hands on his apron while he walked to the front of the store. "Now, what can I do for you?"

"I've just been to the schoolhouse to talk with Ben and Zeke Wheeler." Sam's eyebrows went up in a knowing manner and Clark was reminded of just how small the town was.

"And you wanted to talk about Satan's Hound," Sam finished.

"Sure do," grinned Clark. "You started out ahead of me. How about waiting while I catch up to you?"

"Ezra ran into the Sheriff up here this morning so I heard the whole thing." He finished stacking some cans on the counter. "But I'm not the feller to give you the lowdown on the Hound. You need to go see Boo. He knows a lot about the Hound–maybe even had an ancestor involved or something. Anyway, he'll tell you the story better than I could."

Clark grinned, "He can sure tell the stories."

"I'll say he can. He's got about half the boys in the county all fired up to join the cavalry with his stories about Jeb Stuart."

"I wouldn't doubt it. You know the stories sound glorious to a young fellow. Of course, the reality might be a little different."

"Ain't it always the way? Cept when they told me stories when I was a courtin my dear, sweet wife. They told me she was the meanest girl in the county but I didn't believe 'em. That's one time when the stories were true," Sam chuckled. "Don't tell her I told you."

"Your secret's safe with me."

Sam snorted. "Hell that ain't no secret just the truth that ain't got the courage to be spoke."

"Thanks for your help, Sam."

"Didn't do anything but you're welcome to it. Thanks again for the help unloading the wagon."

Clark nodded and waved, swung up on to his horse and headed south toward the home of Benjamin Oliphant Olivier or Boo as he was known.

# 3

**Tuesday Noon**

About three miles out of the village, Clark took the northeast fork of the road that led to the large plantation house that was the home of one of the region's most illustrious families. Mr. Hugo Olivier had come up from New Orleans about seventy years before with more money than most folks could imagine. He was rumored to be the illegitimate son of a famous Louisiana planter or a river pirate—take your pick. With his famous pile of gold he bought up most of the good farmland and started raising tobacco.

For the next thirty years or so, the Oliviers had done well and lorded it over the rest of their neighbors who barely eked out a living in the best of times. The war ended their prosperity and the lives of two of the three Olivier boys who both died somewhat ingloriously. Hugo, Jr. died from dysentery and Lemuel was killed in a duel over a prostitute in Richmond. The other son, however, had done the family proud. Col. Benjamin not only survived the war but came home a hero–having whipped the Yankees every time he faced them.

Ben was one of the last to come home from the war because he went with every one of his surviving soldiers to their home to see what he could do to help them get their lives restarted.

When he came home, he found what most planters did—a homestead in ruins. He responded the way most of the others did, too. He sold off most of the land except for the house and a few acres that he sharecropped. Ben had a flair for oratory, however, and because of this; he was elected to the legislature. He was also given command of the area militia so unlike many of his contemporaries, he actually began to recover financially. Within a few years, he acquired enough cash to enable Mrs. Olivier to get her snoot back in the air—at least a little bit. But he never forgot the war and every year he gave a big barbecue for all the surviving Confederate veterans that wanted to come. The numbers declined every year but the finale was always the same, a chorus of Dixie at midnight on the anniversary of the day of Robert E. Lee's surrender.

As Clark rode through the wide, elm-shaded alley that led to the Olivier mansion, he spotted Grant first. Grant was an elderly, dignified black man with gray hair who worked on the Olivier place. Grant was also a bit of a character. He had grown up on the plantation, too, but on the wrong side of the pedigree—and his name used to be Amos. After the war, he had stayed on but had changed his name to Grant (in honor of the Union general by the same name) just to annoy Boo.

On this bright morning, Grant was sweeping the leaves off the front porch. He also did all the cooking and drove the Oliviers whenever they needed to go somewhere—which wasn't often, anymore.

"Mornin' Grant. Boo receiving visitors today?"

"Reckon he is, Doc. But he's got company. Mr. Corcoran. It's their battle day."

"I'd forgotten about that. What are they doing this year?"

"Chess. If they get any older, they be flipping coins."

Clark laughed. If Boo was an "unreconstructed" rebel, Mark Corcoran or "Cork" was the worst sort of Yankee. The worst sort of Yankee, by definition, is one that stays. Originally Cork was part of the occupying army in Knoxville. While he was there he had met, fallen in love with and married Priscilla, one of Boo's nieces. At the wedding, Boo and Cork had discovered that they had fought against each other at an indecisive battle, which both sides claimed to have won. The wedding ended in the best southern tradition with a fistfight on the lawn of the church—which was also inconclusive. Since that time, the two men had met every year on the anniversary of the battle to refight it. For years, they repeated their original fistfight. But as they got older, the fistfight became a wrestling match, then arm-wrestling and now, apparently chess was the way to determine the winner.

"Any violence yet?"

"Not yet, but there's still time. Come on in." Clark followed him into the house. As they passed, Clark saw Mrs. Olivier was sipping tea in the parlor from a tiny porcelain cup. She was formally dressed in a gown that billowed out around her, and her eyes glanced languidly at Clark.

"Good morning, Mr. Ammons," she said.

Clark walked two steps into the room and bowed formally. "Good morning, Mrs. Olivier. How are you today?"

"Fine, thank you. Have you come to see the Colonel?"

"Yes ma'am. I need to find out about a local legend."

"Well, I'm certain he can help you. Grant, will you take Mr. Ammons to the drawing room?"

"Yes, ma'am." They walked down the hall to the next room. Two elderly gray heads swiveled as Grant opened the door. Boo raised his hand in greeting, "Morning, Doc." Cork merely grunted his greeting. Between them was the chess board. "I need to apologize for the unsociable behavior of my guest but this is serious business here. We're refighting the battle of Hatchie's Bridge–"

"Matamora."

"And it takes all his effort just to remember that it's his turn."

Clark grinned. "How's it going?"

"Well I definitely have the bluebellies on the run. He will be mated in a few turns."

"Rubbish," snorted Cork. "Your own general is dangerously close to capture. Within a few turns, you will be captured, defeated for good and all."

"Until next year, at least. Of course even a victory now will still leave you shy. I'm ahead by two."

"One. You did not win that wrestling match in '84."

"Rubbish. Your memory fails you. It was arm wrestling and I most certainly did win."

"In no way, sir."

"Gentlemen," Clark broke in before that argument escalated. He looked at Boo. "You have the reputation for being an expert on local legends, Boo."

"To many, I am a local legend," said Boo. Cork snorted.

Boo nodded in the direction of an overstuffed chair. "Sit down, please, Mr. Ammons." He turned to Cork. "Captain, I think that we need a temporary truce." He glanced at the grandfather clock in the corner. "Besides it's almost time for lunch. Will you stay, Mr. Ammons?"

"No thanks. I really have to keep moving today."

"Perhaps some other time. Some tea, perhaps?"

"Certainly."

"Grant!" Boo winced. "Grant! Can you come here please?"

The door of the dining room opened and Grant made a dignified entrance. "Yes?"

"Could we have some tea, (pause, pause, pause) please?"

"Yes sir, of course." He closed the door.

"Now, sir, what can I enlighten you about?"

"What do you know about the legend of Satan's Hound?"

"Ah, the hellhound." He considered. "We haven't had a sighting of the hound in at least ten years or so."

"Then you've heard of it?"

"Yes, sir, I have." He turned to Cork. "What year did I first thrash you at chess?"

Corcoran thought. "I think it was about twelve years ago that you shamelessly cheated by improperly castling. Yes, it was twelve years ago."

"Twelve it was, then. One of the Haney boys, I think. He was coming home from his granny's house one evening and swore he saw the beast out on the Chattanooga road. Has there been another sighting?"

"Possibly. Yesterday evening Ben and Zeke Wheeler were hunting up at Squirrel Hollow and they say they were chased down the path by a huge black beast with its face on fire. Ezra Wheeler went up there this morning and he couldn't find any tracks."

"That's the hound all right."

"What sort of rubbish is this?" asked Cork.

"The hellhound," began Boo, "is nothing to make sport of."

"What is the legend, exactly?" asked Clark.

"Let me see. About a hundred and forty years ago, there were only a few families of over mountain men living here. One of them had an Indian wife. Or to be more precise, he had probably traded some hooch to one of the families for one of their daughters. Anyway, one night, he came down from his cabin rantin' and ravin' about a hound that came and took his squaw. He described it as big and black with a fiery face. At first light several of his kinfolk went up to his cabin and searched but they couldn't find any sign of the squaw. They couldn't find any paw prints either. Several of the locals, egged on by their version of Preacher Elrod, decided that the hound was a creature of the devil and that it had been sent by Satan to drag the woman to hell for living in sin. There are a lot of caves around here and one of them often has smoke coming out of it so they decided that the cave led straight to hell. Of course, no one ever led an expedition to find out—least as far as I know."

"Strange that the hound took only the woman," mused Cork. "Since she would have had no more sin than the man."

"I was thinking the same thing," said Clark. "You mentioned a sighting twelve years ago. Have there been others?"

"Every few years, the hound has been blamed for a missing calf or a mauled animal. Every once in a while, someone will claim to either see or hear him. Mamas have used it for years, you know, 'Behave or the hound will get you.' I believe our beloved Preacher Elrod has preached a sermon or two on the topic," his eyes twinkled as he said the last.

"I'm certain of it."

"Of course, my own dear father said he saw it once."

"Really?"

"Yes. He had been out roistering around and came home very late one evening. My mother was waiting for him when he came home and he assured her that if he had not been chased by the hound he would have been home much sooner. He told a fearsome story and it was great entertainment. Of course, as I have grown older and wiser—"

Another snort from Cork.

"I think, perhaps, he was pulling our proverbial legs."

"So how local is this particular legend?"

"Pretty local, Doc. You go more than a few miles from this valley and folks probably have not heard of it. I mentioned the legend to a friend of mine over in Eighteen Mile a few years back and he hadn't heard about it."

Clark stroked his chin. "The original story isn't hard to explain. Probably an Indian in a wolf skin came to get the girl. Superstition, fueled by alcohol could explain the rest. The folks were probably looking for animal prints not moccasin prints and some Indians are pretty good about erasing tracks anyway."

"I thought the same thing. But once a story starts, it has a life of its own."

Clark put down his teacup. "Gentlemen, thank you very much for your patience." He grinned at them. "I'll let you get back to your battle."

"The only weapon I'm interested in now is to use my knife on some victuals. Sure you won't join us?"

"Thank you, again, but I have to be on my way."

"Then, adieu, Doc."

"Captain," he said, rising and waving in Cork's general direction," will you join me in the dining room so that I can educate you in the appropriate use of cutlery."

"I know more about cavalry than you'll ever know," said Cork.

"Cutlery, you old goat," he grinned.

Clark touched his hat and left them arguing on their way to lunch. Clark swung up onto Traveler and rode toward the crossroads. His next step was to talk to Seth Haney. The older Haney boys hadn't been seen in a while. They had gotten a little wild after their ma died and had been in a lot of trouble. Nothing serious but irksome to their neighbors. Then one day, they were both just gone. Rumor had it that they were on the chain gang. Something to do with some drunken sport with a girl over in a neighboring county. Maybe, Clark thought, old man Haney could remember a little something about the twelve-year-old incident. He had another reason for wanting to talk with him as well. The incident had occurred on the backside of his property. He might have heard something that would help.

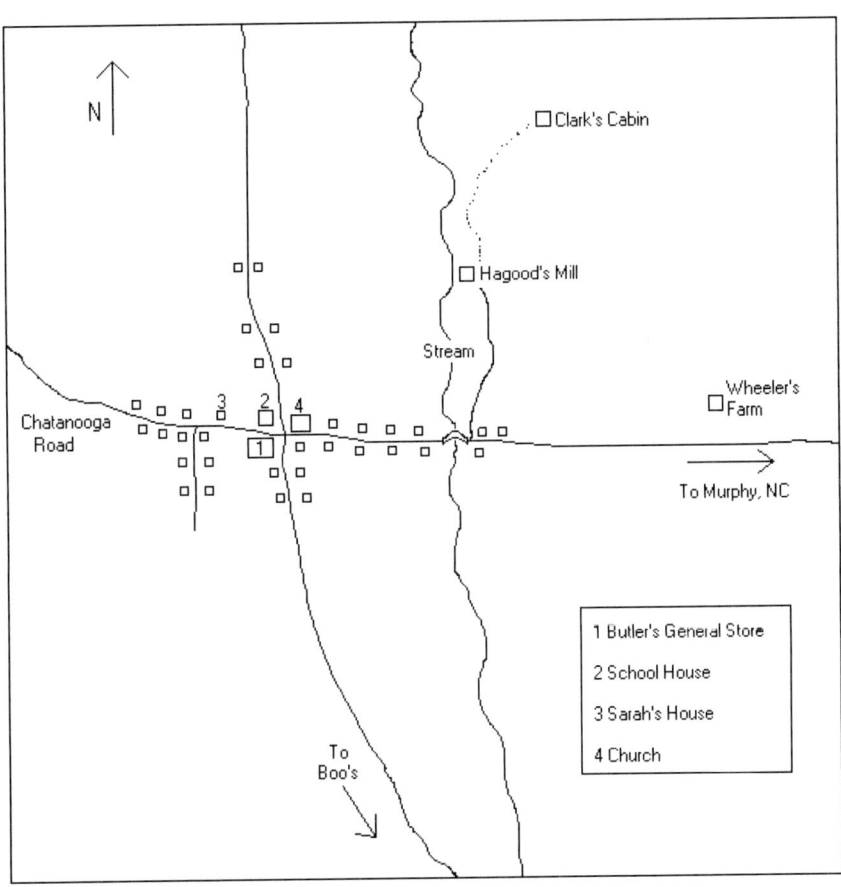

# 4
**Tuesday afternoon**

When Clark reached the crossroads, he turned east and headed past the preacher's house which sat next to the old wooden church. Aggie Elrod, the preacher's wife was hanging clothes out to dry when Clark rode past. She smiled and waved (a little too friendly) and Clark was again reminded of the age difference between the preacher and his wife. Preacher Elrod had to be nearing three score and his wife was just past thirty years. She was the preacher's second wife. His first had died in childbirth. The girl couldn't have been more than sixteen when she married him. He studiously kept his eyes on the road while he called his greeting. He had enough problems with the preacher without encouraging another.

Traveler's hooves clopped across the wooden bridge across the river. Clark cast a glance up the track that led past the Hagood mill and up the old logging road that led to his cabin. He was hungry and he regretted not eating at Boo's. At least he would eat well tonight, he thought.

Both the Haneys and the Wheelers lived out on the eastern side of the village on the Chattanooga Road toward Murphy. As you headed east, the road went up and down (but generally down) and in semicircles around the base of a series of hills. Three hundred yards past the crossroads, the clearing ended and the pine trees grew thick against the sides of the road. Even though it was midday, the full sun barely penetrated the thick pine woods. If you didn't look directly up into the clear, sunlit sky, you would think it was dawn or dusk. After a half hour or so, Clark came to the track that led to the Wheelers. He would stop there on his way back, he decided.

Another couple of miles brought him to the cutoff to the Haney place. He turned his horse in. For a few hundred paces or so, there was no sign of anyone but then he heard sounds of hammering and sawing. Clark came around a small bend and there was Seth Haney's place. Seth was standing in front, hands on his hips, scowling—either at his roof or at the young man on it. Clark was surprised to see that Bruce Haney was hammering a plank in place while his brother Billy was cutting up another plank on two sawhorses in front of the house. The noise of their work had covered the sounds of Clark's horse as he came through the pine-needle covered track so Clark called out as he came closer. "Howdy, Seth. Bruce, Billy. How you all doing?"

The boys stopped working and turned in his direction. Seth's scowl disappeared as he waved, "Hey Doc, how are you? What brings you out this way?" As he spoke, Bruce came down off the roof and Billy wiped his hands on the back of his overalls and all three came forward to shake his hand. The boys looked a lot alike and a lot like every other young man their age. They were lean and both had longish, unkempt hair sticking out from under their hats and scraggly beards. "Here, Doc, let me take care of Traveler for you," Billy said as he led the horse over to a water trough.

"Bruce. Billy. It's good to see you. How long have you been back?'

"Just a few days, Doc," said Billy. Clark decided not to ask where they had been.

"Sorry to interrupt your work, but I've got a question or two for you if you can spare the time?"

"Take all the time you want," said Bruce, while his father shot him another scowl.

"Well, I understand that one of you boys had a brush with Satan's Hound about twelve years back."

"That was me," said Billy.

"What can you remember?"

"Well, I was down at Granny's..."

"That's Lucinda's grandmother," interrupted Seth. Lucinda was his late wife.

"Like I was saying, I was down at Granny's. She was tellin us ghost stories like she did oncet in a while. There was five or six of us younguns there and she told us bout how the hellhound come down and grabbed a feller's wife 'n all. Anyhow I had to git home an it was after dark. I member that as I was walkin through the woods about a mile or so below here I seen it. Least I thought I did. It was black an its face was all glowed up. It scared me so I took off. It chased me for a mile then give up."

"You was a reglar scaredy cat," his older brother contributed helpfully. Billy shot him a look.

"I warn't nothin but a kid," he said.

Clark thought that the old lady's story had probably ignited his imagination but left the thought unsaid. "The reason I was asking is because we just had another visit."

"Really, what happened?"

"The oldest Wheeler boys, Ben and Zeke. Seems they were doing some squirrel hunting in the hollow back of your place last evening and something chased them." The men exchanged looks with their father. "I figured that maybe you'd seen or heard something since it was on the backside of your place. Maybe about supper time?"

The boys looked at their father again. "We didn't see nothin or hear nothin last evening. The boys was out somewheres an I was unloadin this here lumber." Seth ran his fingers through his beard. "Had to run them Wheeler boys off'n my place a time or two but they're good boys—not like these here," he added, with a glance at his sons. They lowered their eyes but said nothing. "Wish we could help you, Doc."

"Do me a favor and keep an eye out and let me know if you see anything out of the ordinary?"

"We'll sure do'er, Doc," said Bruce.

"Come visit any time," Billy said.

Clark turned to leave but decided on one more question. He looked at the boys. "What do you plan to do now?"

"Reckon we'll stay around a while and help Pa. Place needs some work."

"Well, I'm sure your Pa is glad to have you back."

Clark unwrapped his bridle from the post, swung into the saddle, thanked them for their time and headed down the path toward the road. As he rounded the bend the sounds of the saw and the hammer started up again. It was an interesting coincidence that the last participants in the hound saga had just returned when the next episode began. The problem for Clark was that he did not really believe in coincidences. He had received no explanation of where the young men had been for the past year and no indication of where they had been last night. Just that they were out, their Pa had said. Clark had intended to ask where they were but he had held back. It was probably none of his business. And this might also have been part of an elaborate prank. Billy was good with animals. He could train a dog, certainly. He would have to keep an eye on the Haney boys.

It was mid-afternoon when Clark turned down the track that led to the Wheelers. Their place was well kept with no sagging boards or peeling paint. A thin wisp of smoke twisted out of the chimney signifying that someone was home. At the sound of his horse's hooves, Hattie Wheeler appeared at the door wiping her red, chapped hands on her apron. Other little faces peered out around her skirt.

"Howdy Miss Hattie. How are you this afternoon?"

"Fine, Doc."

"How about the rest of your brood? Are you children fine, too?"

The children shyly turned away but they liked being noticed.

"They're fine, too, Doc. I was just peelin taters for supper. Will you stay for it?"

"Thank you ma'am, for the kindness, but I was going to take a look at the spot where the boys had their adventure yesterday. Sheriff Mosley came by the Pilgrim's this morning while I was helping to deliver a calf and asked me to look into it. I went by and talked to the boys this morning at school and I'm sure they saw something, but I'm just not sure what."

"They's sure scared, Doc. I'm afeared myself. I don't know what it means for my family and our kin. We're not lettin the boys out no more, least by themselves. The hound has always been a bad omen round these parts and it could be a sign like the preacher's always on about."

"I doubt it, Hattie. I'm sure that whatever it is we can get to the bottom of it. Is it all right if I go across your land? It's the quickest way."

"O'course. You know the way or should Ezra show you?"

"I can find it. It's the old ridge track, right?"

"Yep. Well come back and stay for supper, if you're able." She turned and started shooing the children back into the house. Clark led his horse through the vegetable patch that began right off their porch then through the cornfield where a few brown stalks of corn hadn't been cut and bundled yet. Once clear of the fields, he remounted. As he headed up the hill toward the track, he figured that he was leaving about the same time the boys had left so he should have just about the same sun.

It was a pleasant afternoon as he rode through the woods. There wasn't much moisture in the air and the sun was warm but not hot. When he reached the cutoff to the Haney place, he considered looking at the ground but decided the later sun would be better so he kept on towards the hollow. Like the boys, he decided that he needed a drink and he thought Traveler might like one, too, so he took them both to the spring. Clark got a few good mouthfuls of the cold spring water and filled his canteen before leading his horse over. While Traveler drank his fill, Clark looked around. He noticed the trampled grass and quite a few apple cores covered now with yellow jackets. That's part of the story the boys didn't tell me, he thought. They stopped and filched a few apples from Seth Haney. I wonder if he saw them and concocted a trick to scare them on the way back, he thought. He might have. He was crazy about his apples.

He led his horse away from the spring back to the track. Without wasting time, he reached Squirrel Hollow fairly quickly. The hollow was dark in there even then and Clark wondered how the boys had managed to shoot anything at dusk. Those boys have keen eyes, he thought. He didn't know it but he tethered his horse at the same tree where the boys had left their sacks. The entrance to the hollow was narrow and he didn't want his horse to get scratched on the trip through the dense trees. Everything looked normal in the hollow. There were no signs of any disturbance and there were the normal animal and insect sounds.

Clark began scouting although he did not know exactly what he was looking for. He could see some scuff marks leading off to the right. Someone had walked that way without picking up their feet and some of the dead leaves had been kicked over. Probably one of the boys. At the base of a tree, he noticed what looked like some sort of small animal lying there. When he walked over to it, he noticed it was a sack. Maybe one of the boys dropped it, he thought. It was a sugar sack. He picked it up, deciding to show it to the boys on the way back.

He walked to the far right of the hollow. Clark's plan was to walk around the edge to see if he could see any signs before he lost all light in the hollow. He had to do it quickly so that he could get back to the spot where the boys saw the dog or whatever it was when the sun's rays were striking the spot at the best angle. The sides of the hollow were steep and it took Clark about a half hour of hard walking to complete the circle. He hadn't seen anything that looked out of place.

He left the hollow, untied his horse and began walking slowly back toward the Wheeler's farm. The sun was almost perfect and in the parts of the trail with sunlight left he could pick out lots of tracks. He saw Traveler's prints as well as four sets of tracks–the boys' jogging steps to the hollow and their hurried steps home. There was another set of bootprints, probably belonging to Ezra when he came up in the morning. There was no sign of any other prints—except for those made by small recognizable animals.

When he reached the cutoff to the Haney place, he bent over at the waist and occasionally crawled on the ground. He saw where the boys had stopped and rested. There were three new sets of prints, here, too. And one more set that was new. One set, probably Ezra's, moving in wider circles away from where the boys said they first saw the hound. The other set of prints came from the direction of the Haney farm. Clark studied the print. There was a noticeable cut in the right boot heel and Clark knew he would recognize it if he saw it again.

*Two sets of eyes watched the man as he picked his way along the track. One knew that he was getting too close. The other stirred–its muscles rippling. The hair on his neck stood up and his ears flared wide. His breathing came faster and a long strand of saliva dripped from his panting mouth. The man beside him gave a slight snick with his mouth and the beast was off and running silently toward the man. Just before the animal reached him, the man looked in its direction but saw nothing. Then it sprang out of the dark thicket knocking him down by its sheer weight. The man screamed and thrust his arms up to ward the beast off. But it was no use. The animal tore at him with his huge jaws and after a minute the fight was over. With a gurgling sound, the man's arms went limp. The animal stood growling over him for a minute. Then, following another snick from his master, the pair tracked off into the gathering gloom.*

While Clark was talking to the Haneys, Sarah had been finishing up her lessons for the day. She had remained after school as she almost always did just in case one of her pupils wanted help and did not want to be seen asking for it. Today, she was hoping that no one wanted her because she had invited Clark for supper and had no idea what she intended to fix.

When school was over, all of the children piled out of the schoolhouse as fast as they could—leaving only one child. She was the only girl in a family of seven children and her mother had little time for the eight-year-old girl sandwiched in between all her rowdy boys. The little girl had no trouble with her lessons but she stayed after school more than most children—more for the company than probably anything else. She was a good student and Sarah could imagine her trying to find a quiet place to do her lessons in the noisy house she lived in.

Sarah pulled a set of paper dolls out of her drawer and played dress-up with the girl for a half hour or so. When she left, Sarah quickly left the schoolhouse and walked next door to her small house. After rummaging around her pantry for a few minutes, she thought she had enough food to satisfy her invitation. She started the dinner and looked at the clock. With a little luck, she might just have time to change and finish dinner before Clark arrived.

The last direct rays of the sun shone brilliantly on an open patch of ground. There were few leaves and Clark could see the long distances between the steps where the boys sprinted down the trail. He noticed the late afternoon calm as the wind died down. And over the stillness came the sounds of sawing and hammering. If I can hear them, Clark thought, they could have heard the boys, if they were there.

As the last light began to fade over the western ridge, Clark remounted and trotted thoughtfully back to the Wheelers. Once again, he dismounted and walked his horse through the vegetable garden. Ezra was sitting on the porch leaning back on a bench, his legs stretched out in front of him, calmly puffing on a corncob pipe.

"Evenin, Doc. Find anything?"

"About what you did, I reckon. No animal prints except for a deer or two and some rabbits. I did find one thing, though," he added, taking the sack from his saddlebag.

"Ever see this?"

"Yep, every time I buy sugar," he chuckled. "Let's see. Ben! Zeke!"

The boys came out on the porch and nodded at Doc. "Doc, here, wants to know if you boys carried sacks like this huntin with you?"

The boys looked at the sack. "No, Pap. We had them canvas bags."

"That's what I figured. Ain't bad enough to lose the squirrels, you got to lose good sacks, too." He paused. "You got any more questions for these rascals, Doc?"

"No, Ezra. Thank you boys."

"Yessir." They walked back in the house.

"What's the matter with the boys, Ezra?"

"Well, I believed 'em when they said they saw somethin but they stole some apples from Seth Haney so they got themselves a whippin."

"I didn't know if you knew about the apples," said Clark.

"Yep. Them boys told me about it. I didn't want to hide 'em but stealin is stealin."

Clark nodded and Ezra continued, "Hattie said she asked you to supper. Won't you stop over?"

"I'd like to Ezra, but I told Miss Sarah I'd stop over there for supper so I'd best be moving along."

Ezra gave Clark a speculative look. "You know you're stretchin this courtin thing out too long, Doc. Miss Sarah might give up on you one o' these days."

"Sometimes I'm ready to give up on myself," he said, somewhat ruefully.

"Well you run along. Stop over when you can and let me know if you find out anything, would you?"

"My pleasure. And thank Miss Hattie for the offer."

Clark rode off towards the crossroads.

# 5

## Tuesday Evening

It was supper time and John "Black" Smith was hungry. He was a big man, almost 300 pounds and most of it muscle. All day, everyday except Sundays, Thanksgiving Day, Christmas Day and the 4$^{th}$ of July, Black labored over his iron. He hefted big pieces and melted them over a blazing hot forge and reshaped them using brute strength and about thirty years of accumulated skill. He was also generally a patient man but hunger had a way of shortening his fuse. Tonight, as he was putting away his tools for another day, he had the misfortune of looking up when he heard hoof beats. It was Preacher Elrod, back from a day of shepherdin his flock, as he liked to call it. There was only one little problem and that was that Black was not one of his sheep.

Like a lot of mountain men, Black had served in the army, but when he returned to the hills, he had never gone back to church. That not only made him a little bit of an oddity, it also made him the prime candidate for Preacher Elrod's proselytizing efforts. Now the big man's rumbling stomach competed with the hortatory rumbling coming from the general direction of the preacher's mouth. "Now, listen here, Black. You heard what's a happenin with the hound. You know them Wheeler boys's chased plumb down the mountain. Seems to me a man oughtta be as close to salvation as he can get in times like this."

Black just shook his head. "Ain't nothin in that building o yours makes me any closer to God than I am right here," he gently tapped his chest. It was a conversation they had had many times. The only difference this time was bringing the hound into it. "Like I told you, Preacher, I'm a believer but I want to believe in my own way—not the way someone tells me to believe. I had nough of that in the army."

"You're just not gettin it, Black," sighed the preacher. "I'm atellin ye that I'm not gonna give up on you. I take your salvation personal. Don't you forget about that hound, Black. Satan's out a harvestin souls. Don't you be part o his crop." He paused when he ran out of wind. "Well, I reckon I'll just pass on."

I wish you would pass on, Black thought. But he waved a cheerful good-bye to him. No sense in goin out of your way to irritate a man of the cloth. He might get religion some day, he thought. But right now he was gonna get supper.

It was completely dark when Clark reached the bridge but his way was lit somewhat by the lanterns burning in the kitchens in the cluster of houses at the crossroads. He was running a little late and it bothered him. When he rode up to Sarah's, she was standing in the door, waiting. She had changed her appearance from this morning. By the lantern light that shone from inside, he could see that the long black dress she wore when she worked had been replaced by a colorful print-covered by an apron. Her dark hair, normally in an austere bun was now down, framing her face and loosely tied back with a ribbon like Clark liked it. She smiled and opened her arms as he walked up the stairs toward her. Her scent was a mixture of lilac water and baking and Clark couldn't decide which one was more pleasing at that moment. They kissed and she took his hand and led him into the kitchen.

"I'm sorry I'm late."

"That's all right. I was a little behind myself. In fact, I had to hurry a little but supper is ready."

"What're we having? I'm starved."

"Poor man. I can see you're wasting away. We're having fried chicken, baked potatoes and greens."

"No bread? I thought I smelled bread baking."

"No bread. But I did make an apple pie."

"An apple pie. My favorite."

"I know. That's why I made it." Sarah served dinner and as they began to eat, she asked, "What's going on with the Wheeler boys? I heard some story about Satan's Hound? What's that all about?"

"They've got a legend around here about a satanic hound that takes sinners to the devil. The Wheeler boys had gone hunting and on the way they filched a few of Old Man Haney's apples and when they were chased by something—I'm not sure what—they decided it was the hound."

"Goodness. It sure sounds like your kind of problem, Clark. What else did you learn?" Talking with Sarah helped Clark to put things in order and he liked the way her mind worked. It was neat and orderly and her approach had helped him to solve little puzzles before.

"I wanted to talk with you about it because there are a few strange things about this incident."

"Such as?"

"For one thing, there weren't any paw prints. I'm pretty sure that the boys thought they saw something but animals make prints. The ground was soft enough for them but there weren't any." He paused. "Then, there's the Haneys. The older boys, Bruce and Billy, are back. Have just been back a couple of days. That's especially interesting because the last sighting of the hound was about twelve years ago by Billy Haney."

"That is an interesting coincidence," Sarah raised a quizzical eyebrow.

"And you know how I am about coincidences. One other thing, too, I stopped by the Haney's today and asked them if they had heard anything on Monday evening. The incident occurred on the back of their place. They said they hadn't heard anything but there was a set of footprints leading from their place back to the spot where it had happened. There was a crack in the right boot heel, by the way."

"You said that Billy was the last to see the hound?"

"I asked them about it. Billy had been visiting his

mother's grandmother and she told them the story about the hound, then he saw it on the way home."

"Let me see," said Sarah. "That would be Mary Abbott, Lucinda's grandmother on her mother's side. Her mother was a Haskell, I think."

"How do you know all that?"

"She was the only one of Lucinda's grandmothers living. One of the first things I did when I came here was to learn who was related to whom. You really need that information to sort out what people mean."

"Why is that?"

"A lot of conversation is based on old animosities. You ought to know that by now. Everyone here dislikes someone and everyone related to them. I don't know why and I bet they don't either, but it helps to know it."

Clark nodded. "You're a genealogical encyclopedia."

"I'm probably one of the few people here who knows that I wasn't just insulted. What are you going to do next?"

"Well I found an old sack in the hollow. The Wheeler boys didn't lose it. It looks like a sugar sack. I'm pretty sure it came from Sam's store but I'll check just to make sure. Sam told me today that he thought that some of his sugar was walking out on him. Maybe I found one of the bags for him—although it's empty. Other than that, I'm not sure. This just might turn out to be a joke. You know, the boys are late so they make up a story to get out of trouble. Who knows?" He had been eating and his plate was remarkably empty so he remarked on it. "Did you say something about apple pie?"

"Indeed I did. And we have some coffee to go with it." Sarah took the plates from the table and returned with two pieces of pie and coffee. "It's strange that the trouble started about the time those Haney boys came back, isn't it? Why did they leave anyway? Bruce was through with his schooling but Billy still had a year to go. He needed it, too."

"Well, you know the rumors. Something about a drunken brawl in a neighboring county. And something about assaulting a girl. But I didn't ask. I think I will talk to Tom Mosley about it, but I don't want to jump to any conclusions. A whole lot of people have been tried and found guilty around here—without the first scrap of truth—at least in the court of public opinion. I'll have to keep an eye on them, though. I'm really in no hurry, I guess. It's just kind of interesting."

"I know. You enjoy a good puzzle. Can I do anything to help?"

"You certainly can. Do like you've done before and write down your impressions. I'll keep you posted on what I find out. And you can keep your ears open when you talk with folks. This might even be the start of a practical joke. You know, someone like Ray Potter might start it up just to see how people react."

"He might at that. Tell me," said Sarah, "how you would react if I took your hand and led you into the sitting room for a while?"

"Try me." She did.

Clark was content and full as he swung into his saddle later (but not scandalously late) that evening. The stars were twinkling brightly and there was a chill in the air. You can smell cold weather coming, he thought and buttoned up his coat. There would be frost soon—maybe tonight if the breeze didn't pick up. There was only one lamp still burning in the few houses between Sarah's and the turnoff to his cabin. After crossing the bridge, he turned north up the track to Hagood's Mill.

The road was good down on that end. Bobby Hagood put down several tons of crushed rock every year so that folks could get their wagons to his mill. At this time of the evening, the mill was quiet and dark. The big wheel was just a giant shadow. There were no lamps on in the Hagood house so Bobby and his brood had gone to bed.

After passing by the mill, the road quickly became a track and then a trail. At one time it had been a logging road. Load after load of hardwood had been cut down and carted to the mill where it was sawed up into boards. That was when Bobby's pa was alive and running the mill. When they cut down all the hardwood they could get to, they had closed the operation leaving a few cabins and some roadbeds throughout the region. One of these cabins was Clark's. It was perched on a hillside on a flat place scraped out of the side of the mountain. On a clear day, Clark could see at least five miles across the valley. Now as he approached it from below, his cabin and small barn were just indistinct shadows—not even recognizable because they were fitted snug up against the rocks of the cliff.

He walked Traveler into the barn, struck a match and lit the lantern. He took great care in grooming his horse. If you perform veterinary services, folks judge you on the care of your own animals. Besides, Clark really liked dealing with animals. They never complained. Before leaving and taking the lamp with him, he gave Traveler an apple from the barrel near the door.

When he reached his cabin, he hung the lamp over his small kitchen table and lit another lamp and hung it over his chair. Other than his bed, his chair was his most important piece of furniture. It had been quite a chore to get the two heavy pieces of furniture up the hill and since that was before he knew anyone, he had to do it by himself. But it had been worth it. Many pleasant hours had been spent, sitting there, reading or even occasionally, writing.

Before sitting down, he looked at his fiddle hanging over the fireplace and his bookshelf. The bookshelf won. He took a copy of *The Hound of the Baskervilles* and laid it on the table next to his chair. After sitting down, by habit, he reached for a shelf ledge under the table for his pipe and leather pouch of tobacco. He opened the pouch and the sweet smell of the tobacco rose pleasingly to his nose. Like fresh ground coffee, pipe tobacco was something that smelled better raw than cooked. He loved them both anyway. He carefully filled the bowl, adding a pinch at a time and gently tamping each down. He took a modest private pride in his pipe-filling abilities. He liked his pipe to burn straight through without going out. It ruined a pipe to have to keep lighting it. He took one of the wooden matches and struck it against a lump of Georgia marble that served as a paperweight. The match flared instantly and its sulphurous fumes were quickly replaced by the more aromatic smell of burning tobacco. He took several brisk puffs and then one more long one to make sure the pipe was well lit, sat back in his chair and picked up his book. He had read everything by A. Conan Doyle he could get his hands on. For some reason, this particular story seemed to fit the current situation perfectly.

While Clark was reading, Sarah was busy cleaning up from dinner and thinking. She thought about her work and she thought about Clark. While the two may not have seemed to go together, they were intertwined in a way that was hard to untangle. Sarah loved her work and she loved Clark. More than this, she knew that Clark loved her. Yet, for both of them, love did not mean marriage. At least not right now. She was not certain why Clark had not committed, they had touched on the topic once or twice but she had not pushed—mainly because she had her own conflicts about the subject. In her part of the world, teaching jobs were for single women. Marriage meant the end of the opportunity to teach and inspire and help people that she really cared about. It was a hard choice, but since Clark was not forcing her to make it, she would let it rest, for a while anyway.

# 6
**Wednesday Morning**

Wednesday morning dawned crisp, clear and bright with the first frost of the fall. As always, Clark was up with the sun. He yawned, stretched and swung his feet onto the cold floor. He began his mornings the same way he ended his days, by washing up. In the fall and winter, this meant stinging cold water. He splashed the water in the bowl noisily. After dressing, he went into his kitchen and lit his stove. He put the coffee pot on as well as a separate pot of water he would use to shave with after breakfast. He also put a skillet on the remaining opening to heat up while he did his morning chores.

Clark went to the barn and scooped out a bucket full of chicken feed that he spread around the yard for the chickens. While they were eating, he gathered the eggs and put them in a basket. He returned to the barn where he fed and watered Traveler, as well as the old mule he used for plowing and his milk cow. While the cow was eating, he sat on the milking stool and squeezed out a large bucketful of milk. Then he carried the pail and the eggs to the tiny springhouse that sat over a pile of rocks where the spring spilled out of the hill. He poured the milk into the container and noticed that he had plenty, way too much, in fact. He drew a little off for his coffee and put all the eggs but two on the egg shelf and returned to his cabin. The Hagood boy had taken good care of his animals yesterday, he thought. He decided to leave a nickel for him when he went out for the day.

The water was hot and so was the skillet. He cut off a piece of cured ham and laid it in the hot skillet. It sizzled pleasingly and Clark flipped it once or twice, and then set it on a plate on the stove to keep it warm. He cracked two eggs and poured them into the skillet, scrambling them quickly in the hot ham grease. After the eggs were done he scraped them onto his plate, as well. Then he cut two biscuits and laid the cut halves down in the skillet, browning them quickly. He also put these on his plate. The only thing left was to pour the coffee, which he did. He ate everything quickly using his biscuits to mop up every last bit on his plate. He washed the last bite down with his last sip of coffee. A good way to end a good meal, he thought, when everything ran out together. He lifted the other pot and poured the water into his shaving bowl, and then he put the dirty dishes into the remaining water to soak. He figured he would get to them later.

With all his chores done, he used his shaving time to think about what he needed to do. Several of his neighbors needed to see him so he would spend the day working but he could still probably find a few minutes to think about the puzzling events of Monday evening. He toweled off his face and put on his coat. He collected a pail full of milk, which he put into a collapsible canvas container. He had decided to take the milk to the school. Then he saddled up Traveler and rode down the trail where he left a nickel and his thanks for Cal Hagood.

Clark's next stop was the schoolhouse. He had to get rid of the sloshing pail of milk. When he reached the schoolhouse, he walked up the front steps and, as he had done many times before, gently tapped on the door and walked in.

The children were just getting into their seats and Clark stood for a moment admiring Sarah's profile as she wrote the day's lesson on the blackboard. After a moment, she turned and gave him the warm smile he had last seen when they parted the evening before. He smiled back and set the pail of milk on the floor. "Sorry to interrupt but I had some extra milk so I brought it for the children."

She walked over to him and said, "That was thoughtful of you. Are we going to church together tonight?" They usually did, but she always asked.

"We are. I'll stop by in time to walk with you."

Sarah moved closer and asked quietly, "Dessert after?"

Clark smiled, "Why not before, too?"

"You ask too much, Mr. Ammons," she said with a smile.

"See you this evening. Study well," he said with a wave to the class.

During the morning, he visited the farms of several of his neighbors. He treated his "patients," which this morning consisted of a couple of horses, a cow and one bull that really needed to be shot and put out of its misery. Along the way, most of the conversation was about the crops and the weather although a few folks had an anxious question or two for Clark about the hound incident.

It was about noon and he was out at the Pilgrim place (checking on the new calf) when he heard galloping hoof beats. Someone was coming in a hurry. He stopped what he was doing and went outside the barn to see if this somehow concerned him.

The rider was Charley Pell, Sheriff Mosley's lone deputy. Pell was a long, lean, hawk-nosed man whose previous police experience was in the army. Today, he would not have passed Tom Mosley's muster because his shirttail was hanging out and his cap was pushed way back on his head. When he saw Clark, he reined up and jumped off his horse. "Doc, I'm glad I found you. We got trouble."

"What's the matter, Charley?"

"It's Bobby Dunstan. He went out huntin on Tuesday about noon and didn't come home. His wife got nervous and asked us to go lookin for him. Figured maybe he'd twisted a leg or somethin. Anyway, Miz Dustan said he was headed out Round Mountain Road so this mornin I took a few boys and we headed out that way. I found his horse tethered at the base of a trail that leads off Round Mountain so I followed the trail and then I seen him. He was layin there, dead as could be. His eyes was wide open but I knowed he was dead cause of the way his throat was all tore up. I sent up to the county seat to get the coroner but the sheriff wanted you to take a look at him."

"Why?"

"Cause of the way he died. Looks like a huge dog killed 'im, but we wanted you to look. We got his body in the Johnson barn. It was the closest place."

"OK, Charley, let me get saddled up and I'll be right with you." Clark said his good-byes to the Pilgrims and followed Pell back to the Chattanooga road. As they rode, Clark asked, "Any idea how long he's been dead?"

"Don't know, he's not in too bad a shape so he was probably killed sometime yesterday."

They didn't talk again until they reached the Johnson house. A wagon and four horses were tied up out front. As they got nearer, Clark could hear a woman's sobs intermingled with the lower buzzing of men's voices. A man on the porch called out, "Hey, Charley, see you found Doc. Hey, Doc. We got him in the barn. His widder 'n younguns is inside. Preacher Elrod's in with 'em but he ain't doin no good. Miz Elrod's here, too. Sheriff's in the barn."

"Thanks," said Clark, "I think I'll go on out to the barn and take a look, first. I'll be inside directly."

Clark and Charley walked over to the barn where the sheriff greeted them at the door. "Wanted you to see 'im before he gets any worse." I've seen a lot worse, thought Clark, but he didn't say it.

Bobby Dunstan was laid out on the floor. Clark kneeled down at his feet and began a careful inspection. He had some dirt on his boots but his right heel wasn't marked—not that he thought it would be. He looked at his jeans then he examined his arms and his hands–paying careful attention to his fingernails. Then he looked at his torso, throat and head. He stood up and looked at the Sheriff and Deputy Pell. "He was killed by a dog or wolf of some sort. Dog, I think. Black and stood about this high," he indicated a height of about four feet.

"You sure?"

"Pretty sure. I found some black hairs on Bobby's clothes and under his fingernails. The method of killing indicates a dog not a bear or other animal—like a mountain lion, for instance. The way his throat is torn and the other bite marks also indicate a dog's tooth pattern. By the size of the bites I can also estimate his size."

"The hellhound," said Charley.

"I wouldn't say that. Let's close that barn door and get it dark in here, Sheriff. I want to check something." When it was dark, glowing phosphorescent spots appeared on Bobby's hands and on his clothing, face and neck.

Pell gasped, "What does it mean, Clark?"

"Probably that this man was killed by the same dog that chased the Wheeler boys. You can see where the glowing spots are that something rubbed off onto him. His hands are covered and there are spots on his face and neck. So it means that a human applied it, unless the animal got into some special kind of fungus around here, which is unlikely because it's poisonous to animals. That means the dog is real and he was set on this man. And that means Bobby was probably murdered."

There was silence in the barn for a minute or so while Charley went and opened the door. "I wonder why someone would want to kill Bobby," mused Mosley.

"No telling. Maybe because he got too close to something. The way the Wheeler boys might have gotten too close to something."

"Too close to what?"

"I'm not sure yet. There are one or two other puzzling things about this."

"What are they?"

"Well, a dog likes to hold his prey down with his paws. Bobby doesn't have a single scratch mark on him. That's kind of unusual." He turned to Charley. "Did you check the spot where you found him for paw prints?"

"Not really. We were so shook up when we found him that we just carried him off of the mountain." Clark nodded.

"I think I need to go up there myself." He turned to the Sheriff. "That is, if you want me to keep working on it."

"Of course, I'd appreciate your help." He paused. "What are we going to tell folks?"

"Offhand, I'd say we need to tell them he was killed by a dog, but <u>not</u> a satanic hound, a real-life flesh and blood hound." He paused. "Not that it will do any good, but we'll try it."

Charley covered up Bobby's body. "I guess we need to get him buried as soon as possible," said Charley. The sheriff nodded. "The coroner'll be here later this afternoon to certify the fact that he is legally dead. Then, Preacher Elrod can get 'im properly buried."

Clark turned to Charley. "Where, exactly, did you find him?"

"Head out Round Mountain Road. Go about a mile or so 'n you'll see an oak tree that was struck by lightening. If you look just past it on the right there, you'll see a trail heading up the hill. We found Bobby's horse tethered in there. Go up the trail about five hundred paces or so and that's where we found the body."

Clark shook his head.

"What's the matter Doc?"

"I don't know but that doesn't seem to make sense. If he set out at lunchtime on Tuesday he would have been there by early afternoon. It's not a half hour by horse from his house to that spot. But if the dog was painted, it probably meant that Bobby was killed at dusk or later, so he should have been a lot further in. It just doesn't make sense. Well, I'll look at it." He turned to the sheriff. "Tom. I have a question for you. The Haney boys have returned to our community. I saw them at their house yesterday, but they've been gone for a while. What happened to them?"

"I'm not really sure. It happened over in Jefferson County. I know that they spent some time on the chain gang. Judge John would know why. You say they're back, huh?"

"Yep. I don't want to jump to any conclusions, though." The Sheriff nodded and Clark turned and walked into the Johnson house where he found Mrs. Dunstan and four of their five children. The oldest had joined the army and wasn't around anymore. As with all sudden deaths, the children just bore a kind of stunned look. It hadn't sunk in that their daddy wasn't ever coming home again. Mrs. Elrod was holding Mrs. Dunstan's hand and speaking to her in a low voice, saying the things that people always say at times like that. Preacher Elrod was talking to the group of men who helped to bring the body back. "You see, what I've been asayin," he was saying. "There's evil here. Satan's work." The men nodded glumly as Clark walked up. "Preacher. Gentlemen."

"What'd you find, Doc?" one of them asked.

"He was killed by a dog. A real flesh and blood dog that had been painted with some sort of glowing compound to make it fearsome." He turned to the Preacher. "You really shouldn't put Satan in this."

"Don't you believe in the power of Satan in this world?"

"I do, but I think in most cases, he has human helpers. He certainly has, at least in this case."

"What makes you say that?" asked one of the men.

"Like I said, the dog was painted up. That means that someone painted him. And if someone painted him, that someone probably trained him and uses him. Someone probably set the dog on Bobby. The men (except for the preacher) nodded at the truth of his statement. Clark turned to Preacher Elrod. "I'm asking you not to cater to the people's fears." The preacher stared at him but said nothing. With a curt nod, Clark walked over to Mrs. Dunstan and the children. Mrs. Elrod stopped talking to her and looked up at Clark, expectantly.

Clark kept his eyes on Mrs. Dunstan and said, "I'm sorry to interrupt but I wanted to say how sorry I am. Bobby was a good man and I'll do everything I can to see that justice is done." Mrs. Dunstan looked up through swollen, tear-stained eyes and nodded. Clark kneeled and hugged the children and left.

With a last glance at the preacher, Clark walked out of the house and headed towards Round Mountain Road. After a few minutes of riding, he came to the fork in the road that became Round Mountain Road. To the best of Clark's knowledge, there was no "Round Mountain," so the name of the road must have meant "a road around the mountain." The mountain, itself, was known as Bear Paw. No one knew why. Perhaps it vaguely resembled a bear's paw or maybe when the first settlers got there, a lot of bears were there. Clark thought it would be interesting if it really was "Bare Pa" and referred to another, perhaps funnier incident.

After riding down Round Mountain for a mile or so, he had located the oak and the trail. The trail was steep so Clark tethered his horse in the same area that Bobby had probably used and walked up the trail approximately five hundred paces and looked around. Up the trail another twenty paces or so, he spotted an area that was slightly scuffed up. That must be the place. Charley Pell's legs must be just a mite longer than mine, he thought.

As he had done on the ridge track, Clark dropped to his hands and knees and began looking intently at the ground. He looked for boot prints that matched those Bobby had worn but he couldn't find any. At least not at the spot where he had fallen. He also looked for blood but there wasn't any. A throat wound like that would have severed the carotid artery and bled intensely. But there was no blood. The evidence was pretty clear. He had been killed elsewhere and brought here. Whoever had killed him had moved him almost to the base of the trail. Why? Clark thought he knew the answer: to be found quickly without much of a search. Why? Because there must be something up here that no one was supposed to see. Having the body found would also serve another purpose. It would help to scare people. To keep them out of the area. Like the Transylvania count that staked out dead people on his border to scare invaders. Whoever had done it probably hadn't thought about the possibility of the glowing substance being observed.

Now that he knew the body had been moved, he could try to find where it had been. The sunlight was bright but there were no tracks. No claw marks on the body. No paw prints. No tracks. Clark looked around the area. He could see faint signs of the ground being brushed. He followed the brush marks to a small stream where the brushing ended. He walked along the creek for several hundred yards in each direction. The going was tough because there was dense plant growth in spots that grew almost to the water's edge.

At various spots along the side of the bank, there were sheets of solid rock. He examined each to see if there was a scrape mark from a shoe but there was nothing to give away which of these places the men had used to carry the body. And there must have been two of them. Either that or a mountain of a man. Bobby Dunstan was not a small man. And he would have been the deadest of dead weights and difficult for two men to carry—let alone one.

Clark was pretty sure that they had not come back out of the creek on the north side. That meant they had come from the south side of the creek—back in the direction of Squirrel Hollow. The way he reckoned it, he was about six miles almost due north of there–as the crow flies. About six miles of hard walking up and down the hills if you could go straight or as many as twenty miles of walking if you followed an old deer tail or logging track. Any way you looked at it, it was a lot of territory to search.

He walked back to where Bobby's body had been found and took a final look around. The sky was blue and out across the valley he could see a hawk soaring, trying to find an updraft. The beauty of the day was not lost on Clark—even in these sad circumstances. He just wished he had the ability to fly over the area like an eagle. Maybe he could spot something that way. He thought about the hot air balloon at the county fair. Too bad the fair's not going on, he thought. With a shrug he walked down the trail, untied his horse and rode down Round Mountain to the fork where he headed toward home.

# 7
**Wednesday Evening**

Preacher Jeremy Elrod stood in front of his mirror, combing his stringy gray hair. He was vain about his looks, although no one really understood why. His face had never been handsome and with age, it had become even less so. Yet, he always took meticulous care of his appearance; combing his hair, slicking it back and dressing as well as a preacher could (on the meager wages he earned). A lot of folks thought he worked so hard on his looks because of his young wife but the older folks knew better. He had always been vain.

For years his dream had been to be a politician, a governor or a senator or something of that ilk. As a child, the candidates at the political stump meetings in the county seat had mesmerized him. He noticed how they could whip the crowd up into a frenzy or crack them up with a joke with seeming ease. He was impressed with the power of speech making and more importantly, with the speechmakers. They were admired and sought after and wherever they went, there was always a crowd of folks around them including quite a few pretty girls. That's the kind of work I want, he thought to himself.

He read a lot of speeches as a child—even some from notorious Yankees such as Abe Lincoln and Danicl Webster. He went around giving parts of the speeches to anyone that would listen. He had a good memory but his speeches were like a musician who knew the notes but not the rhythm. He said the words in order but, often out of context, and with no real feeling behind them.

By the time he was about twenty or so, he had a clear plan. He would run for a local office, be elected, and quickly move up through the ranks. But somehow, politics didn't seem to be his long suit. His first race was a close one but he lost. He lost several others in quick succession, as it became clearer and clearer that he was running only to get elected—and not to do anything.

Finally, Jeremy suffered the ultimate indignity. He lost to a man that had died a week before the election by a wide margin. That, more than all the other failures, finally convinced him that, perhaps, God had another plan for his life. And what better plan than to become a preacher.

It was almost as good as being a politician only you had to be a little more careful with the ladies. So young Jeremy had been licensed to preach by a local congregation and when a vacancy occurred just down the road in Hagood's Mill (some scandal involving the former preacher and the former pianist), Jeremy had talked his way in and he had been talking ever since.

With his pulpit, he was now ready to begin moving people as he had seen it done. The only problem with Brother Elrod was that he was only good at shouting. Despite his long years of service, he seldom reached people in the way that old time evangelicals had done it. Possibly this was because the people in Hagood's Mill did not know genius when they saw it. Possibly it was because Brother Elrod, truth to tell, was not really a good speaker.

Now, with over 30 years of preaching under his belt, he was still hoping for a chance to make a speech that would move people and be remembered like Cotton Mather or his less famous father, Increase Mather.

That's why the hound incident meant so much to him. With this kind of thing going on in the community, he might just get the kind of reaction he had always craved. With a final pat of his hair and a tug at this tie, he left his mirror and went in to supper. I'm gonna raise the roof tonight, he thought. They're gonna get some Holy Ghost preachin, whether they need it or not.

As he made his way back into town, Clark's thoughts returned again to the Haney boys. They had showed up just as the trouble started. They had been troublemakers before they left. They certainly knew about the legend. But were they killers? The death of Bobby had changed the situation from a simple prank to murder. You had to be a certain type of person to kill. Clark knew, though, that even decent people could kill, given the right set of circumstances.

He stopped at Butler's General Merchandise and showed Sam the sack he had found in the hollow. "I think I found part of your missing sugar," he said. Sam examined the sack. "It's probably mine, all right. Where'd you find it?"

"Out at Squirrel Hollow. It was just laying on the ground."

"Funny you should mention sugar. The Haney boys were in here today and they bought a whole bunch of sugar. Just about cleaned me out, again."

Clark looked at Sam speculatively. "There's a lot of uses for sugar, of course, especially during canning season, but one other use does come to mind."

Sam nodded. "Moonshine. Interesting that those boys are back just about the time our troubles start up. Terrible thing about Bobby Dunstan, isn't it?"

Clark agreed. "Well, I've got to run. Church and Miss Sarah are waiting on me."

Sam grinned. "Church and a she-devil are waitin on me. See you there."

It was almost six o'clock before he was able to get back to his cabin to wash and put on his almost-Sunday best. He didn't dress all the way up for Wednesday night service and few of the other men in the community did either. Occasionally, a fellow would come in his work clothes. As he hurried down the track he noticed that the Hagood family had already gone so he knew that he was running late, for sure. The Hagoods were not the most prompt people in the area. When he reached Sarah's house, she was dressed and waiting on the front porch. He hastily jumped down and tied his horse up. "So much for dessert before..." she said.

"Sorry about being late," he said, taking her hand and setting off briskly in the direction of the church. "But my day changed dramatically. Did you hear about Bobby Dunstan?"

"No. I did notice that his children weren't in school today. What happened?"

"He was killed by a dog. Probably last night."

Sarah stopped. "Oh, no. By a dog? Are you sure?"

"I'm sure. Deputy Pell came and got me from the Pilgrims' about noon. They had found his body and carried it to the Johnsons'. He had been killed in the woods off Round Mountain Road. He had his throat torn open. And he had marks on him that glowed in the dark. You see what this means."

She nodded and they began walking again. "Someone painted the dog and someone set the dog on both the Wheeler boys and Bobby Dunstan."

"That's the way I read it. Two main questions remain: Who? And Why?"

"What are you going to do now?"

"Tomorrow, I plan to go down to the county seat to check on what really happened with the Haney boys. Tom didn't really know because it happened over in Jefferson County but he thought that Judge John would know."

They had reached the church and the sound of the old piano being unmercifully flogged by Miss Mary Owens could be heard as they entered during the opening hymn. Miss Owens proudly claimed that she played by ear and to Clark, it always sounded as if she banged not just her ear but her whole head against the keys. Her playing was imprecise, to be kind about it. Truthfully, she was awful, but it would be unchristian to tell her so.

Because they were late, all of the back pews were filled in the best church tradition, so they had to walk almost to the front to find a seat.

After the hymn, Preacher Elrod rose to his feet. He wore his preachin' outfit, a black frock coat, black pants, white shirt and black string tie. His hair was slicked back and his seamed face gleamed a sickly white in the lantern and candlelight. Surely, Preacher Elrod was on a mission.

"Tonight," he began, studiously not looking at Clark, "I'm agonna bring a word to ya'll from the Book o Rebelation." Clark's groan was almost audible. Sarah caught his disfavor and elbowed him in the ribs. Clark could tell what was coming and he didn't like it. "The scripture readin is from the leventh chapter, verse seven. 'When they finish their testimony, the beast that ascends out of the bottomless pit will make war against them, overcome them and kill them,'" he shouted. "Friends, we're living in the time o testimony. The beast done come out o' his bottomless pit—an pay attention to this—he will make war gainst them an kill them. That ain't Brother Elrod a' talkin to ye, it's the word o' God right here," he raised the Bible, "in His Book."

For the next thirty minutes or so, Clark fidgeted in his seat while Preacher Elrod expounded on his theme. Clark stood with the other members of the congregation to sing the final hymn to the ruptured melody and rhythm of Miss Owens's piano playing. As the congregation filed out, Clark said, "Sarah, why don't you go outside and wait for me a minute. I want to have a word with the Preacher."

"Clark," she began, "don't be mean to him. He doesn't know any better."

"I'll wait till everyone else leaves so I won't embarrass him but I have to get this off my chest. He's not helping at all."

"Okay, but save some of that passion for me."

Clark grinned. "Yes, ma'am."

Sarah left but appeared to be so deep in conversation with one of the other ladies that she didn't see the Preacher's outstretched hand as she walked past. Clark had calmed down considerably but he was disappointed to see so many of the people warmly congratulating the preacher as they left the church.

When there were only the two of them left, Clark walked slowly down the aisle. The preacher looked in his direction and for a moment, there was a look of consternation on his face. He looked like he was going to leave without talking to him but instead he turned and went on the offensive.

"Now Doc, I know what you're gonna say but it's right here in The Book. The word 'o God... ," he tapered off.

"Preacher, I know what's in The Book," Clark began gently. "You can find a lot of things in there but as far as I can tell, the main theme is about love. You picked out a passage on fear and you took it out of context and you're using it to scare people."

"But they's evil in this world, Doc. My job is to lay it out for 'em so's they don't lose their souls to Satan. There's evil loose in the hills, Doc."

"Preacher, you're a community leader here. You have a responsibility to these people. There is certainly evil in these hills, but not a hellhound. The real evil is ignorance and the superstition that feeds on it. You're preying on their fears. Shouldn't you use your position to help lift them rather than try to hold them down?" He held the Preacher's eyes then walked out in the churchyard.

Sarah was standing with a group of ladies when Clark walked up to join them. "Doc Ammons," one of them asked, "will you be joining us at the church social this Saturday? Won't you come and bring your fiddle?"

"Yes ma'am, I'll be there. I'll even bring my fiddle, if you promise to fry some chicken."

"I didn't know you liked my chicken so much but I'd be proud to bring some. Bring your fiddle now, hear?"

"Yes'm." He turned to Sarah. "Miss Sarah, you ready?"

"Certainly, Mr. Ammons. Good night, ladies." She linked her arm through his for the short walk back to her house. "I'm jealous," she teased.

"Jealous?"

"Certainly, you bragged on Etta Mae's chicken. If it had been brighter, you would have seen her blush scarlet from head to toe. She'll probably go straight home and start frying. Poor woman. She doesn't know how shallow and self-serving your compliments are. I have half a mind not to give you that piece of pie I saved for you."

"Please forgive me. Shall I go down on one knee and beg your forgiveness?"

"Wait till we're inside. I want you to preserve your public dignity." They walked up the steps and into her house. Sarah lit a lamp in the kitchen and then the stove.

"One thing I need to ask you," said Clark.

"It's a strange time to propose but go ahead."

Clark grinned. "Better wait to hear what I'm proposin'. Actually, I wanted to ask you if you knew of any active feuds. You know, between the Haneys and anyone else like the Wheelers or the Dunstans and their kin?"

Sarah set the apple pie on the table. "No. In fact, I think the Haneys and Wheelers are distantly related. I'm not sure about the Dunstans, though, but I can't think of any active feuding except for the Owens and everyone else. Even that one is kind of simmering. No one has died in years from it. Why do you want to know?"

"I'm just trying to find a reason for Bobby's death and the attack on the boys. Old Man Haney ran the Wheeler boys out of his apple orchard but I guess that blood is thicker than apples in these parts," Clark grinned. "I did find out that the sack came from Sam's store but that doesn't mean anything unless I can connect it to something. Anyone could have lost it up there. Other people hunt there. But Sam did tell me that the Haneys had been into his store today and just about cleaned out his sugar supplies. There are still those footprints that lead to the spot where the Wheelers had their adventure and back to the Haney farm. It may mean nothing but there is an arrow pointing in that direction."

Sarah changed the subject as she poured the coffee, "What did you say to the preacher?"

"Nothing much. I just politely reminded him that he had a responsibility as a community leader to help lift the people and not hold them down by encouraging their superstitious beliefs. In fact, he told me that there was evil loose in the hills and I answered that the greatest evil here was ignorance and the superstition that feeds on it—or something to that effect." Clark sat back smugly.

"What a wonderful little speech. You need a scribe to write down all these gems."

"So I thought." They looked at each other for a moment and smiled.

Sarah cleared away the dishes and put them in a pot on the stove. "Should we go into the parlor?"

"I thought we just had dessert." Sarah smiled brightly as she took his hand and led him away from the table. "You're not going to wash the dishes?" Clark asked.

"I thought that I'd just let them soak."

"That's always best," he agreed.

A little while later, after his second dessert, he left Sarah and went back to his cabin.

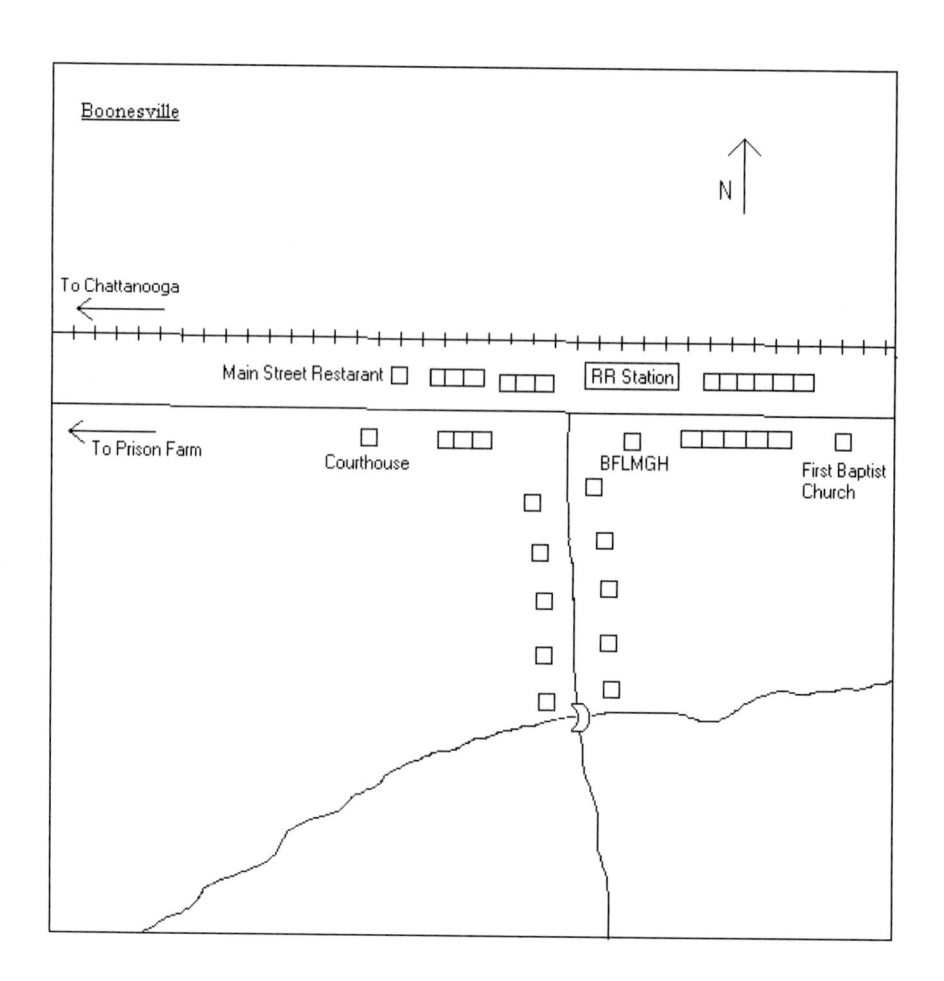

# 8
## Thursday Morning

Fifteen miles or so down the mountain from Hagood's Mill is the City of Boonesville, which has special significance for two reasons. The first is that the railroad company ran out of money there so the rail line goes there and no further (not that anyone could fathom a reason why it should have gone any further, anyway). The other significance is based on the fact that Boonesville is also the county seat of Jackson County. Now the uninitiated might think that it was named after Daniel Boone, the famous trailblazer. In fact, the venerable Boone might have wandered around there at some point. He had flirted with bankruptcy in quite a few places in Tennessee on his way to frontier legenddom and that might have been one of them.

But the town was really named after Jeremiah Boone, a squatter who could not really trace his parentage on his father's side so he adopted a famous last name. After all, he reckoned, if you're going to pick a name, why not pick a good one? Boone had left a community further east where people would never let him forget that he was either a bastard or another miracle virgin birth and hacked out an existence on the top of the ridge, defending it against Indian attacks and tax collectors until his death in 1832. (To hear him tell it, the Indians were significantly more civilized than the tax collectors.)

While Boonesville looked like civilization to the people of Hagood's Mill, it looked like the beginning of the wilderness to the folks living in such civilized places as Chattanooga. One wag even suggested that the term "boonies," originally came from that town.

After Clark had done his chores and checked on his patients that needed attention, he and Traveler headed "down the hill." For the first few miles, the road was not straight. It wound around the hills through pine forests with occasional stands of hardwood visible in the distance that the loggers had missed or just given up on. Occasionally, there were large patches of ground that were just about empty, only a few scraggly pine trees left standing and some hardwood saplings. Large erosion gullies often split these open fields with mud over the trail in spots and gouged out dry drainage ditches lining the road in other spots. When you could see it, the bright morning sky was brilliant. In the other places, the road was in an almost perpetual shade. The snow would linger for days there during the winter.

As the road wound lower, the trees thinned out some. Homes and ploughed fields could occasionally be seen as the steep rocky slopes gave way to rounded rocky hills. The farms were small but larger than the small patches you could farm up the hill and seemingly were more prosperous. Some houses were made of stone and occasional fieldstone walls lined the road.

Clark made this trip at least once a month. He purchased his vet supplies in Boonesville, as it was the closest railhead. The packages would be held there for him by the station manager or passed along to the drugstore where he would pick them up. He also received his books that way. He regularly telegraphed his orders to a company in Atlanta, which would then ship them up to him. When he first arrived, there were only a few books in the small library in the town. He liked to read so he spent a lot of his cash money buying books. He kept the ones he liked—the others he gave to the library. According to the local librarian, he had increased their books by about a third since he came.

He reached the bridge across the river on the outskirts of town by about one o'clock. The road went up a hill passing by a series of two-story red brick houses. In these houses lived some of the most important people in the county. At the top of the hill was the main street. The businesses (thirty-one to be exact) lined the street with the courthouse on one end and the First Baptist Church on the other. A casual observer could see that the spire of the church was just a "leetle bit" taller than the dome of the courthouse—although both impressive structures were made out of the same red brick.

The gray-green clapboard train station was almost in the middle of the two and directly at the head of the road Clark was on. The train provided regular service to Chattanooga and then on to Atlanta and all points south (and north, if you were fool enough to want to go there). Clark reined in at the train station. He walked through the waiting room where the old pot bellied stove belched out hellish heat past the ticket counter to the stationmaster's office.

"Afternoon, Mr. Drawdy." Clark addressed the elderly stationmaster. He didn't know his first name. The sign simply read: *StationMaster: Mr. Drawdy* and the old man had never bothered to introduce himself, if in fact, he was Mr. Drawdy at all, and not just too cheap to change the sign.

"Afternoon, Mr. Ammons," he wheezed. Clark had never seen him without a lit cigarette dangling from his lips.

"Anything for me?"

"Let's take a look." Drawdy led Clark back into the freight area. He walked through the racks past a few pieces of luggage and down to the end of the row. "Here you are. One parcel from Excelsior in Nashville and a package from H.B. Hayes & Sons, Publishers in Atlanta."

Clark handed him two bits for the storage fee and picked up the two small crates. The contents would fit easily in his saddlebags. "Can I borrow a crowbar?" he asked.

Drawdy shuffled over to a table and picked up one of the small crowbars and handed it to Clark. Clark wrenched off the tops of both crates. From one he pulled the vet supplies he had ordered. From the other came three books. They were bound in rich brown leather and smelled crisp and new. He flipped through them. With any new book, he wanted to drop everything and immediately begin reading it, but he resisted the temptation. He would savor them later. He thanked Mr. Drawdy for his help and walked back out to his horse where he carefully put his supplies and his books in his saddlebags.

His mission now was to find the Judge and to eat lunch. And despite the fact that the lunch hour had expired a while ago, he thought he could do both in the same place. The county's elected officials had a habit of eating, en masse, at the Main Street Restaurant. And their lunches had a habit of starting about 10:30 and running till about 3:00. He rode his horse down the main street raising a small cloud of red dust until he reached the restaurant, which was just across from the courthouse.

He tethered his horse out front, not surprised to find that it was still crowded. When he entered, he looked around for the person he needed. On one side of the room, the county supervisor was in conversation with the county auditor. The county treasurer was involved in an apparently tense conversation with the president of the local bank. At the very back of the restaurant, sitting in a separate seating alcove was the person Clark was looking for, Judge John Bolingham. Judge John was a roly-poly, round-faced, affable man who had been appointed judge about a year after Clark had moved to the area. He had replaced an ancient, addle-pated man who had once sentenced himself to jail for thirty days for contempt of court. Judge John's table was piled high with dirty dishes and, as was often the case, fawning lawyers surrounded him. Today, in fact, most of the county's lawyers were at the table, laughing just a little too loud at one of the judge's stories. John looked in his direction as Clark walked back through the restaurant.

"Clark, come on back here and sit down!" he bellowed.

Clark pulled up a chair as several of the men moved their chairs to make room. "Annie," the judge yelled, "Where you been? Got a starvin' man, here. Come on over here and take this man's order and clear away some of these plates, will you?"

The waitress came over and obediently began clearing plates. After a few trips she remembered that the Judge had given her two orders and asked Clark, "What kin I get fer ya?"

"Ham steak, greens, biscuit and iced tea please." She left with yet another load of plates.

"Well, Clark, what brings you down the hill to civilization?"

"We're having some problems up our way Judge and I wanted to talk with you about them."

"What's goin on?"

"One of our people, Bobby Dunstan, was killed by a dog on Tuesday and a couple of our boys were scared the other evening by a black hound with a burning face that chased them down the ridge trail."

"Bobby Dunstan?" asked the judge. Clark nodded. "He was a good man. Served on a jury for me a year or so ago. Why didn't he just shoot the damn thing?"

"I don't know. He had his gun. He was hunting in an area off Round Mountain Road. My guess is that he was frozen, you know a huge hound with a glowing face comes out at you in the twilight you might react quickly enough, then again you might not."

The waitress brought Clark's food and he began to eat.

"You say some boys saw it?"

Clark nodded. "But not the same night. A night earlier. The description of what they saw ties into a local legend we have up there about Satan's Hound. Have you heard of it?"

Judge John's eyes glinted in the dim light. "Seen him a few times myself," he paused. "During a weekend drunk or whenever I come home late and have to face Mrs. Bolingham." The lawyers competed with each other to laugh the loudest. Clark decided that the county attorney won that round. "No," the judge continued seriously, "I've never heard of that one. What's it about?"

"A hellhound supposedly took a settler's squaw more than a hundred years back because they were living in sin. It had a fiery face and left no paw prints and kind of worked itself into the local lore as a punishment for sinners."

Judge John turned to look at one of the men, "You better stay out of Hagood's Mill." They laughed. "Maybe I should, too, come to think of it." Some weasel-faced attorney that Clark didn't know led the laughter on that one. The judge addressed the rest of the men, "Any you boys heard of that one?" General head shaking followed. He turned to Clark, "Well, finish your lunch and we'll go across the street and talk about it." He turned to the group at the table. "All right if we hold court a little later to let me talk with my pal here?"

"Of course, your honor," said the county attorney, edging back into the lead in apple-polishing. The rest of the group nodded or grunted their assent.

"Say," said the Judge, "did you boys ever hear the one about the hound dog, the rabbit and the old farmer?" The men shook their heads no, they hadn't. "Well, neither have I. I was hopin' you had. Sounds like it would be funny." Red-faced laughter followed that one. Clark had eaten quickly and now pushed back his plate to signal that he was through. Judge John rose and they all rose with him. "Who's buyin? Am I buyin?"

"I'll get it, Judge," weasel-face magnanimously offered.

"I'll get my own check," volunteered Clark.

"He wouldn't hear of it," said the judge.

"Of course not," said weasel-face. "Any friend of the judge's is a friend of mine." He put out his hand. "Hiram Snell," he offered.

"Nice to meet you, Mr. Snell." Clark returned. "I'd really like to pay for my own."

"Nonsense, my pleasure."

Clark shrugged and followed the judge out of the restaurant across the street to the courthouse. Several groups of people stood outside studiously not looking at each other. These were probably the people looking for justice in Judge John's court. They walked past the various groups through the large waiting room and up the marble steps to the third floor then down the hall to an unmarked green door. The judge used his key and they entered. This was not the official judge's chambers but his private office where he did most of his work. The judge sat down behind a small desk cluttered with papers, books opened to various pages and quite a few partially smoked cigars. He waved Clark to the only other chair in the room. He patted his coat. "Care for a cheroot?" he said handing one over to Clark.

"Much obliged," Clark answered taking the cigar. Both men bit off the ends and spat them on the floor. Each lit a match and held it to the end of the cigar, puffing until the end glowed red.

The judge leaned back contentedly and expelled a long stream of smoke. "Tell me about it."

"Like I said, one death. I'm pretty sure he was murdered."

"Murdered? I thought you said a wild dog killed him"

"I said he was killed by a dog. I'm pretty sure he's not wild. He's black, stands over four feet tall and has at least one master—probably two. When they found him, Bobby had some sort of phosphorous on his hands and head. I'm pretty sure that someone painted the dog to make him glow to jibe with the legend. Then there's the fact that Bobby was carried to where he was found." The judge raised one eyebrow. "No foot prints including Bobby's anywhere near where they found him. And no blood. And no paw prints."

"No paw prints either?'

Clark shook his head. "No and none up where the Wheeler boys had their scare either. Of course I can think of several ways to do that." He didn't continue and the Judge didn't ask.

The judge thought for a minute. "You said he probably had two masters?"

"Bobby was a big man. And he was dead. And he had to have been carried a long way because I couldn't find any signs of where he had been killed." He paused. "Which brings me back to another reason I came. Bruce and Billy Haney showed up back home just before all our troubles started. We heard rumors that they had been on the chain gang. Any truth to the rumors?"

The judge nodded. "Yes. Let me see, it was about a year ago or more—county fair time over in Jefferson County.

They had come down to the fair. Apparently they got into some bootleg liquor. Anyway they found their way back into town and took a local girl off in the woods. She went willingly enough at first. Well, something went wrong and she put up a bit of a ruckus and someone heard it and got the sheriff. When he got there, the boys were fighting each other. The girl was unconscious—without a scrap of clothing on. Seems she passed out then the boys started fighting over who would have a go first. Lucky for them they got arrested when they did. If they'd have raped her, her Pa would've killed 'em." He grinned, "Of course, he and his boys seem to spend about half their time fightin over the honor of their women. Anyway, the boys got a year on the chain gang. Must have served their time if they're back home."

He paused, "Which reminds me." He rifled through a pile of papers on his desk. "This might have a bearing as well. We had an escape last week that might be important." He read from the telegraph, "Alton Neddles and Johnny Goss escaped off the chain gang near Pigeon Forge." He looked up. "They were serving a life sentence for murder. Some of their friends ambushed the guards. We lost one warder, two were wounded and these men got away clean. Neddles has got kin up your way so they warned us to look out for them."

"Do you have a description?"

"Sure do." The judge handed him the telegram. "There'll be wanted posters with their likenesses here soon but this is what we have."

"These descriptions would fit about half the young men in the county."

The judge nodded. "The posters will be along soon. What does the sheriff think about all this?

"He doesn't know part of it. I planned on telling him what I saw after I spoke with you. He asked me to look into it when it was just the Wheeler boys and the hound legend. And he told me to see what I could find about Bobby's death because he's tied down with all the rowdiness."

The judge nodded. "We've got an outbreak of rowdiness right now." He raised his voice. "I think we got some spirits among us and I don't mean the hellhound." Clark smiled. The judge was getting back into character.

"I think I'll go along and report to the sheriff. Do you know where he is?"

"No, but check out at the prison farm."

Clark thanked the judge and they walked down the stairs together. As Clark left the courthouse, he heard the judge, his voice raised, asking, "Ya'll lookin' for justice? Well, here I am." Clark chuckled and headed across the street for his horse.

The prison farm was located about three miles out of town and to get there, you just followed the road in a southwesterly direction toward Chattanooga. The road paralleled the railroad track for most of the way. As he rode, Clark heard the steam whistle of the 4:00 o'clock train as it headed into the tunnel way down the valley. Clark had always lived near a railroad track until he moved to the mountains and he missed the sounds of the train. He especially liked to hear them late at night. As a child he used to lie awake as long as he could, listening for the sounds of the trains and making plans for all the places he would travel to when he was older.

He had seen a lot of the world in a few short years and spent a lot of time on trains. Enough to take most of the wanderlust out of him, but not all. He was quite content with his life now, he decided as he rode along.

When he neared the prison farm, he heard the sounds of work. Sounds of hammers on rocks clanged as one group of prisoners made big rocks into little ones. Other men worked in one of the fields gathering the rustling corn stalks together. Cattle were being herded into another pasture for the night. Here and there, men armed with shotguns kept an eye on the prisoners. For the most part, though, the men at the county farm weren't all that dangerous. They were serving short sentences for public drunkenness or brawling and so weren't likely to rabbit off. There's not much point in running from a thirty-day sentence, most figured.

Clark called to one of the warders as he rode past, "Is the sheriff here?"

"Yessir. He's in his office down at the prison."

"Thanks," Clark tipped his hat and rode on. In another minute, he rounded the bend and came to the prison. It was a short squat, gray stone building with barred windows. Even the sheriff's office had bars. Inside it was oppressively hot in the summer and cold and damp in the winter. The men slept eight to a room in bunk beds, barracks-style. The mess hall was a separate building about fifty feet behind the prison. It was made of the same gray stone and also had barred windows.

The men worked hard to stay out of the building. Many would volunteer for overnight hard labor assignments to get to sleep out under the stars, chained together, rather than have to spend the night inside. Clark had been there many times—mostly to work on the animals and occasionally to see the sheriff. Clark hitched his horse and walked in through the "visitors" entrance.

The warden was in with the sheriff so Clark sat down in the uncomfortable wooden chair provided for visitors and waited.

About five o'clock, the door opened and the warden, Billy "Deke" Sutton, walked out. He was an ugly man, short, squat and scarred but his face broke into his contagious grin when he saw Clark. "Hey, Doc. You should've come on in. Me'n the sheriff wasn't doin nothin but joshin each other. How you been lately?"

"Fine, Deke, just fine. How about yourself?"

"Everything's about the same here, Doc. Still the county's least popular innkeeper."

Clark grinned, wished him well and went into the sheriff's office. Despite the appearance from the outside, Sheriff Mosley had a fairly pleasant office. His desk was clean, the walls were always painted and there was no dirt on the floor except for the occasional spots of tobacco juice where a visitor had missed the spittoon. Tom used the cheap labor to keep his place spotless. He was neat by nature and had served under a strict disciplinarian on the Chattanooga police force and he applied most of what he had learned.

Tom welcomed him with a warm greeting but there was a worried frown on his face. "Clark, I've been thinking about what you said yesterday about a murder. We haven't had a murder up there for about ten years and that was the result of a drunken brawl. You sure about it?"

"I'm even more sure now, Sheriff. I went up to where Bobby's body was found. He wasn't killed there. He was killed somewhere else and moved, probably by two men. Men who trained a dog to kill and painted up his face to match the local legend."

"How do you know he wasn't killed there? I'm not doubting, you understand, I just want to know what you saw."

"No foot prints—even Bobby's anywhere around the body. No paw prints although, according to the legend, the hound isn't supposed to make them, anyway. No blood—and there should have been with a wound like that. And the area was swept. Someone went to great lengths to not make a trail. They came from somewhere south of a little creek that runs up that way, though, I'm pretty sure. My guess is that they're holed up somewhere near Squirrel Hollow."

"That's a large area to search and there's a bunch of caves back in there, too. What are they doing back there?"

"I don't know. I have a suspicion that it might be tied into the disorderly problem you've been having lately. I think we've got some moonshining going on back in there. But it also might be tied in to a jail break."

"You know about that?"

Clark nodded. "Judge Bolingham told me about it. I saw him this afternoon before I came out here looking for you. It could be that these fellows are hiding out back in there somewhere. Or it could be the Haneys are cooking up a little something back in the hills. Or it might be nothing to do with any of them."

"It sure is a puzzle. You know when it was just those boys, I thought it might just be a prank but with all this... " he shrugged.

"Well, there's something going on back in there and I aim to find out what. And we know now that it has nothing to do with any demon hound. This is a man-made situation here." He paused. "You told me yesterday that you wanted me to keep looking into it. With a murder it's official now. I'd like to see it through but should I?"

The sheriff leaned back in his chair for a minute. Then he sat up and pulled open his top right hand drawer. He pulled out a Bible and handed it over to Clark. "Put your left hand on the Bible and raise your right hand." Clark did as he was told. "Now, repeat after me: 'I, Clark Ammons, accept this commission as a deputy sheriff for the County of Jackson in the State of Tennessee for the time specified by the duly elected Sheriff.'" Clark repeated it.

"By the powers vested in me by the State of Tennessee and the people of Jackson County, you are hereby appointed as a deputy sheriff, without pay," he added, with a grin, "until such time that you are released from that duty." He paused. "You all right with that?"

"Sure."

"Want a badge?"

Clark looked at Tom and grinned, "I don't need a badge."

"Well, like I said, I've got my hands full. We've got an official problem and now you're official." He smiled. "And don't get any ideas about running for sheriff. I plan to die in this job." He paused. "But not soon."

"It was the furthest thing from my mind."

"Okay, Deputy. Looks like we've got several problems here but it's going to come down to searching the woods. How big an area, you figure?"

"Well, my place and the Wheelers and the Round Mountain junction border the probable western end. Round Mountain Road looks like the northern border and the Chattanooga-Murphy Road looks like the southern border. The eastern border is still undefined but I'm pretty sure that the town of Eighteen Mile is it. But we've got at least a hundred fifty square miles, as the crow flies, in that area. More really because it's hilly." He paused. "I need to take a trip around the area and just talk to folks to see if they can point me in a direction...and then, I've still got to make a living."

The sheriff pulled a pocket watch out of his vest and looked at it. "Speaking of earning a living, you got to be back first thing in the morning?"

Clark shook his head. "Not really, why?"

"Well, why don't you come on up to the house and stay for supper. We can even put you up for the night. What do you say?"

Clark thought about it. A hot meal he wouldn't have to fix and clean sheets he didn't have to wash and pleasant company besides. "Sure, Sheriff. If it won't be an imposition on Mrs. Mosley?"

"Oh, Mrs. Mosley'll make you sing for your supper. She had a great time on your last visit. I'm sure she'd love to see you again."

"Well, if you're sure." The sheriff was already standing and putting on his hat. Being a man who understood subtle gestures, Clark did likewise.

The two men rode back into town along the railroad track. Occasional gusts of wind sent cinders up into their eyes. The sun had set and the night was clear with millions of stars twinkling brightly in the cool air. When they reached the center of town, they turned down the road Clark had ridden up earlier in the day. When they reached a sturdy two-story red brick house, they turned in and rode down a short path to the back of the house where there was a small stable. A man had been alerted by their hoof beats and was waiting when they led their horses into the barn. With a brief word of thanks, they handed their horses over and went inside the house.

As expected, Mrs. Mosley was glad to see Clark. She looked like a slightly smaller version of her husband in the way that people who are married a long time tend to get. She was short and stout with a round face and like her husband, her face often gleamed with a shine of perspiration. Unlike her husband, she dabbed daintily with a little white lace handkerchief. This evening her face lit up and she rushed up to him. "Oh, Mr. Ammons, I am so glad to see you. Did you bring that wonderful singing voice with you? Give us a hug."

Clark hugged her dutifully and even gave her a peck on the proffered dewy cheek. "You look like you're doing well, Mrs. Mosley. I came prepared to earn my victuals, ma'am."

"Clark, you're welcome here any time you're in town—singing or no." She paused. "But it would be fun to sing a few of the old songs after dinner."

"We'll sing all your favorites."

"Oh, good." She turned to Tom. "Let's get you men washed up. Lucy's got dinner ready and I'm anxious to get to it."

They did as they were told and returned quickly to the table. The cooler weather had heralded the start of barbecue time and the meal that evening had chopped pork as its centerpiece. Mrs. Mosley came from somewhere where they used vinegar in their sauce—South Carolina, Clark thought—and he had become partial to it. Along with the pork, Lucy, the housekeeper, had fixed baked beans, cole slaw, biscuits and iced tea, as well. For dessert, she brought out a peach pie. It wasn't quite as good as Sarah's apple pie but it was very good. When they finished dinner, Mrs. Mosley shooed them away from the table. "Lucy will get it cleaned up. Let's go into the parlor."

The Mosley parlor held only four pieces of furniture—five if you counted the bench for the piano. The other pieces were an overstuffed sofa, an overstuffed chair and a grandfather clock, which, by the way, had been made in England in the early 1700s and was a family heirloom on her mother's side. (If you ever got her started, Mrs. Mosley could trace her pedigree back through the Daughters of the American Revolution and, of course, the United Daughters of the Confederacy, but Clark tried to never get her started.)

The sheriff excused himself to go out on the porch to smoke a cigar because Mrs. Mosley did not permit the smelly things in her house. The sheriff also did not have a great interest in music—possibly because Mrs. Mosley loved it so much and possibly because he had a tin ear.

So Clark was left alone with Mrs. Mosley for the better part of an hour. She liked some of the old ballads so they sang "Barbara Allen," "Lord Thomas and Fair Elinore," "The Foggy, Foggy Dew" and "Pretty Polly." Then they sang some of the old hymns such as "The Seven Joys of Mary" and "Old Hundred."

About 9:00, the sheriff rejoined them. He pulled his pocket watch out and remarked to his wife, "I think the neighbors are trying to sleep—not that your music wouldn't lull them off to dreamland. Clark has to get back early in the morning and I'm getting a bit sleepy myself." He yawned—pointedly.

"I was just thinking the same thing. Why just a few minutes ago, I asked Lucy to get the guest room ready for Mr. Ammons. I'm sure its ready now."

"Well, in that case, I think I'll turn in," said Clark. "Good night Sheriff. Thank you for the wonderful evening of music, Mrs. Mosley."

"The pleasure was mine."

When Clark reached the top of the stairs he turned left and went to the last door on the left, which he knew to be the guest bedroom from previous trips. Lucy was just finishing turning down the bed linens. A pitcher of hot water, a bowl, soap and some towels were laid out on the nightstand next to the bed, as well.

"Good evening Lucy. Thank you for getting it ready for me. And thank you again for supper, it was delicious."

"No trouble, Mr. Ammons. You remember that breakfast is at 8:00?"

"Yes, ma'am."

"You remember that I'll bring hot water up at about 7:30?"

"Yes, ma'am."

"Need ennythin else?"

"No, ma'am."

"G'night, then," she turned and walked out of the room closing the door gently behind her. Clark washed up and then took out one of his new books. He opened it and read a few pages and then decided that he was too tired to really enjoy it so he closed it without marking his page and went to bed.

# 9

**Friday Morning**

Clark rose in luxury in a real bed in a real house. It was a feeling he had seldom known since he was a boy. He luxuriated in the feel of the sheets and the smell of breakfast cooking while he was still in bed. He looked at his pocket watch that he had left open-faced on the nightstand next to the bed. It was much later than he normally rose—a little after seven o'clock. His mind immediately snapped to what he had to do that day and to the puzzle he was now "officially" working on.

He still had the pesky need to earn a living and a list of several farms he had to visit that day to check on mending patients. After that, he planned to see Sarah to put her encyclopedic knowledge of local relations to work. Then, well maybe then, he would go home and play a little fiddle to get ready for the promised performance on Saturday evening.

He allowed himself one more stretch then he sat up and swung his legs out of bed. It wouldn't do for Lucy to find him still in bed when she was up working. He put on his clothes from yesterday—something he hated. He had spent too many days in the same clothes at one point in his life. He did have a change of drawers and stockings, which he always carried in his saddlebags. After dressing, he opened one of his books and was leafing through it when Lucy tapped quietly on the door.

He called her in and she placed the pan of warm water on the stand and reminded him that breakfast would be at 8:00. When she had gone, Clark shaved and then used the soapy water to wash up. Feeling better about himself, he went downstairs to breakfast. The sheriff was already down, as well, smoking his first cigar of the day out on the porch. Mrs. Mosley was not yet up and would apparently be having her breakfast in bed. At the thought, Clark had quick flashes of his own mother, propped up on her big satin pillows—eating her breakfast and talking to her children—all of them gathered around her on the big bed.

Clark greeted the Sheriff when he clumped in off the porch—his heavy boots scuffing across the floor.

"Well, Clark," he boomed. "Not exactly up with the chickens this morning."

"No, Tom. The comforts of your home should be enjoyed fully so I did." They sat down at the table and Lucy set several steaming plates before them. Bacon, eggs, biscuits, grits and red-eye gravy were the fare, along with coffee.

As the sheriff hefted a bite, he asked, "What are you going to do?"

"Got to go see some of my patients this morning. Then I thought I would try to find out who's related to the Neddles out our way. Judge said that they had relatives but I don't know who they might be. Any ideas?"

"Not really. That's not my part of the county. I know some of the families but not nearly enough—as my electoral record in that part of the county testifies." He paused for another forkful. "Supposing you do find some relatives, what then?"

"Well, for starters, I can ask around a little. Most of those folks pay attention to the comings and goings of their neighbors. Someone may have seen something. And it's possible that someone might give something away if I talk to them. I can use the legend of the hound to ask a few questions without really asking them. And I can do a little looking around in the woods. It's really too much ground to cover, but if I can narrow it down some, I'll know better where to look."

Mosley considered. "Clark, I value you as a friend—not to mention my slim one vote majority. If you go pokin around up there, you might stir up a hornet's nest. Don't push too hard. If you get an inkling; get word to me or Charley Pell. Don't risk yourself. I wouldn't be able to live with myself or Mrs. Mosley, if I got you killed. Remember the folks will kill to protect their family. Alton Neddles maybe a cold-blooded killer to us but he's Uncle Al to someone up there—maybe a whole bunch of someones."

"I'll be careful but you know I have to find out who's behind all this. And besides, proving that there is a human element will help me win a little battle in my community."

"Well, I've warned you." He said, shoving back his plate and standing. "A word to the wise..." He let it drop.

As Clark set off, Lucy handed him a small package wrapped in oilpaper. "What's this, Lucy?'

"Some barbecue, biscuits and peach pie. Figgered a man who cooks for hisself probly is hungry mos of the time."

"Thank you very much, Lucy. You take good care of folks." She almost smiled as she turned and went back into the house.

The morning was cold and beautiful. The sun glinted off the frosted grass and the air was crisp and clean once he got out of the wood and coal smoke in town. As he climbed the ridge he heard the sounds of the train as it pulled out of the station.

As he rode along, he considered the puzzle. He now had two coincidences to deal with—a pair of escaped prisoners and the return of the Haney brothers. Both could be responsible for raising the hound legend. The convicts would like to keep people out of the woods to keep from being found. He wasn't sure though that the Neddles even knew about the legend. He would have to find out.

The Haneys, well the Haneys might be in a "spirited" way and out to keep their activities from prying eyes as well. And there might be other reasons. I just don't like coincidences he thought. Most things have a rational cause and he would have to find this one.

It was late morning when he got to the first of his stops. Micah Sutter's horse was mending well but Micah was full of questions about Bobby Dunstan. Was it true he was killed by the hellhound? Had the Wheeler boys seen it? Did it herald the end of the world as the preacher said? Clark answered the questions without showing his irritation or much of it anyway

This is what comes from ignorance, he thought. Clark had seen plenty of ignorance. There never seemed to be a short supply of it—no matter how much people used. That was a good thought, I should write that down, he thought, and quickly forgot it.

It was the same all day long. Good people forgot about everything else to talk about the sensation of the hound. Because of everyone's desire to talk, his visits took him longer than he expected.

It was almost four o'clock when he got to the schoolhouse. The children had left some time before and Clark wondered if Sarah would be there or at her house next door. He decided to try the school first. He walked up the steps and tried the door. It opened so he went inside—still not necessarily expecting to find her. He was pleased to see the light of an oil lamp. It was still daylight outside but the mountains cast long shadows over the school and it was fairly dark inside. Sarah looked up from her desk when he entered. He was not expected so she turned with her school marm look—half expecting a student that had slipped back for a little help with their homework.

On recognition, though, the school marm went away and Clark's lady was there instead, smiling at him. "Clark, what a delightful surprise. I didn't see you on the road last night. Did you get home?"

"No, I went down to Boonesville and spent the night there."

"It's all so dreadful. All of the children were talking about poor Bobby and I couldn't keep their minds on their lessons so I just sent them home early."

Clark nodded. "It's been the same all day for me, too. Everyone is all riled up about it." He changed the subject. "I stayed for supper at the Mosley's and they invited me to stay over so that's where I was."

Sarah lightened, "I think I should be jealous of that woman, too."

Clark grinned wickedly. "She did have me seated beside her for a spell last evening. She likes music and she plays the piano and forces me to sing. It's a tough life."

"You bear up remarkably well." She paused and changed the subject back. "Did you learn anything in Boonesville?"

"I learned the true story of what happened to the Haney boys. They were involved in a drunken indiscretion with a young lady over in Jefferson County and they spent a year on the chain gang over there for their troubles. And I also found out that we might have something else to think about."

"And that is?"

"They had an escape off of the state chain gang, near Pigeon Forge. Two fellows, Alton Neddles and Johnny Goss. One of them, Neddles, is supposed to have some kin up here. Any idea who that might be?"

Sarah thought for a minute. "Let me see." She looked past him to the back of the room apparently at a map of the 45 United States and Territories but Clark knew better. Her brows were formed in concentration and he noticed a certain stillness as she systematically went through what she knew. Clark did not disturb her but amused himself by watching her. After a moment or two, she looked at him. "There might be one or two families that live out on Round Mountain Road. I seem to remember something about one of them being kin to the Neddles. The Cooper woman, I think."

"Amazing." Clark shook his head.

"Does that help?"

"A lot. At least it gives me a place to start."

"So what are you going to do now?"

"Sheriff asked me the same thing. Oh, by the way, I'm temporarily official."

"You'd better explain."

"Well, this thing is a lot bigger than a legend and now a man has been killed and that means that someone would go to jail if anyone is ever caught. I asked the sheriff if I should keep working on it so he deputized me 'for a time as specified by the Sheriff and without pay. So, like I said I'm temporarily official."

"What does it all mean?"

"Nothing, really. I'll just do what I had planned on doing and I'm supposed to report in to the sheriff if I find anything. He said that Mrs. Mosley would never forgive him if anything happened to me."

"Neither would I." She paused. "So what next?"

"I guess that I'll go out Round Mountain and start talking with folks. I might try and ride all the way around—you know—down the Chattanooga Road to Eighteen Mile—then back on Round Mountain. I'll talk to them about the Wheeler boys and the hound legend and that might allow me to find out one or two other things I'm curious about—like how widespread the hound legend is. If the Neddles family has never heard of it..." He let it tail off.

"Is there anything else I can do?"

"Like I said, keep your ears open. Now especially, news of strangers out Round Mountain way would be interesting." Clark stood and put on his hat. For some reason, they had both always felt strange about touching in the schoolhouse. While they had been talking, Sarah had finished packing up her things and they went outside together.

As he walked her home, Sarah said, "You know, Bobby Dunstan's funeral is tomorrow."

"I thought it would be. I'm not going. You know, just in case the preacher says something I'd have to be sore about."

"Maybe it is best. I've taught his children so I'm going. I'll let you know how it goes." She brightened. "When are you picking me up tomorrow evening?"

"When does it start?"

"Dinner's at six, the music starts whenever."

"I'll be here at 5:30, to help you get your food together. What are you fixing?"

"What else? Apple pies."

"You're a great lady."

"Time you noticed." Clark smiled, swung into his saddle and headed down the road.

It was almost dark when he reached his cabin. He had to light the lantern to get his chores done. After taking care of his animals, Clark went inside to take care of himself. He had eaten the lunch Lucy packed for him which was more than he often had so he wasn't very hungry. He knew, though, that he would be hungry later if he didn't eat anything. Then he would have to interrupt his music to eat.

He compromised and decided to eat something that was easy to fix. He cut off a hunk of cheese, and then cut two pieces of cornbread. He put on the pot for coffee. Next he cut each piece of cornbread in half. He put the piece of cheese between the top and bottom of the first piece. The second piece he covered with molasses. He waited until the coffee was ready and then he sat down to eat. When he put the first bite in his mouth he realized how hungry he was. He ate the cornbread and cheese quickly. For a minute he considered another piece of cornbread but decided against it. He ate the second piece of cornbread more slowly-deliberately chewing each bite and washing it down with coffee. When he was done, he was full. It was enough.

He stood up and was confronted with the pot of dirty dishes, still soaking where he had left them two days ago. With a sigh, he began washing them.

When he was finished, he thought about a pipe. It would be good but you could not play the fiddle well with a pipe so he decided against it. He hadn't touched his fiddle in almost a week. He took it down from its resting place, got out his tin of rosin and carefully rosined his bow. Then he plucked the strings and twisted the knobs, carefully tuning each string. When he was satisfied with his instrument, he played several tunes that he thought he would play the next evening. He started with the slower ones to get his fingers and his bow moving in harmony. When he was certain that he was warmed up, he played a few of the faster tunes.

When he looked at his pocket watch, it was almost ten o'clock. He had played longer than he thought. Time went by quickly whenever he was playing. It was interesting, he thought, how time and music interacted. Some of the tunes he played were hundreds of years old, he suspected. But basically unchanged. How many people had played those tunes over the years? How many had sung them? Or heard them or whistled them? He thought about a long, unbroken chain of people dating back beyond the written word—the music telling their stories and holding them together as a people. It was nice to be part of that chain.

He put up his fiddle and meticulously filled his pipe and lit it as he thought about the music. The aromatic smoke filled his cabin and mixed with the occasional draughts of wood smoke to provide a comfortable, known scent. His father's pipe, wood smoke, an oil lamp and a good book curled up in a chair in the corner on a cool evening were more great memories of his childhood.

He looked at his new books and at the bookshelf but it was too late to start a new one now. His eyes were heavy and bed beckoned. It wouldn't be as nice as the Mosleys' or others he had known over the years but it was better than a lot of places he had slept. And it was his. He washed, lay down and quickly fell asleep.

# 10

## Saturday Morning

The fall church social at the Hagood's Mill Baptist Church passed for the high mark of the social season in Hagood's Mill. (In fact, it was the only social event scheduled other than a tea party given by Mrs. Olivier that no one in town was invited to. Her friends all came from Boonesville, and further away.)

For the men of Hagood's Mill, the church social started at about 6:00 on Saturday evening and ended when they went home. For the ladies of the community, however, the church social started several days before and often ended several days after it was officially over when all the cleaning and washing was finally done.

But for the ladies, it was a good excuse to put on church clothes without having to hear the preacher. And because food and music were involved, attendance was normally higher than at church so that meant that you saw a few more folks. And if anyone had visiting relatives with them, they would tag along, as well, so you could get news from other parts of the world.

Normally, the talk would be about the harvest. This was the only time in the year when many of the folks would have cash money. If they were lucky, they sold a few sheaves of tobacco and might even have enough money to go down to the county seat and buy a few things. If it was a good year (and those came around every so often), a family might even have enough money to take a train trip to Chattanooga or even Atlanta where you could spend a lot of money very quickly on frivolous items such as a second pair of pants or a new hat.

If it was an election year, some of the county luminaries would probably drop by and pump a few paws and kiss a few babies. One year, an obscure candidate for governor even honored them with his presence. This year, however, the mood was somber. A violent death in the community put a damper on things in a way that a bad crop failed to do. But it was a harvest festival, the only time of plenty, and most folks were grimly determined to have a good time.

Saturday morning dawned cold and gray. The few men who had chores associated with the social were already doing them. The social hall had to be set up and a gang of men, led by Bobby Hagood, was already there, moving tables around and doing the heavy lifting.

As a bachelor, Clark was spared from this chore, mainly because he didn't have any woman haranguing him about helping. Sarah, however, was not spared in the same way and she was up well before dawn, putting pies in the oven.

When Clark walked outside to start his own chores, the wind came from the north and there was a damp coldness to it that smelled of winter. He did his chores quickly while the coffee water was heating—anxious to get back inside for a while at least. After eating, he put on his warmest coat and an extra pair of stockings before heading out for the day. He had a long day of riding ahead as he intended to "circle the problem."

It was not much brighter than it had been at dawn when he rode down past the Hagood mill and reached the Chattanooga Road where he turned east—toward the town of Eighteen Mile. He rode past the cutoff to the Wheelers and then past the Haneys where he cast a speculative glance down their silent lane. There were no more homes out that way for about three miles. He covered the distance in silence, save only for the sounds Traveler made as he clopped quietly down the trail. Clark stayed burrowed inside his coat as the cold wind gusted over him.

He reached the next farm a little after nine. He was not surprised to see no one out working. Smart folks found something to do inside or in the barn on a day like today, he thought. This farm belonged to the O'Kellys, Jimmy and Sallie. They farmed about twenty acres; ten of tobacco and the rest was corn. There were a few brown tobacco plants visible from the road and in the distance, Clark could see a few bundles of corn stalks. The O'Kellys weren't a part of the Hagood's Mill community. They went to church over in Eighteen Mile, if they went at all, and bought their supplies from the General Store down that way. He only knew them because once they had brought their son to him with a broken arm and he had set the bone for the boy.

Their house was a little better than some. It was two stories tall and had two chimneys, one on each side of the house. Smoke was curling over out of one of them and dropping down toward the ground before being whipped away by the wind—a predictor of snow, but not always a good one.

Clark tethered his horse and walked up on the front porch. His footsteps had alerted the folks in the house and the door opened as he reached to knock. Jimmy O'Kelly, a genial young man of about thirty, opened the door and invited him inside. His wife, Sallie, offered him a cup of coffee, which he accepted.

"How's that boy of yours doing?" Clark asked.

"Fine, just fine. His arm's as good as new. You done a good job, Doc," said Jimmy.

"Nothing to it, but you're certainly welcome." He paused. "I hate to bother you folks but we're having some strange doings up our way and I wondered if you knew anything about it."

"What kind of things, Doc?" Jimmy asked.

"Well, we had a man killed by a dog last week and a couple of our boys were chased by one, as well."

"A wild one?"

"We don't know but I don't think so. Have you folks ever heard of a local legend about a satanic hound?"

Jimmy and Sallie looked at each other. "No," said Jimmy. "Is that what this is all about? Is there something out there, Doc?"

"Nothing like that. I'm sorry to rile you folks up but we have this story and I wondered if you had heard about it?"

Jimmy looked at Sallie. Sallie shook her head, "Heavens, no, Doc. Ain't never heard of such."

"No, we ain't heard of no story or nuthin like that. But I have heard the bayin of a hound a coupla times over the past weeks. And come to think of it, we did hear what sounded like a wagon headin down the road from your direction late one night. I thought it was awful late for carters to be on the road."

"When was that?"

"Reckon it was last Saturday, maybe. What's it all mean?"

"Don't know. Maybe nothing. There's no truth in the legend—of that I'm sure but a man was killed." He paused. "And there was an escape off the state chain gang last week. Fellow by the name of Neddles is supposed to have kin up our way somewhere. You heard of them?'

The O'Kellys shook their heads in unison.

Clark nodded. "I thought so but I wanted to ask." He stood up. "Thank you for the coffee. You might want to keep your eyes open—just in case."

Jimmy walked him to the front door and went outside with him. "You don't put no store in them old wives tales, do you?'

"Nope."

Jimmy relaxed. "Neither do I, but... " he let it trail off.

"Don't worry, but keep your eyes open."

"I'll do it."

Clark found pretty much the same thing at the other scattered homesites he passed on his way to Eighteen Mile. One or two folks thought they might have heard something from someone about a hound but no one really knew. Boo was right. The legend was really local. And no one else in that direction had heard or seen anything suspicious, either. The trouble must be back up his way, Clark thought.

Another seven miles or so down the road where Round Mountain Road rejoined the Chattanooga Road, was the little town of Eighteen Mile. Clark wasn't sure what it was eighteen miles from. Eighteen Mile was a little more substantial than the Hagood's Mill community. They had a cluster of houses, a general store, two churches, a bigger school and another small cluster of houses. When he reached the center of the Eighteen Mile Community, he went to the general store of Herman Lynch. He had traded with him on occasion and had stopped there to ask directions to some of their outlying farms so the two men knew each other.

As Clark tied his horse up outside, he saw the usual crowd of men that gathered around on Saturday mornings to discuss the usual topics: the crop, the weather and politics. If they had a problem with their preacher, they would discuss religion, too. Mr. Lynch had provided a fire for the men by pitching parts of old crates into a barrel and lighting it. The men took turns standing around it, warming their hands and occasionally turning around to warm their hindquarters. As he walked up to the group, he was recognized by a few of the men and he knew several others, by face, if not by name. He gravitated to a spot next to someone he knew, Bobby Lee. He had doctored Bobby's horses on occasion. Lee hailed him as soon as he walked up. "Howdy, Doc, what brings you out our way?'

"Morning, Bobby. We're having some trouble up around Hagood's Mill and I just wondered if you folks had any thing to speak of down here."

"What kind of trouble?"

"A dog chasing some boys through the woods. Another case where a dog apparently killed a man. Anything like that here?"

"None that I know of, but let's find out." He raised his hand and his voice, "Hey, fellers, some of you know Doc Ammons from over to Hagood's Mill." Some heads nodded. "They've been havin some strangeness about dog attacks and Doc here wants to know if any of you've seen anything?"

Several of the men shook their heads. "Nothin to speak of," one of them said, "cept for the scaped prisoners that's supposed to be heading our way. One of them Neddles boys, the way I heard it. Maybe theys over your way, too."

"We've heard. In fact, they're supposed to be some Neddles living in this area. Any of you folks know about that?"

One of the men spoke, "There a whole passel of 'em living out Round Mountain Road between here and Hagood's but they mostly keep to themselves." He looked around to make sure of his audience. "Don't even come down here much."

Sarah was right, thought Clark. "Where is that, do you know?"

"Out of town about five miles heading west, back your way, there's a hollow out there. Five or six houses of 'em but they're not very friendly. I'd steer clear of that bunch if I was you."

"Thanks for the advice," said Clark.

Herman Lynch had come out on the porch while the men were talking to find out what all the commotion was about. "Doc, step on in here a minute when you're through, would you?" Clark finished his discussion with the men and went inside. Herman had a potbelly stove going full blast and some men were sitting next to it, playing checkers.

Lynch said, "Clark, I heard you talkin out there about dog attacks. I ain't heard nothin bout that but I might have somthin for ya."

"Go on."

Herman said in a low voice, "A couple of strangers was in here t'other day and just about cleaned me out of sugar. Might be them convicts settin up a still back in the woods. They headed down the Chattanooga Road toward Hagood's Mill."

"Did you know them?"

"Nope. They was two of 'em, youngish—but they both had beards and was kind of scraggly lookin."

"Could one of them have been the Neddles boy?"

Herman scratched his chin. "Could've been, come to think of it, but like old John was a sayin outside there, they mostly keep to themselves up there. I doubt that I've seen Alton more'n three or four times in my life. Not that I wanted to see any more of them folks." He shook his head. "I just don't know. Anyway, I wanted you to know."

"Thanks, Herman. Mind if I buy some cheese and crackers off you?"

"Now that I can handle."

Clark bought enough for lunch and then headed down the road, this time back in the direction of Hagood's Mill on Round Mountain Road.

Clark ate the cheese and crackers as he rode, interspersing it with an occasional bite of apple or swig of water from his canteen. He stopped at several of the homes he saw along the way. No one had seen or heard anything and no one had heard of any hound legends.

After riding for about five miles, Clark started looking for a track that led off into the woods. He saw a well-used trail that led off through the trees and decided to follow it. He would have to be careful, he thought. After a few hundred yards, he came to a cluster of rundown cabins and shacks. Smoke came out of most of the houses although all of the chimneys appeared to be leaning dangerously and missing quite a few bricks. Some of them were just tin stovepipes stuck up through holes in the roof. The houses weren't much to speak of, either. Some of them were just tarpaper shacks. Obviously, the Neddles were not an affluent bunch.

A couple of poorly dressed boys were aimlessly tossing rocks at a tin can they had set up on a stump. Other than that there was no one in sight.

Clark got off of his horse to be less threatening. "Howdy, boys. My name's Ammons and I wondered if any of your folks are around."

The older boy looked at him. "Yessir." He turned to the other boy. "Go fetch Pa." The boy ducked into one of the cabins without saying a word. "He don't speak," the older boy said by way of explanation for the boy's poor manners.

Clark nodded and said nothing. In a minute, a scraggly looking man, dressed in overalls with no coat appeared on the porch—armed with a rifle.

"What can I do fer ya?" he asked.

"Name's Ammons. Clark Ammons, from over Hagood's

Mill way. We're having some troubles with dogs over our way and I was wondering if you folks were having the same kinds of troubles."

At this, the man visibly relaxed. In fact, he leaned his rifle against the porch and walked out to stand with Clark. "No, Mr. Ammons, we ain't had no problems with dogs here."

"Ever hear a tale about a legend of a hellhound?"

The man nodded. "Reckon I might have. One of my aunties told us stories and one of 'em was somethin bout a hellhound. Tryin to skeer us, I reckon. Cain't member zackly what it was all about."

"Two boys were chased by a dog and we had a man killed by one the other day," said Clark. "So it's not just a legend."

"Zat a fack? Well, tell you what, we see'm round here, we'll kill 'im fer ya. But like I say, we aint seen nothin like that round here."

"Well, I'm sorry to bother you and I appreciate your time. By the way, who am I speaking with?"

The man stuck out his hand. "Sorry bout that, I'm Ziggy. Ziggy Neddles."

"Nice to meet you," said Clark. "Thanks again for your time. I'll be on my way." He walked back to his horse and rode out of the hollow and back to the road—glad to be out of there. He had found the Neddles and they had heard about the legend. But Ziggy didn't mind talking about it. Even offered to settle it for him. He didn't seem to have any concern about it so it might stand to reason that the Neddles clan wasn't behind the hound legend. Either that or they were good at lying.

But while he had been standing there, Clark couldn't help but wonder if the convicts had been in one of the houses, guns trained on him while they talked. The Neddles man had been wary of him, sure enough. He would report that little incident to the sheriff, he thought.

He stopped in at a few more houses along the way. One or two were dark with no one seemingly at home. One of them might have been the Coopers that Sarah had mentioned but Clark wasn't sure.

All of the people had heard about Bobby Dunstan's death but none of them seemed to know anything about the hound.

The last place he stopped was at the Wilkersons. He knew the Wilkersons pretty well. They had a farm about a mile up the road from where Bobby Dunstan had taken his horse off the trail.

Over the years he had worked with several of their animals and even mended a few broken bones for humans in their house. When he got there it was mid-afternoon and they received him warmly and invited him in for coffee. They had heard of the hound legend and all of the other recent troubles. Mrs. Wilkerson looked like she really wanted to tell him something but as long as her husband was in the room, she kept pretty quiet.

After his coffee was done, he allowed himself to be escorted outside by her husband, Loyd.

"Your wife looks a little nervous, Loyd."

"She's all het up about this stuff, Doc. Don't pay her no never mind."

"Well, be careful and let me know if you folks see anything," said Clark.

"We will," Loyd said.

When Clark had ridden away, Loyd went back inside. "Why didn't you let me tell him?" she asked.

"Ain't none of our bidness," said Loyd. "I'm hungry, woman, get dinner on the table, will ya." It wasn't really a request.

# 11
**Saturday Evening**

Clark arrived back at his cabin in plenty of time. After seeing to his animals, he meticulously scrubbed, using heated water and he also shaved again. He dressed in his fiddlin' outfit which consisted of black pants and a shirt with wide sleeves that wouldn't interfere with his playing. A string tie and a black coat completed his outfit. He took down his fiddle and spent a minute tuning it. He even played a song or two—just to limber up. Then he rode down the hill.

The Hagoods were getting ready to go, as well. He could hear Bobby's wife, Abigail, fussing at some of her brood inside. Two of the Hagood children were already sitting in Bobby's wagon waiting impatiently for their parents. Clark waved and told them he would see them at the church.

In a few minutes he was at Sarah's house. She did not look like a schoolmarm when she answered his knock. She was wearing a brightly colored print dress and her hair was down but loosely tied back with a ribbon. They kissed when Clark entered but then she led him quickly to the kitchen where two racks of freshly baked pies were waiting. "You know, these people really don't need all these pies. I think one rack will do," said Clark.

Sarah scolded him with mock severity, "If I didn't know you I would think you were just plain selfish. Instead, it's much worse. You're still trying to sweet talk me about my cooking because of the fuss you made over Etta Mae's chicken."

"In fact, Madam, I had forgotten completely about her chicken. I was merely being selfish but even in my selfishness, my basic goodness shone through. I was, after all, willing to share half."

Sarah smiled. "Get moving sir. The church social waits for no man—or woman either for that matter." Sarah blew out the lamps in her kitchen and they carried the pies out the back steps and across the backyard toward the church social hall.

As they arrived, they could hear the sounds of activity. Children made lots of noise as they played in groups outside the social hall. Their noise competed with the sounds of laughter, sometimes raucous, that came from the little knots of men that had formed around the door to the social hall.

There were no signs of any women. All of the women and most of the teen-aged girls were inside the social hall putting the final touches on the evening meal. Clark accompanied Sarah inside—a large open room with rough wooden planks for flooring and open rafters above. He paused only long enough to deposit his burden of pies, politely tip his hat to a few of the ladies idle enough to notice and left.

Back outside, he scanned the various groups of men looking for the one with either the best information about local happenings or the best stories. He settled on a group that did not include the preacher. When he joined the group, amid a chorus of "How ya doin, Doc?" the subject was, as expected, the recent death of Bobby Dunstan and the hound legend. Most of the men had been to the funeral that afternoon and all agreed that it was a sad occasion, all right. Not that anyone could remember a really happy funeral.

"What all is agoin on, Doc?" asked one of the men. "First, the trouble with them Wheeler boys, then Bobby a dyin, then escaped prisoners—an I don't know what all."

"I think some of it might be connected," said Clark.

"How do you figger?"

"Well, I don't believe that the hound is a Satanic creature. I think he's a flesh and blood hound—with human masters."

"But we heard he didn't leave no tracks," one of the other men said.

"That's pretty easy to arrange. Prints can be erased." Several men nodded. "But the real proof is the fact that Bobby's body was moved."

"Moved?"

"Yep, he wasn't killed where he was found. No footprints. No blood. So he was carried to the spot where he was found. And there were marks of phosphorous or something on his hands and face where he had touched the hound. So the hound is real, someone has painted him up to match the legend and there has to be a reason why whoever it is doesn't want people in the woods."

"Whether from Satan or no, I ain't sayin, but the hound is real, all right." Mark Rampling spat a stream of tobacco juice on the ground. "One of my dogs was killed." He paused to allow everyone to stop talking and look at him. When he was certain he was the center of attention, he continued, "Went coon huntin last night. Me'n some fellers, went up to Hound's Tooth Ridge. We'd set our dogs out 'n built us a fire and was waitin for 'em to get on a trail." He spat. "Well, they was huntin and yelpin and carryin on when we heard a sound that set the hair up on the back of my neck." He paused for dramatic effect. "It was the bayin of a hound. Weren't no normal hound, though. Anyway, them dogs just shut up. Ain't never heard nothing like it. They just got total quiet." He spat. "Well, after a minute or so, we called 'em back in. They all came 'ceptin Old Blue. Some of you fellers knowed Ole Blue." Several of the men nodded. "He was a good'n—had a nose for coons. Well, after that howl didn't none of us want to stay out there but I didn't want to go without Ole Blue so we stayed a spell 'n after a few minutes, there was a rustlin in the bushes and a whimperin and Ole Blue come limpin into the clearin. Poor feller, he was bleedin fierce 'n his left ear was tore clean off." He spat again. "Well, I bundled him out on the back of my horse 'n we lit out from there. When I got him back to my place, I looked him over real good. He had been bit several times. His back leg was crushed." He turned to Clark. "We would've called for you but I didn't think he was gonna to make it. He didn't." He spat. "Died first thing in the mornin right after sunup."

"Where did it happen?"

"At the base of Hound's Tooth Ridge. We had gone down the Chattanooga-Murphy Road east—past Haneys. We made our camp a few hundred yards north of the road. You know the place. The dogs was maybe another few hundred yards—maybe as much as half a mile further in. Northeast as best as I could figger by the sounds they was makin."

Clark nodded. "That can't be more than a mile or so from where the boys saw the hound but on the other side of the mountain from where Bobby was killed." He paused.

Ray Potter broke the silence (and the mood). "Well, I lost me some livestock this week, too." Several of the men grinned. "Tell us what happened, Ray," one of them asked.

"Well, you'll remember my prize hog, Sweet Sue? The one my daughter won that Blue Ribbon for at the County Fair last fall?" Several men nodded—either in agreement or encouragement. "Well, when I seen her on Thursday, she was just as fine as she could be. Rootin around just has happy as a pig in..." He paused, remembering that he was at a church social. "Anyway, she was happy. Well this mornin when I saw her she was just plain dead. All cut up in little pieces, like."

"What happened, Ray?"

"Bacon," he answered. Laughter broke out in the gray darkness.

Abigail Hagood, Clark's neighbor, appeared at the door of the social hall. "Men, your womenfolk have the food all laid out. Come on in." The children raced to the door and the men let them in front so they could take a last puff or spit out their tobacco cuds.

Inside, the air smelled of a huge variety of cooked foods. "Thanksgiving's a mite early this year," one man said when he saw the spread. When everyone was inside, Bobby Hagood rapped a spoon against a pan. "Everyone, I'll ask Preacher Elrod to say a word." The preacher stepped behind a lectern at the far end of the hall and looked up into the dark rafters. When everyone was quiet (and with a quick glance at Clark), he began, "Heavenly Father, we thank you for the rich bounty you have set afore us. We just ask your blessin pon us. Help us to see your signs 'n to open our hearts to your messages. We just praise you in Jesus' name, Amen."

"Amen," several people said.

Clark had been looking for Sarah and he found her standing in a corner. She was in the middle of several women who fell silent as he approached. He bowed to them. They curtsied to him in return. Etta Mae's greeting was more pointed. "My chicken is in the blue bucket, Mr. Ammons."

"My first stop," he said. Sarah took his arm. "I just need to set my fiddle down and we can get some dinner. What was that all about?"

"What was what all about?"

"You know, all talking stopped when I came over."

"Oh, they were talking about you. I just didn't want to admit it," she smiled. "You think too much of yourself already." She paused, "But not quite as highly as I think of you and I was telling them so. One or two of the ladies thought that you might be trifling with me... after all these years of dalliance. I asked them why it wasn't possible that I was just trifling with you? It was good fun," she concluded.

They walked down the food line together. On tables in the middle of the room were all sorts of dishes. The meats were first: roasted chicken, fried chicken, turkey, baked ham, fried ham, roast venison, pork chops, and some fried steak. The vegetables were next: roast corn, creamed corn, green beans, green peas, greens, black-eyed peas, candied yams, fresh squash, roasted potatoes and fried potatoes and baked potatoes. Then the desserts: berry cobblers, pies—apple, peach, pecan and sweet potato and churned ice cream.

Clark and Sarah each took a little from everything—especially dishes that hadn't been tried yet. Clark made sure to get some of Etta Mae's chicken and Sarah's pie.

There were long tables on the left and right of the food tables in the middle. Clark and Sarah sat at a table with the Hagoods. The room was full of the sounds of conversation and laughter as well as the sounds of forks scraping on plates and bowls. By the time the last in line were seated, the first in line would be heading back for seconds. There were never any leftovers. No one would take a plate home with any food on it.

Over the hum of conversation, one of the Hutton men leaned over and asked, "What's really going on?" As Clark leaned forward to speak, everyone at the table stopped talking. Clark repeated his earlier explanation. By the end of the evening, he had it memorized. He gave his little speech a dozen times or more. While he was explaining the situation in terms of human events, he noticed that the preacher was doing his best to explain it in other terms. Clark was disappointed to note that some of the same people sought both of them out. I'm not swaying them with my logic, he thought. At least not enough to keep them from seeking other answers. Within forty-five minutes or so, most of the food was gone and people began to drift away from the tables. Several of the men began moving the tables away from the middle of the room. They left the benches in place along the walls of the social hall.

Several of the local men played instruments. Banjos, dulcimers and fiddles were the most popular. The most exotic was a tuba, played by Johnny Gaines. Johnny had been in the army band. When he mustered out, for some strange reason, he brought his tuba home with him.

A group of players from over Chattanooga way were the excuse for the evening. Between the four of them, they played the accordion, banjo, bells, dulcimer, fiddle, guitar, and piano. They would play five or six songs then take a break. In between, the locals would take the stage. The evening included a wide range of songs: folk music, church music, military music, and even some of the popular sheet music that was making the rounds of the big cities.

Johnny Gaines played the first break—his three song

tuba repertoire rattling the windows in the place. Clark was the second intermission of the evening. He got a lot of stomping and hand-clapping, but, of course, no dancing. Not even square dancing in this Baptist community. Sometimes, though, the folks would join in on a well-known chorus.

At about ten o'clock or so, things started to break up. The guest musicians had been invited to Boo's to spend the evening. They would ride down to the county seat and catch the train to Chattanooga in the morning.

Clark walked back into the kitchen where Sarah was putting all of her pie racks together. As Clark knew, there was no pie left. He carried her cooking articles back to her house and stayed until she had lit lanterns. He kissed her solidly and with feeling.

She pressed into him and he enjoyed the way she felt, firm but soft. It didn't make sense but that was the way she felt. As he was getting ready to leave, she handed him a sack. Inside was a complete meal, including a piece of Etta Mae's chicken and her apple pie.

Because of the lateness of the hour, he left quickly so that the stragglers could see him leaving. They had raised enough eyebrows in the community without trying. As he rode up the trail to his cabin, he saw there was still light in Bobby Hagood's house. One of the Hagood children called to him from the barn as he rode past. He had at least one witness that he had gone home at a reasonable time.

He took care of his animals and headed into his cabin where he lit a lantern and the fireplace to take the chill off. The weather had turned even colder as the day had given way to a crisp, clear evening. It would be very cold in the morning but probably no snow, it was just too cold, he decided.

He hung a pot on the iron hanger in his fireplace to let the water warm that he would use for washing. While it heated, he decided to do a little reading. He opened *The Hound of the Baskervilles* and began to read. He was startled by two sounds: the sound of his water boiling over and splashing into the fire and the baying of a hound.

The boiling water he was sure of because it continued to splash and sputter. But had he heard the hound or dreamed it? Clark couldn't be sure. He looked at the book lying open against his chest where he had been reading. Maybe I dreamed it, he thought. He laid the book down and lifted the boiling water off of the fire using his hat to hold the scalding handle. He liked hot water for washing but not that hot.

He was trying to decide whether to take a tub bath. It was Saturday night after all, or just to wash as usual when he heard it again. This time he was sure he had not been dreaming. It was distant and he couldn't be certain which direction it came from. But it was the baying of some sort of hound.

He walked outside and stood on his porch hoping to hear it again—hoping to get some idea of where it came from. He heard a rustling sound in a pine thicket close to his small barn. He walked back inside, and took his shotgun off the rack above his fireplace. Then he lit his lantern and began walking toward the thicket. He held the shotgun in his right hand, his finger on the trigger, the shotgun leaning back against his right shoulder. If something came at him, he would have to drop the lantern to aim it or else he could lay it over his left arm if he didn't have time. If he had to shoot that way, he probably wouldn't hit it but he might scare it.

The bushes rustled again. There was no mistake. Something was in there. He headed toward the thicket. His heart was beating strongly and his chest was constricted—his breathing shallow. Every sense was on the alert—his hearing, his seeing, and his sense of smell. Then he saw it, two eyes reflecting the lamplight—about chest high. He was just about ready to fire when it moved farther into the lamplight and he caught full sight of the possum. "You were almost dinner," he said aloud. But far off, somewhere in the hills, he heard the baying of a hound.

# 12
## Sunday Morning

Clark rose, took care of his animals, ate and dressed for church cheerfully. Rampling's coon dog story was another piece of the puzzle. He would have to go to Hound's Tooth Ridge and see if he could find anything. He was looking forward to a beautiful day outdoors. In this mood, he rode down the trail. He was passing the Hagood's when Bobby hailed him.

"Mornin' Bobby. Beautiful day isn't it?"

Bobby looked at him solemnly. "The day is." He paused. "Clark, did you hear anything last night?"

"Heard a hound baying off in the distance. You hear the same?"

"Sure did. And another thing, too. Just after, I heard a hoot owl outside my window." He paused.

"Which means," said Clark, "that an owl was hunting for the mice that got into your grain, Bobby. Don't let this thing get to you."

Bobby nodded. "Well, you know how kids 'n womenfolk are sometimes. My wife made me bolt the door and my boys 'n' I took turns setting up with my shotgun loaded and ready."

"I had a little adventure of my own last night. When I heard the hound I went outside and heard a rustling in the bushes. I was getting ready to shoot when a possum stuck its head out at me. Abigail would have had a fit for sure if she'd have heard me shooting up here."

"She would at that," Bobby chuckled. "All the same, Clark, this thing worries me. People are starting to talk and their imaginations are running wild. Even worse, I've seen signs that some folks are beginning to suspect their neighbors. Last night, one of the women remarked that old lady Hankins had given her children the evil eye."

"The evil eye? I haven't heard that expression in years."

"Neither have I. That's what bothers me. Something like this, if it's not quickly solved, can really cause hard feelings."

"Well, I'm doing what I can."

"I know it. Just be as quick as you can about it."

Clark waved and rode Traveler on down the hill. When he reached Sarah's house, she was dressed and opened the door promptly when he hitched his horse and walked up the stairs. "I have enough coffee for two. We still have time, don't we?" she asked brightly.

"I believe we do," he said as she led him by the hand back into the kitchen. She had baked some cinnamon bread—another of Clark's favorites and the smell of the coffee and cinnamon wafted gently throughout the house. She poured the coffee and sat down. "Did you sleep well?"

"Not really. I was reading and I guess I fell asleep. I woke up when I thought I heard the baying of a hound."

"Did you?"

"I wasn't sure. I heard a rustling outside so I got my shotgun and a lantern and went out to investigate. I nearly had dinner for us."

"What was it?"

"A possum. He was just staring at me from inside the thicket out next to my barn. So I was outside, just standing there feeling stupid and I heard it for sure then—a dog of some sort. It was distant and I'm not sure where it was but it came from somewhere southeast of me—in the general direction of Squirrel Hollow."

"Or over near Houndstooth Ridge."

"Could be. I had planned to go out there this afternoon and look around anyway. Now I'm sure I will."

"Well, you be careful."

"I will be." He took a bite of bread and washed it down with his coffee. "Bobby heard it, too. He also heard a hoot owl about the same time. Seems Abigail made a big fuss about it. They kept a lantern lit, barred their door and stood watch with a shotgun handy." He chuckled, "I was going to scold him for his behavior but then I remembered my own possum scare."

"Well, you did right to be careful. We know that there is something out there. And it's killed twice—if you count Mr. Rampling's coon dog." She cleared away the dishes.

Clark stood, "I guess that we better get going. I don't want to miss whatever the preacher will say to get my goat this morning."

"Clark, don't make a scene. He means well."

"He probably does but he's going about it the wrong way in our Book."

"Our Book?"

"Yep, the one he preaches out of and the one you and I believe."

She smiled. "Well, you just turn the other cheek, Mr. Ammons. That's in there, too."

They walked out the front door this time, through the cold morning sunshine to the front of the church. As always, people were gathered outside. Friends and neighbors catching up even though most of them had seen each other last evening. When people are isolated, they seem to lean on each other more, he thought. He had spent some time in cities and the people there just didn't do so much of this sort of thing. Several of the folks complimented Clark on his playing but they didn't tarry too long outside. It was cold and the hour was approaching.

Sarah and Clark entered and sat together—this time about halfway down. Old Miss Owens's fingers stopped so the sounds of the piano mercifully stopped, as well. The first blessing of the day, Clark thought uncivilly.

The preacher read some scripture and then launched into a sermon, which Clark ignored without dozing. It might be sacrilegious, but he had figured out a long time ago that the only thing this preacher contributed to his Biblical understanding was to point out things that Clark was sure God never intended. In this way, the preacher showed light by being exceedingly dark himself.

Instead, he spent his time thinking about what he knew. He drew a mental map of everything that had happened—from the boys episode to Rampling's coon dog and everything in between. He decided that he would need to make a real map. He liked the idea because it would help him to cut down the area he would need to search.

About the time that Miss Owens began to torture the guiltless piano for the final hymn, Clark came back from his private thoughts. He would not only go out to Hound's Tooth but he would also stop by and check on the Haneys again.

As they left the church, Sarah asked, "Get it figured out?"

"The preacher's sermon?" Clark asked disingenuously.

"You didn't pay the least bit of attention to his sermon—which was pretty awful, by the way. A series of unrelated scripture verses, taken out of context, and held together by Jeremy's logic—which is flawed, as far as I can tell."

Clark grinned as Sarah went on. "I know when you're actually listening to his sermons because you fidget and clench and unclench your hands and your jaw. You were out in the woods this morning. Did you come up with anything else?"

"One thing I am certain of is that you are much too observant," said Clark. "I did remember one thing that maybe you can help me with."

"What's that?"

"I didn't get to tell you all this last night at the social but yesterday, I rode all the way to Eighteen Mile and back, talking with folks. I pretty much confirmed that the hound legend is very local. I did have an interesting run-in with some of the Neddles, who indicated that they were vaguely aware of it, by the way. But the most interesting event involved the Wilkersons. Mrs. Wilkerson seemed to want to tell me something but she never did. I don't know if it was anything important, but it might have been."

"Her husband is a bit of a brute, I think. Maybe I can get her to talk with me."

"That would be good but don't make it obvious."

Sarah looked at him. "I am a very subtle person, Mr. Ammons. Look at how unsuspecting you have been of me."

Clark grinned. "Come to think of it, you're a lot more subtle than I am."

"Did you find out anything about the convicts? It seems to me that you need to find out whether they are behind this or whether it's some of the local folks."

"You're right. Like I said, old Ziggy Neddles recollected that he had heard the legend. If he had, the rest of them probably have, too. But he didn't try to hide their knowledge. In fact, Ziggy said he'd kill the dog for us if it came out his way. He seemed pretty unconcerned about the dog." He paused. "I'm more interested in the Haneys. In fact, I'm headed back to the Haney place as soon as I get out of my Sunday duds. I want to know where those boys were." They had arrived at Sarah's house.

"When will I see you?"

"In a day or so. I expect to be spending a lot of my time out in the woods. For a while, anyway. But I will want to know what you find out from Mrs. Wilkerson."

"I'll go there this afternoon."

"That's good. Be careful and get home early."

"You, too."

Sarah smiled and Clark kissed her affectionately, but chastely, and walked back to his horse and rode off toward his cabin to get into some more suitable clothes for prowling around the woods.

Sarah took off her hat, gloves and cloak and put them away. That outfit was for winter Sundays, only. She had a less formal cloak that she wrapped around herself for the short times outside during the week. She busied herself in the kitchen—warming up some leftovers for lunch.

Even alone, she ate off of the china her parents had given her. The plates had originally been her grandmother's and Sarah had eaten off of them many times when she was a girl. GrandPa had died when she was about five so she had only vague memories of him. She remembered him as a large man who smelled of cigars but who always hugged her and had her sit in his lap while he told her stories. Her grandmother had lived until just a few years ago. Sarah had just received her teaching certificate when she heard that her grandmother had died. She had been so happy about getting her certificate but her GrandMa's death had taken some of the happiness out of it.

Her grandmother had encouraged her all of her life. When she about ten, she had received a different kind of birthday present from her. A book. Sarah had been disappointed at first. GrandMa often sent her dolls or doll clothes and sometimes even pretty things to wear. She had laid the book aside when it came. A few weeks later, though, her GrandMa had asked her how her reading was going. With a little guilt, she admitted that she had not started it yet.

When her grandmother left, she had begun to read. It was slow going but it was wonderful, too. She had read it straight through—asking her Mother and Father about the hard words and what some things meant. Within a few days she had finished and when her grandmother asked about her reading she proudly told what she had read. Then something even more wonderful occurred, her grandmother began giving her lots of books. And Sarah had the best present she could ever hope for, she had become a reader.

As she got older, her grandmother sent different kinds of books on all kinds of subjects. On their visits, she and her grandmother would talk about them—about the things she had learned and the places that the books had taken her. Reading had expanded her notion of the world and of her role in it. It was largely because of this that she had decided to teach—to bring the gift of words to others.

The china was a reminder of that great lady. Today, as she finished her meal, she turned her thoughts to the problem. Clark thought that Mary Wilkerson might know something. She lived out Round Mountain Road near where Bobby Dunstan had been attacked. And she might know if any of the Neddles kin lived out that way, as well. What reason was there for her to visit the Wilkersons? Then she had it. One of the Wilkerson daughters, Molly, was having some trouble reading. Now she had a reason to go.

She quickly washed and put away her dishes. The she put her Sunday best back on, selected a simple book from her bookshelves and set out for the Wilkersons.

Clark had ridden up to his cabin and fixed a quick lunch for himself—a hunk of cheese, some cornbread and a cold slice of salted ham—washed down with a glass of cold milk. He didn't want to go through the steps required to light his stove. He wanted to get out to Hound's Tooth Ridge while he still had plenty of daylight left and he had a stop to make on the way. When he reached the Chattanooga Road, he tuned left and headed east.

The day was very bright but it wasn't much warmer than it had been in the morning and there was a thin line of clouds on the western horizon. When he reached the cutoff to the Haneys, he turned Traveler down the path. There was no work going on—not that he expected any. Seth and the boys had quit coming to church when Lucinda had died. But they wouldn't be working on Sunday in any case. There were no signs of outside activity at all but a billow of smoke came from the chimney so Clark knew that someone was there.

The sounds of his horse had been heard this time and Seth Haney, himself, walked out on his porch as Clark rode up.

"Beautiful day, ain't it?" he asked.

"Sure is, Seth. How are you today?'

"Fine, Doc. Will you come in and have a cup with me?"

"Be pleased to." Clark walked up the steps, shook hands with Seth and followed him into his house. The Haney house still looked like a woman lived there. Seth hadn't changed anything in the house although the things were a bit scratched and beat up. Even Clark noticed that everything could use a good dusting.

Clark sat down at a heavy oak table in the kitchen while Seth put a pot of water on. Then he joined Clark at the table. "What brings you out this way?"

"You remember that I talked with you about what happened to the Wheeler boys?"

Seth nodded. "Well, we've had two other hound instances."

"I'd heard about poor Bobby Dustan. Had his throat ripped out, they say."

"Yep. That was Tuesday evening when he was killed."

"You said they was two?"

"That's right. Friday evening Mark Rampling and some others were coon hunting out at Hound's Tooth Ridge and they had a dog mauled. Said they heard the baying of a hound, then, too. Your boys do some hunting and fishing. I wonder if you folks saw or heard anything either of those evenings? Hound's Tooth Ridge is not too far from your place, either."

Seth scratched his bearded chin. "Well, I can't speak for my boys cause they was out both of them times but I didn't hear nothing. O' course, I'm partial deaf so I might not've heard nothin anyway." He rose and poured them each a cup of coffee and sat back down. "You put any store in this hound business?"

Clark shook his head. "A demon hound, no. A dog painted up to scare people? Yes. I'm not sure why or who, though." He paused. "You say your boys were out. Any idea where they were?"

"No. Not to speak of. They was just out. They've been more gone since they came back than when they was gone. You know how young boys are. Reckon they don't know nothin cause they didn't say nothin but I'll ask em when they get back."

"They're not here now?"

"Nope. They went to visit some kin. Should be back before nightfall."

Clark drained his cup. "Appreciate your hospitality, Seth. Reckon I'll be on my way." He stood up and Seth did, too.

"Where you headed?"

"I'm going up to Hound's Tooth to see if I can find anything up there that will help me find out the 'why' and the 'who.'"

"Well, good luck, Doc." Seth had walked him to the door and remained on the porch as Clark unhitched his horse.

"Give my regards to your boys, Seth."

"I'll do it." Clark waved and headed back down the track. It sure was interesting that the boys were always out in the evenings. Clark thoughtfully turned his horse east toward Hound's Tooth Ridge.

Sarah had enjoyed her walk out Round Mountain Road. The air was cold but the sun was warm and she was warm in her clothing. Several of her neighbors had called cheerily to her. Everyone had reminded her to be home well before dark. Womenfolk needed to be indoors—especially now, they warned her. The day was so cheerful that she almost forgot the recent sinister events. In less than an hour, she had reached the Wilkersons. Two boys were outside playing at sword fighting with sticks. Both were her students and they immediately stopped their playing and ran over to her. "Hey, Miss Sarah, how are you? Come to pay a visit? Ma's inside. Come on in." They walked her to the door—opened it and shouted, "Hey, everyone, Miss Sarah's here."

Mary Wilkerson came out of the kitchen, followed by Molly and her little sisters. "Howdy, Miss Sarah," said Mary. "We was baking some cookies. Would you sit down? Would you like some tea? Boys, take Miss Sarah's things and hang 'em up on the peg, will you?"

"How are you, Mrs. Wilkerson? Girls?" Sarah kneeled and asked the two younger girls, "Are you going to come to school with your brothers and sisters?"

"Yes, ma'am, they are. And we're all fine. Loyd's out back in the barn. Not working, mind, just piddlin.'"

Sarah sat in one of the chairs while Mary disappeared into the kitchen. The children sat on the floor.

"Molly, I brought something for you." She took the book out and handed it to her. A worried frown crossed Molly's face.

"Readin's hard, Miss Sarah," she said.

"That's why I brought you this book. It's about a little girl just your age. I thought it might be more fun to read than your lessons."

"Fun?" The thought had never occurred to Molly.

"Yes, Molly. Reading can be fun. With a book you can go places and see things and learn about different people."

Mrs. Wilkerson returned to the room with two mugs of tea and a plate of cookies. The children looked expectantly at the cookies.

Sarah took one then the plate was passed around. The boys took theirs and headed back outside. Sarah continued, "Molly has been having a little trouble with her reading so I thought it might help if I gave her a fun book to read—rather than just her lesson books."

"That's mighty nice of you. Did you thank Miss Sarah?"

Molly lowered her eyes. "Thank you, Miss Sarah."

"Read the first two pages and copy the words you don't know. We'll spend a minute working on it after school tomorrow."

"Yes, ma'am."

Sarah turned to Mary. "How are you folks holding up out here with all the things going on?"

Mary nodded. "Clark was by here yesterday. It's plumb scary, I tell you. Loyd won't let none of us outside after dark. That man was killed up our way, you know."

"Yes, ma'am." Sarah paused. "I was wondering if you had seen or heard anything unusual around here."

Mary cast a quick glance at the back door. "My oldest, Loyd, Jr., said he saw a girl walking out in the woods," she said quietly.

"Where did he see her?" asked Sarah.

"She was up there," she pointed out a window. "He seen her walkin, carryin somethin. Wern't no trail or nothin. Just in the woods. Bout a mile or so east of here. Loyd didn't want me to say nothin about it but someone needs to know."

"Did Loyd, Jr. know her?"

"Thought he's seen her but he didn't know her name."

"What did she look like?"

"Accordin to the boy, she was tallern me and she had hair like mine. He said she was wearin a blue dress. But he said she didn't look like a Mama or nothin!"

"What did he mean by that?"

"She didn't have no wrinkles," said Mary and they both laughed.

"How long ago was it that he saw her?"

"Last Sunday mornin it was. Loyd, Jr. didn't want to go to church so he run off at daybreak. When we got back from church he was here. Loyd give him a hidin an he told us what he done and what he seen. Of course, since all this come up, we don't let the younguns even play in the woods no more."

Sarah nodded. "That's very wise." She paused. "Who lives out this way? I don't really know any of the folks that live past you over the hill?'

"Well, we got some Neddles down the road apiece." She paused. "I think that the Coopers live up at the next place an she was a Neddles fore she married. I think her Pa give them that place." She paused again. "I was thinkin it might've been her that Loyd, Jr. saw."

Sarah nodded at that. I was thinking the same thing, she thought. "I thought that there were some Neddles kin out this way."

Mary nodded. "The Coopers ain't like the rest of them, though. They moved out from the rest of 'em. She seems like a nice sort. She come over a time or two—to talk. But Loyd don't like me talkin to any of 'em."

"Thank you, Mary. You've been very helpful." She turned to Molly. "Please read the assignment and we'll talk about it tomorrow."

Mary walked her to the door. "Come for a visit any time." And she added quietly, "Don't let on that I told you."

Sarah nodded. "I'll be back," she said with a final glance at Molly. She put back on her hat, cloak and gloves and waved to the boys who had resumed their play and left. She was glad to have been able to get some information for Clark. She stood at the road trying to decide whether to go further out Round Mountain to talk with Mrs. Cooper, Annie May, she thought her name was, or whether to head back toward her home. It was later than she thought and the sun's rays were causing long shadows to fall across the valley. With a mental shrug, she turned and began to walk down the road.

*The man watched the young woman as she walked down the road. She was good enough he decided. Even better, she didn't seem to be paying much attention to what was going on around her. She appeared to be thinking about something. This'll be easy he thought. He stepped out from behind the tree and walked silently behind her. The setting sun cast long shadows across the road. It was already fairly dark. He knew there was no one coming behind him and he could see no one on the road ahead. He had closed to within a few feet of her before she even heard him. As she started to turn, he grabbed her under the waist with his left arm and put his right arm over her mouth and nose and carried her quickly off the road and into the bushes. She tried to scream and kicked her legs but she was out of breath and the most important thing was to breathe but she couldn't and then he set her on her feet and as she gasped in a breath, she felt his fist against her head and a light exploded inside her eyes and then everything went black. The man stuffed his bandana in her mouth and tied it behind her head. Then he bound her hands and feet as she lay sprawled on the ground. He slung her over his shoulder and headed up through the woods. He enjoyed the feel of her warm body where he held her. This is gonna be good, he thought, real damn good.*

# 13

## Sunday Afternoon

After about another fifteen minutes or so of riding, the trees thinned out and a panoramic view opened up as the mid-afternoon sun bathed the little valley in brilliant sunshine. Up ahead on the left (or north) side of the trail was Hound's Tooth Ridge, its jagged peaks roughly resembling a dog's lower jaw. Over the years, the ridge had been a favorite spot for different activities at different seasons. For years, the hills had no name but after the lumberjacks had done their work, the jagged tops of the hills became more visible and hence the name.

In the spring, a lot of young couples often snuck up there to find a little privacy. The girls called the place "Spoonin Hollow" but so many hurried marriages started there that some of the young men of the community had begun calling the place "Shotgun Ridge." Come summer time, a lot of families would head out that way because you could always find an open patch of ground to eat on and a waterfall or two for the younguns to cool off in—and drownings were rare in the shallow pools so Ma and Pa often got a few minutes to themselves.

In the fall, hunting took over as there was a pretty good population of deer and because the area was a large one, lots of people could shoot at deer and only rarely hit another hunter. And once the weather turned colder, and most of the snakes were in their holes, coon hunting took over as another favorite pastime.

Coon hunting is the male equivalent of a tea party, although none of the men involved would agree with that assessment. It's more about talking and drinking (not tea, however) than it is about hunting. What makes it a great sport is that the dogs do most of the work. Men who coon hunt put great store in their dogs and most coon dogs get better treatment than the hunter's wives; to hear the wives tell it, anyway.

For the uninitiated, a good coon hunt involves making a fire, drinking and talking, and setting your dogs out in the woods at night looking for raccoons. While you're fortifying yourself with a chillbuster or two, the dogs are running around the woods trying to get on the scent of a coon. When they get it, they take off after him, ideally running him up a tree. When the luckless coon is treed, the dogs start baying and the hunters interrupt their drinking long enough to find the tree, then one of the men will shoot it down. Hunt over. Unless they decide to repeat the process.

Clark never really understood the sport, although he went with the men every so often—the first time to see what it was all about and after that not to appear standoffish.

Clark rode on another half hour or so until he reached the path at the base of Hound's Tooth that Mark Rampling said he had taken. He left Traveler tethered and walked up the path. The sun came through the bare branches and that, combined with the effort required to get up the path, made him warm. A few minutes of walking brought him to the campsite the men had used. A circle of rocks, used many times over the years, contained a pile of ashes and a few pieces of charred wood. Rusting tin cans littered the site as well as quite a few empty bottles. Quite a few pints of corn squeezings had been consumed there over the years, he figured. Clark wondered about drinking heavily on Saturday night and listening to a temperance sermon on Sunday morning through the fog of a hangover.

He searched methodically. He began by selecting a wedge that began at the fireplace and extended out away from the road. He walked a straight line out from the fire. He was going to walk a thousand paces in a northeasterly direction then turn and walk a thousand paces easterly then complete the triangle by walking southwesterly back to the fire-ring. In that way, he thought he might stumble across some clue.

He knew he probably wouldn't find any hound prints. Footprints, maybe, but they wouldn't mean anything unless he could track them back to a source. Clark picked out a distant peak along the line he wanted to follow and then picked out a tall tree along the same line and started walking. The first few hundred paces were easy going but as he got further back into the woods, the grade rose sharply. Briars and dense thickets barred the way and the going became tough. When he finally counted a thousand paces, he was at the saddle between two humps of rock—the peak he used for a guide was directly in front of him.

Clark was pretty certain that no one would try to cross in that direction. You would go around that mess. Again, he sited another smaller peak to the east and headed for it. The grade was fairly level along that line with small dips and rises. The vegetation was also not quite as thick so he made much better time. This direction ran roughly parallel to the Chattanooga road. He had almost reached his thousand paces when he saw it. He hadn't expected it but he knew it as soon as he saw it. There was a narrow trail, snaking its way along through the woods. He forced himself not to get excited when he spotted it. It could, after all, be nothing.

He struck the trail at a right angle. The sun was shining from his back so he had decent light. The trail was fairly new. Without stepping on it, he examined it. One, no two, shod animals—mules—had walked down the path—led by a man wearing boots. Whoever it was didn't lift his left leg quite as high as he needed to so there was a slight scuffing on every step. Nothing that you would necessarily notice if you watched—but a very distinctive print—easy to recognize if you ever saw it again. He noticed something else—the mules had been heavily laden when they came down the trail and much lighter when they returned. Something was being packed out of the hills using this trail.

That explains the attack on the dog, he thought. Someone had to move something down this path and the coon hunters were too close. About a half a mile, Clark reckoned. Clark took a good look at the sky. He didn't have a lot of daylight left. Two hours at best. He decided to try to follow the trail back into the woods as far as he could.

He thought knew about where it would hit the Chattanooga Road. He would go out that way—rather than back to the campfire.

He walked slowly through the brush and small trees that lined the path. He was careful not to leave any signs of his presence. No sense in giving away the fact that the trail had been discovered. He walked about two hundred paces before he came to a creek. The trail ended there.

Clark looked up the creek to see if he could see any obvious signs of a path out of the creek bed. He didn't expect to see any. Whoever it was knew a few tricks. But there was a trail somewhere up there. With enough time, Clark could find it. He looked at the sun and several peaks to fix his position and the general direction of the trail. With a little luck, he could now drastically limit the area of his search. He retraced his steps and then walked parallel to the trail in a southeasterly direction.

About two hundred paces shy of the Chattanooga Road, Clark saw where the footprints went back into the creek. Smart, Clark thought. The creek cut across the Chattanooga Road at this spot. Clark suspected that he would see wagon tracks on the road pulled off to the side of the creek. The mules could be unloaded there with no evidence of a trail leading off the main road. And wagon tracks at the stream would arouse no suspicion. Any number of folks would let their animals water there. Whoever it was knew a few tricks all right—quite a few tricks. He reached the spot where the stream cut the Chattanooga Road. Sure enough, there were the wagon tracks.

Congratulating himself on a good bit of reasoning, Clark turned west down the road. He wanted to get Traveler, get home and try to put together what he now knew. He hurried because the sun was definitely getting low on the horizon.

About the time that Clark was making his discovery, the Haney boys returned from their visit. They had spent the afternoon visiting some relatives over in Eighteen Mile.

Seth greeted them bluntly on their return. "Clark Ammons was by here today asking after you two."

"Really? How's he doin?" asked Billy.

"He's fine, I reckon. He was telling me about some more hound doings. And askin me where you boys were a few nights last week."

"Why's that?" asked Bruce.

"Don't rightly know. I guess it just seems strange to him that you boys are out whenever anything happens around here."

"We didn't do nothin," said Bruce.

"All the same, you'd best mind your Ps and Qs. If Doc thinks you're up to something, he can get you into a heap o trouble. He's great friends with the sheriff, you know."

"We know it," said Billy. "But we ain't done nothin."

"All the same, I don't like it. We'll have to see what we can do. You boys might want to think about goin off again. I'll have to study on it." He walked into the barn. "I think I'm goin to go up back for a while."

"But we ain't done nothin," they yelled at his back. With a look at each other, the boys quietly remounted their horses and rode off.

Clark walked briskly down the Chattanooga Road until he reached his horse then rode at an even brisker pace down the road. Traveler was in a mood to stretch his legs and Clark let him go fast. They went thudding down the road, past the Wheelers, all the way to the track that led up to his cabin. When he reached the cutoff, he reined up and they slowly climbed the road past Bobby Hagood's. No lamps were lit so the Hagood family had gone back to church. Clark regretted not getting home in time to go to church himself but he had found out a lot.

He led Traveler into the barn and brushed him down and covered him with a blanket. He fed the rest of his animals and made sure that all was as it should be. He went inside, lit a lamp in the kitchen and his stove. He also lit the fireplace. It would be cold tonight. He was very hungry. And very tired. He had had a long day. He opened a can of beans and emptied them into a pot. He cut off some bacon and laid it in the frying pan. He cut up a couple of apples. He would fry them after draining off the bacon grease. He dipped out a half pot of cold water, scooped out some coffee and dropped it in the pot and set it on the stove as well. The beans wouldn't take much effort—just a stir now and then. The coffee would fix itself.

Clark liked his bacon browned and this would require some attention. He used a fork to turn it over and lay it out flat in the skillet—then watched until it browned just enough. The beans were heating up and the coffee water was close to boiling when he took the bacon out of the skillet and laid it on his plate. He poured out the bacon grease into an old tin can and then put the cut apples into the pan, coating them with sugar and cinnamon. The apples browned up and the sugar burned in spots on the hot skillet. The smells of the bacon, beans, coffee and apples were so good. He was tempted to eat a bite of something but he knew that he would wait. He wanted to eat everything together.

He finished cooking and spooned everything out onto his plate. He poured his coffee and took a sip. He was hungry and impatient. He couldn't make his map until after he ate.

After eating, he poured the last bit of coffee into his cup—being careful not to pour in too many grounds. He took out a piece of paper and filled his gold fountain pen. His fiddle, his books and his gold pen were the only luxuries he allowed himself. He sketched a map of the area—orienting north. Then he began marking the map. He put an X next to the ridge track that ran behind the Haney's and labeled it with the date of the boys' scare. He did the same thing with the attack on Bobby Dunstan and the spot where Rampling's dog was attacked. To be fair, he also put an X out on Round Mountain Road in the general vicinity of where the Neddles lived and marked the date the escaped prisoners might have reached this part of the world. He also labeled the trail he had found.

Finally, he drew lines along the general direction the trail had taken. He had done a decent job of narrowing the area of his search. But it was still a big area. He picked the map up off of his table, walked over to his chair, sat down and laid the map in his lap. He looked at the points he had identified.

With the exception of the attack on Bobby Dunstan and the Neddles place, they were all very close to the Haney farm. He thought about putting another X on the Haney farm and labeling it "Haney boys return," but he was still not sure that they were involved. He needed to spend some time out on Round Mountain Road. And some time seeing to his real work, which was taking care of animals, he reminded himself.

He stood up and walked to the window. It was completely dark outside. He thought about the things he needed to do in the morning. As always, several neighbors had asked him at church to come look at an animal. He had promised them he would. He mentally mapped out the visits he had to make—starting with the one furthest away and working his way back home.

He was thinking about this, not really paying attention, when he noticed that Traveler was making a strange noise. Several other animals were making sounds as well. Maybe there was some wild animal out there, like a deer or another possum. Then, things got very quiet. There was a stillness in the air that stirred a memory. It was almost like the feeling he got before battle when he sat there gripping his rifle with sweaty hands, his mouth dry and no amount of sips from the canteen would help that dryness. He cast a casual glance at the window. Then he dove forward straight to the floor. I'll feel stupid, he thought, if...He never finished the thought because his window shattered over his head spraying him with broken pieces of glass and the bang of a shotgun and the noise of the pellets spraying his room joined to make a huge racket.

Like all the times before, once the shooting started, training took over. As soon as he hit the floor, Clark was crawling on his hands and knees toward his rifle leaning against the corner. He grabbed it, chambered a round and took the box of ammo off the shelf. He stuffed a handful of cartridges into each pocket and crawled into the next room which was dark. There had not been a second shot and it was possible that whoever it was thought they had gotten him. Right now, the shooter was probably thinking—did he fall before or after I shot him? If Clark was lucky, the shooter thought he had hit him and was gone. If Clark was very lucky, the shooter would come up to the cabin and check. Either way, Clark wasn't going to expose himself and be shot at again. He crawled to the window of the darkened room, unlocked it and slowly swung it open enough to get his gun barrel through. He knew that the movement could not be detected under the darkened porch.

Clark was listening intently. He was at a distinct disadvantage. His eyes were not adjusted to the dark—and could not be because of the light in the other room. He couldn't go in there and snuff out the lamp because it would expose him to more fire. He had a good view facing the right side of his cabin. It was fairly open there and he thought he would see anyone trying to circle in that direction. He counted on his animals in the barn to his left to warn him of a continuing presence on that side. He didn't think that anyone was on the back side but he wasn't sure and it bothered him. He hadn't made a sound—he had been listening intently for several minutes. If he was dealing with untrained people, he had a trick that might work to flush them out.

He thought he knew generally where the shooter was—if he hadn't moved. He eased himself up to the window and took careful aim at a spot about thirty yards away at the base of an oak tree. He took a deep breath, closed his eyes and gently squeezed the trigger. The report filled the room and as soon as he fired, he was on his feet, leaning against the side of the window, staring out. He was rewarded by not one but two gun flashes. A big boom from the shotgun at the base of the tree and the high whine of a rifle from off to the left in a clump of bushes. Shotgun stood to fire. Rifle was probably kneeling. Several rifle shots and two more shotgun blasts thundered into his house—breaking more glass. By that time, he had already chambered a new round and was crawling quickly toward the rear door of his cabin. He was in trouble if there was someone out there, too, but he doubted it. Within fifteen seconds of firing his shot, he was outside crawling toward the barn. Once inside, he could get to the roof and get both of the shooters if they hadn't moved yet.

He reached the barn and climbed the ladder to the hayloft above. From there, he slipped out onto the roof and inched his way to a spot about three feet from the edge. He was probably about thirty feet away from Rifle—and about seventy-five feet from Shotgun. He would fire a shot at Rifle first. Shotgun would not be surprised by a rifle shot from that direction and might return fire in the direction of the house. Then Clark could pot Shotgun.

He was siting the probable spot where Rifle was and getting ready to shoot when two shot gun blasts sounded on the trail below. All was quiet, then a voice called, "Clark, you all right?" It was Bobby Hagood. Clark didn't want to answer and give away his position. "Clark, we're comin and there's more of us on the way."

At that, there was a stealthy rustling where Rifle had been and Clark was pretty sure that the shooters had gone. He called out, "Bobby. It's Clark. I'm all right."

"Thank God. What's goin on up here?"

"Meet me at the thicket and I'll tell you."

Clark carefully crawled across the roof and slipped into the barn and down the ladder. He circled cautiously to the rear of his cabin and went quickly out across a patch of open ground, then into the thicket. Two dark shadows squatted on the ground. "Bobby, is that you?" Clark whispered.

"Yeah, it's me." Bobby Hagood was there with his double-barreled shotgun.

"Cal, you come with your papa?"

"Yessir, Doc." His oldest son, Cal was there, too, a rifle clutched in his hand.

"You're both brave men," said Clark.

"What 'n the Sam Hill's goin on up here? At first, I though maybe you'd seen another possum but when I heard the other shots, I knew something else was going on. Sounded like a battle."

"It was a small one. I was standing in my cabin and something worried me. Old Traveler was making some strange noises. I dropped to the floor just as the first shot came through my window."

"Why, Clark?"

"I'm not sure. I was out looking around this afternoon. I guess someone saw me." Suddenly it occurred to him what that meant. Maybe someone had followed him home but probably whoever it was knew him—and they knew where to find him. He was pretty certain that no one had followed him home. "Cal, you should've stayed home. Both of you should've. But let me tell you, I'm grateful to both of you."

"Cal wouldn't stay. I sent Caleb down the hill to round up some more men but Calvin said he was comin no matter what." He paused. "What are you goin to do now?"

"I need to board up my cabin." He spoke to Cal. "Cal, would you take care of my animals for a few days?"

"Sure, Doc. You goin away?" He paused. "Not that I'd blame you."

"Well, I'm going, but not away. They know where to find me but I don't know who they are. I'm a sitting duck. I'm going to take some gear and camp out while I'm getting to the bottom of this. It'll be harder to keep track of me and I won't have to worry as much about being shot at."

"Cal and I'll help you board up the place. After that, you can spend the rest of the evening at our house and in the morning, Cal will get your animals and take them down to our place. You can pack up and leave then." As Clark thought about it, half a dozen or so men rode up the hill. Several were carrying torches. At their head rode young Caleb.

"Pa, Cal! Are you all right?" He jumped off his horse.

"We're fine. So's Doc. But we had a regular battle here."

"What happened?" one of the men asked.

"A couple of men came up here and shot up Doc's place," Bobby answered.

"Let's go take a look," said Clark. He led the men across the open space to his cabin where the lamp still burned. The men brought their torches and looked at his cabin. The two windows on the front were gone. Several bullet holes riddled the door and others had penetrated the walls in other places. The men looked at the damage. They went inside and looked at the rest. "Sure made a mess o' your place."

"It can be fixed," Clark walked over to a wall where a picture hung—riddled by shotgun pellets.

"Doc is gonna go out looking for the fellows that did this. He's goin to board it up."

"Let's get at it," someone said. The men went into the barn and cut some wood into pieces and covered the two broken windows. They also nailed the front door shut as well. Clark would get what he needed in the morning. Clark saddled up Traveler and they rode as a group as far as the Hagood Mill. Abigail Hagood was waiting on the porch when they came down the hill. "Thank God you're all right," she said. She hugged and kissed all three of her men. Cal took it the worst—averting his eyes and shrugging. She looked at Clark, "I'm glad you're all right, too, Mr. Ammons," she said.

"Abby, we boarded up his place so I invited him down here for tonight," said Bobby.

"Cal, you can bunk in with Caleb tonight and give your bed to Mr. Ammons."

"I wouldn't think of throwing Cal out of his bed. That young man saved my life. I'll just put my bedroll down somewhere if that's all right."

"Well, if you're sure..." she didn't sound sure. "Put it down here on the rug in front of the fire. At least you'll be warm."

"Thank you, Ma'am."

"And I'll fix a good breakfast in the morning. Do you like buckwheat cakes?"

"Yes, ma'am, I do."

"Well, that's what we'll have then. Sleep well."

Clark shook hands with the three Hagood men—thanking them again for their bravery. As he put his bedroll out on the floor and prepared for sleep, he couldn't help but wish they'd come just a minute or two later. And despite himself, he couldn't help but notice that the Hagood men had carried the same weapons as those used to shoot at him. He slept fitfully on the Hagood floor that night.

# 14

**Monday morning**

As Sam Butler approached his store that morning before daybreak, he was surprised to see a man on horseback in front of his store. Everyone in the community knew that Sam never opened until daybreak so this man must be a stranger, he thought.

Sure enough, he did not recognize the man. He called out, "What can I do for ya, Mister?"

The man swung down from his horse and approached Sam with his hand outstretched, "Name's, Bobby Evatt." They shook. "I live out Round Mountain, about seven miles or so from here. I'm sorry to trouble you, Mister... ?"

"Butler. Sam Butler."

"Mr. Butler. My niece, Laney Sue Evatt, turned up missin last night and we're out looking for her."

"What happened?"

"We don't rightly know. She was visitin her granny's and her folks expected her back by supper time but she never come home."

"Any chance she run off?"

"She didn't have no reglar beau or nuthin. So we're worried about her."

"What does she look like?"

"She's seventeen year, over five foot, with long dark hair an she's a purty thing. Ain't never hurt no one. She was wearin a blue dress. Will you put the word out down here, in case she shows up?" He quickly told Sam a few more details.

"O'course. I'll tell everyone who comes by today about it and maybe we can help you find her. Have you talked to the sheriff?"

"Went by Deputy Pell's before I come here."

"I guess you're doin everything you can. We'll look out for her."

The man nodded, then waved, remounted and headed down the Chattanooga Road, in the direction of Eighteen Mile.

What a world, thought Sam. It wasn't the only bad news he heard that morning.

Clark had his promised buckwheat cakes, courtesy of Abby Hagood, then he went up to his cabin and packed several days worth of clothes and food. He also took some tools with him. He went out to the barn and lifted down the small regulation US Army tent he would stay in. It brought back memories—not any good ones. He also took his rifle, shotgun, pistol and several boxes of shells. He would not be caught without weapons. His final act was to nail his back door shut. To any visitor, it would appear that Clark was gone—for a spell, anyway.

He loaded everything on Traveler and they headed down the hill. His first stop was at Sam Butler's store. Sam had recruited a new helper, so he was at his accustomed place behind the counter. When he saw Clark, he blurted, "Heard you had a war at your place last night."

"Sure did, Sam."

"Well, looks like you came out of it all right."

"If Bobby and Cal Hagood hadn't come up the hill, I might've been a grave fellow this morning," said Clark.

Sam chuckled, but then became solemn himself. "You know, there was some other trouble last night, too."

"What happened?"

"Seems a girl, Laney Sue Evatt, from out Round Mountain Road, disappeared last night. One of her kinfolk was in here first thing this morning, asking after her."

"Any chance she ran off with a fellow?"

"Nope. Seems she didn't have a beau. Leastways, none that her family knew about."

"What does she look like?"

"Well, her uncle said she stood about this tall," Sam indicated a little over five feet, "had long brown hair and was seventeen years. Accordin to her uncle, she was a pretty thing but he probably wouldn't have said she was ugly, even if she was."

"When did they notice she was missing?"

"She had walked down Round Mountain to visit her granny yesterday afternoon. They reckoned she'd be back by sundown at the latest. When she wasn't back by about eight o'clock, they sent someone down to her granny's. The old lady said she left about six o'clock. Should've been around then that she either took off or was taken." Sam paused. "You're lookin thoughtful. Do you think there's any connection between this and the hound business?"

"Could be. Or it might be connected to those escaped prisoners. I'm trying to keep an open mind about it. I need to get my arms around all of it. I'm pretty certain there's something going on back in the hills but there's too much area to search unless I can narrow it down some."

Sam nodded. "Folks here are gettin scared. Everyone knows about your place getting shot up. And now, there's the girl's disappearance. I've had a couple of men already say they ain't lettin no one out o' their houses—at least from sundown to sunup. Preacher Elrod didn't help any last night with his sermon. He went thunderin on for almost an hour about 'Satan among us.' He hasn't been this worked up in years. It's getting bad, Clark."

"I know. And that attitude is exactly what the folks behind all this are counting on. Getting people scared and keeping them out of the woods. Well, that's exactly where I'm going," he paused. "But I have to take care of a few sick animals first."

"Let me know what I can do to help." Clark thanked him and left the store.

Before setting off to make his first visit, Clark stepped across the road to the schoolhouse to look in on Sarah. He stepped inside just as the first few children were arriving. Sarah looked at him as he came in, then wordlessly grabbed him and pulled him into the cloakroom. She hugged him firmly (a first in the schoolhouse) and looked him over anxiously as she asked him, "Are you all right? I heard that someone was shooting at you last night."

"I'm fine. Mad but fine." She hugged him again then stepped away from him. "I have some news for you," she said.

Clark smiled at her and she went on, "I wanted to help so I visited the Wilkersons out on Round Mountain. Their daughter, Molly, is having some trouble reading so I took her a book and gave her an assignment. While I was there, I talked to Mrs. Wilkerson. You said that you thought that she wanted to tell you something. You were right. Their son, Loyd, Jr., had seen a girl carrying something in the woods last Sunday morning. He described her to his Ma as being tall with long, dark hair and that she wasn't a Mama. He knew this because she didn't have any wrinkles." She smiled at Clark. "I was running over the people it might be and one person came to me—you remember that I thought that Annie Mae Cooper was a Neddles? Well, Loyd, Jr.'s description would fit her pretty well—despite the fact that she is a Mama."

"That's an important bit of confirmation." He had a worried look of his own now. "Did you hear about that girl that disappeared up Round Mountain way?" Sara nodded. "She fits the description, too." He paused. "When did you get home last night?"

"About six o'clock. I was going to go see Annie Mae, but it was getting late..." She let it drop.

"Still, you were out there too late. It could have been you that disappeared. You've got to promise me that you won't go out there again. At least not alone."

She smiled. "I'm glad you're so concerned about me. I promise. You know I had already thought about that. I still wonder, though, whether the Evatt girl ran off or was taken off. And whether it was her that was carrying things back into the hills—or maybe, Annie Mae Cooper."

"Me, too. It gives me something else to think about and a few more points on my map." He changed subjects. "Since they know where I live, whoever they are, and I don't know who they are yet, I've decided to leave my house and camp out. It will make it easier for me to search for them and I won't have to worry about being shot."

Sarah looked concerned, "So I'm not going to see you for a while."

"Just a few days or so. Like you said, I really need to focus on finding the escaped prisoners, if they're up here at all."

"Hurry up and find out then so things can get back to normal."

"That's why I'm doing it this way. I will check back every day or so, too. If you need me for anything, you can leave a message with Sam at the general store."

"Most of the things I need from you I'd be embarrassed to put on paper—let alone leave with Sam," she smiled, "But it is nice to know how to get in touch with you." He hugged her again, smiled, and went back outside as Sarah turned her attention to her students.

By lunchtime, he had visited every place he said he would and turned his thoughts to his ginseng spot. Soon after arriving in the hills, he had learned about ginseng as a cash crop. He searched it out in the wild and also grew a small patch. But the real value was how Clark used the patch. It was his quiet spot—even more remote than where he lived.

He was careful about its location and always took a slightly different route to his patch so he never made a path. In fact, there was only one other person who knew about it and not because Clark told him, either. After about forty-five minutes of circuitous walking, Clark reached his spot. He surveyed his patch. There was really nothing to do but he dropped to his knees and began plucking out weeds and digging up tree roots and thinking—turning everything over in his mind the way you would turn over earth in the garden. Somewhere in front of him a strange bird call sounded. He looked up at the sound, but although he saw nothing he knew that he was not alone. Without turning around, he said in a low voice, "Have you come for my scalp?"

A voice sounded almost at his elbow. "No. Despite my age, I have hair enough of my own. Besides, as I have told you before, my people do not take scalps." Clark stood up and turned around. There, standing in front of him was an old Cherokee, his wispy gray hair somewhat controlled by a bright polka dot bandana knotted around his head. The bandana contrasted with the faded denim work clothes he always wore. Clark hugged the old man. "Gray Eagle, how do you do it?"

"I have tried to teach you. You must be in harmony with the sounds nature makes. It doesn't hurt to be very old and have to move very slowly either."

Clark grinned. "You are a truly old Indian."

Gray Eagle grinned back. "If the only good Indian is a dead Indian, soon I will be a very good Indian. What problem brings you here, my son? There is no real work to do."

Clark nodded. "I came here to think. A man has been killed. A young woman has disappeared. There may be escaped prisoners here in the woods. The sheriff has asked me to help him find the answers. Last night, two men came up to my cabin and took a few shots at me. At the root of it all is a legend of a hellhound that has been a part of this area for over a hundred years." He paused. "So I came here to sort it all out."

Gray Eagle nodded. "This is serious. But perhaps I can help. Last week, on Saturday, it was, I saw a young woman walking in the woods in the area of the caves. She was carrying a basket. She was a great distance away and I am not certain exactly where she was going. Perhaps it is she who disappeared."

Clark was immediately interested. "Could you see what she looked like?"

"Sadly, no. When I was young my eyes were like those of an eagle but now...Besides, all you people look alike to me." They both laughed. "I could find where she is going, if she was not the one who is now missing." They both thought about that for a minute.

"You say that she was in the area of the caves?"

"Yes. I have told you many of the legends of my people. I believe I have spoken of the wolf people." Clark nodded so Gray Eagle went on. "They are said to live in caves in this place. My people do not go there. That is why your legend interests me. It is told among my people of a brave warrior who wanted a bride—a fair young maiden that was the daughter of a powerful medicine man. The warrior did many great deeds and presented himself to the medicine man asking for his daughter. For reasons known only to the man, he refused. Perhaps his daughter was not interested and he respected her wishes. One afternoon the girl was out picking berries with the other girls and she disappeared. The brave had taken her somewhere into the hills. The medicine man called for the spirit of the wolf people and one of their kind came out of the caves to the east and killed the warrior."

"So you do not go there because of this legend?"

Gray Eagle smiled. "Also because it is steep and hard to climb. And I have no reason to go there."

Clark asked, "I wonder if our hound legend is a story of something that really happened or if they are retelling your legend—with a dose of our religion thrown in."

Gray Eagle shrugged. "Stories are told to entertain. They are remembered when they teach. My people told this story to instruct young men that they should not take women against their will. Your people may have remembered their story because of some lesson it taught."

Clark understood the wisdom there. Besides, the real point of the story, regardless of its origin, was that it was a cover for whatever was happening now.

"I need to go back out to Hound's Tooth tomorrow to see if I can find where a trail leads. Could you look for the girl?"

"Perhaps my old bones and ancient superstitions can be overcome long enough to help you."

"I would be very grateful. I am camping out until I get the people behind it. How can I find you?"

"You will be around Hound's Tooth?" Clark nodded. "I will find you."

Gray Eagle was looking up into the afternoon sky. He pointed, "There is my brother."

Clark looked out across the valley to see an eagle that glided silently overhead. He watched it soar toward him, catching an updraft. "That's a majestic bird, all right." He turned to where Gray Eagle had been standing but he was alone again. Clark chuckled to himself as he gathered his belongings and began the journey back down the path. Now he had something else to investigate. Was this the Evatt girl or the young woman that Gray Eagle saw—or were they the same person? Was someone hiding in the caves? Clark wondered.

It would be a good place to hide. There were many such caves in that part of the mountains. Clark had been in several of them. Some were very small—others were large enough to hold dozens of men. One of those caves was also said to be the pathway for Satan's Hound. There were many caves and as Gray Eagle had said, they were hard to reach and few people went there. There were too many to search. He would have to count on Gray Eagle to find the girl or the cave or both.

He walked down the mountain to where he had left Traveler. He was anxious to set up a camp before it was dark. There were a couple of possible sites. The best place was out on the Chattanooga Road, back toward Eighteen Mile. There were some streams that led to the creek that came out of the dense woods. He could lead his horse up one of the creeks and make a camp back in there. He would be close to town but hard to find and close to the area he needed to search. He rode back toward the village a little way and then turned south roughly paralleling the stream. About a mile or so back, he hit one of the small creeks and took Traveler up the creek another quarter of a mile. There was a small clearing there and Clark decided to make his camp. He tethered Traveler near the stream and unloaded his gear. He hung his food up in the fork of a tree so it would be off the ground. Then he pitched his tent and placed his bedroll inside. He washed up as best he could in the stream.

The night was cold and Clark considered building a fire, but he didn't want to advertise his presence so he decided to do without. He fed Traveler and crawled into his tent. He lit his lantern, hidden behind a blanket, and made three other Xs on his map—one for the approximate area where Loyd Wilkerson, Jr. had seen the woman, one for the area where Gray Eagle had seen the girl and one for the area where the Evatt girl had disappeared. Three more puzzle pieces, he thought drowsily. Sleep came quickly.

# 15
## Tuesday Morning

She woke up with a sense of dread. Her husband was sleeping quietly beside her and she put her hand on him for her own comfort. Every day was worse than before. Each trip through the woods filled her with a growing sense of dread. She hated the responsibility and resented her kin for putting her in this position. She was doing something wrong, she knew that. And worse, to her way of thinking, she was deceiving her husband. Lately, he had been looking at her with a silent, questioning look. He suspected something, probably the worst. This had to stop soon, it just had to.

With a sigh, she rose as quietly as she could so as not to disturb her man and began her morning chores. She hated it, she just hated it. Something had to give.

When Clark woke up it was so dark he could not see his hand in front of his face. He fumbled for a second with the lantern, lit it then pulled his pocket watch out of his pants pocket and looked at it. Five o'clock. Perfect. He could make some breakfast and be on his way. As he busied himself lighting a fire and heating water for coffee, he decided that he could do one of two things today. He could either scout the area where he found the trail out near Hound's Tooth or try and find out about the girl's disappearance. He decided that she had relatives and the law looking for her so he would go back to Hound's Tooth.

He drank his coffee while he ate a breakfast of cooked salt ham and biscuits. Then he washed his dishes and heated another pot of water for washing and shaving. Even under the worst conditions, he had to be clean. His clothes might not be, but he was. He shaved, then washed and extinguished his fire. He wanted it to be completely out by daybreak. He wanted no telltale of smoke just in case he wanted to use this campsite again.

It was still dark when he led his loaded horse away from the campsite. No one was out although the few houses he passed were showing some light. He turned east and headed down the Chattanooga Road. He wanted to be back in there at first light. When he reached the place in the road where the river cut across he followed the stream north about two hundred paces—to the spot where the prints had gone into the creek before.

He had already decided to go further up the creek—following it along as he looked for places where a person and two heavily laden mules could be brought in and out of the water. He stepped off of Traveler and made a small splash in the creek as his boots hit the cold water. While Traveler drank, Clark walked over to the creek bank. He was expecting to see what he had seen before—footprints and two sets of mule prints. Instead, he saw—nothing. The trail had been swept clean. When they didn't get me on Sunday night, they came here and cleared their tracks. Probably created another path to do their hauling. Smart, thought Clark. It was probably fruitless for him to search but he decided he would, anyway, in case they were careless.

He hopped back on Traveler and rode him up the creek until there was an easy spot to get out. He got off his horse to see if anyone else had used that spot to get out of the creek. They hadn't. Still, he thought that he was heading in generally the right direction. Then he headed toward a small meadow. He tethered Traveler in the trees just outside the clearing where he let him graze. It was highly unlikely that he would find anything now, he thought, but he needed to thoroughly scout the area.

On his previous search, he had figured that the trail probably headed towards Bald Bluff, a big, smooth mound of granite that anchored the western end of Hound's Tooth Ridge.

No trees grew on its southern exposure and it reminded him of Stone Mountain near Atlanta, only it was much smaller. He pulled his map out of his shirt pocket and oriented it with what he saw in front of him. If you followed the probable direction of the trail toward Bald Bluff far enough you would pass near Squirrel Hollow and on over to the area of the caves where Gray Eagle had spotted the young woman.

Since Clark was not on a trail, he wasn't very careful about the footprints he made but he was very careful about sound. The dead leaves and dry twigs underfoot made a lot of noise unless you were careful. Clark practiced some of the lessons he had learned from Gray Eagle. It took time to walk silently and he was no more than halfway to his objective when the position of the sun told him that he it was about midday. Sure enough, his pocket watch confirmed it.

He continued along his original direction always aiming for the eastern side of the mountain and continued looking for signs of a trail. There was no way anyone could take creek beds the whole way. The stream wound around numerous bends and was often choked with low, overhanging trees. The stream was just too hard to use all the way. There had to be a trail somewhere. Whoever it was couldn't take the time to brush it all out. Of course, Clark knew he was looking for a needle in a haystack. He'd gotten lucky that he found it at all. The only thing they had accomplished by brushing part of it out was to prove that they didn't want it seen. And something about that struck Clark as odd. What was it that he was not supposed to see, other than the trail, itself? He trudged on through pale early afternoon sunlight getting closer to the mountain but getting nowhere in his thinking.

He sat down on a fallen tree trunk and ate some dried biscuits and cheese. He had been going up all the way from the Chattanooga Road and from his vantage point, he could see all the way down to the road. All he could see that way was clear sky, brown tree trunks and the occasional pine thicket as the land rolled away under him. Due east was about the same view although he thought he spotted some smoke in the distance. There were a few homesteads out that way.

The only other activity was out to the west at a cliff face. Three or four buzzards were circling. Buzzards weren't unusual and they often found air currents near the cliffs but these birds didn't appear to be rising—just circling. Better check it out. It's probably a dead animal, but you never know, he thought.

He stood up, brushed himself off and began working his way toward the area where the birds were circling. The going was pretty tough. The area was steeper and there were large rocks and rockslides that had once been part of the hill. Every time it rains, part of the cliff comes down, he thought. He saw a high spot at the base of the cliff and headed toward it. When he reached it, he scrambled up its side using handfuls of vines and dead grass to pull himself up. When he reached the top, he stood and looked around. The buzzards were almost directly overhead, flying around in lazy circles some fifty feet or so above him and still a little to the west.

He peered intently in every direction. Then he spotted something. Off to his left, maybe a hundred feet down at the base of the hill next to the one he was on. He couldn't really see but it looked like an arm—the pale white skin visible through the gloom at the base of some pine trees.

She had walked through the woods that morning as she had every other morning recently. Her dress repeatedly snagged on briars and twigs because she knew that she could not go the easy way or ever the same way. Today, she had a sense of foreboding. She had grown up in the woods and had no fear of them. She knew the sounds and smells. But something was different today. She had a sense of being watched. It was nothing that she could put her finger on but it was there. She stopped repeatedly and looked in all directions but of course, she saw nothing. Cussing her errand in low tones to herself, she quickened her pace.

Clark scrambled down from his viewpoint—afraid that he might have some bad news to report to the Evatts. After a few more seconds of labored climbing he reached the spot. He was relieved that the figure was a man's. The arm was up at an odd angle and the legs were twisted unnaturally. The man lay face down. Clark spent a few minutes looking—trying to hold everything in his memory. After he was certain that he could remember every detail of what he had seen, he leaned down and gently rolled the body over onto its back. He was grateful that he did not recognize the man. He was fairly young, about average height, average build and a scraggly beard. The clothing was not unusual either. Just work clothes. He looked at his shoes. The man had scuffed the shoes hard fairly recently. They were not new but they had been well cared for before the present wearer got them. And they didn't exactly fit. They were too big.

He looked carefully at the left shoe to see if there was any abnormal wear—but there wasn't. The right shoe did not have a crack, either. This was not the man who led the mules. The cause of death looked obvious. The man had a smashed skull, a broken neck, and several other broken bones. The signs were like those of a man who had fallen (or been pushed) off of a cliff. Clark looked up.

The cliff face was directly above him. He could also see several broken branches the man must have hit on his way through the trees. They hadn't slowed him down much. He took another minute and carefully searched the man's pockets for anything that might identify him. There was nothing. And no labels inside any of the clothes. If there were any, they had been removed. Clark also noticed that the clothes, like the shoes, seemed to be a little too loose for him. These probably weren't his normal clothes. And someone had gone to a lot of trouble to remove the labels.

It raised a question or two—or maybe answered one. This was probably one of the escaped prisoners—Neddles, he thought, but he wasn't sure.

He looked at the cliff above him–trying to find the easiest way up. There wasn't any that he could see. He picked his way to the top the best he could, cutting his hands on the sharp rocks he had to grab to reach the top. He also barked his shins and scuffed a piece out of his boots. Whoever it was had come from another direction. Only an idiot would climb this hill this way, he thought. When he reached the top, he looked around. There was a relatively flat top to this cliff and in addition to the rocks there were enough patches of earth to read what had happened.

He looked at the approximate spot where the man went off the cliff and looked back. He began a careful search in the general direction of where he thought the man had come from. The cliff top had very few trees for about thirty yards or so. Clark crisscrossed the territory until he found what he was looking for—a footprint. Then he found another. He looked forward and backwards and found several that indicated that two men had walked together across the cliff top. Then one fell or was pushed to his death. He continued to look around—tracing the footprints back to their source—to the spot where they began. He walked back toward the tree line. When he reached it, he saw that one man had been standing. Waiting? Smoking. Cigarette ash and the ends of several cigarettes were lying on the ground.

A separate set of prints then joined him and together they took a death walk. No abnormal wear on the left shoe of the other set of prints, either, so neither of these men had led the mules.

Clark looked out across the view the waiting man would have had, in daylight, anyway. What could he see? What would he have been looking for? Clark looked out across the expanse of hill below him. He had almost the same view he had from the smaller hill below—but with one difference. From there he could just barely make out the

Chattanooga Road. Maybe the man was there looking for a signal from the road. Or maybe he was just out for a smoke? When what happened? A second man joined him. They talked. Walked. Argued? Then what happened?

Another question remained: How far could he follow the men's footprints? The footprints were easy to see. Both had come from a point generally north. He tracked them back for several hundred yards. They had made no attempts to disguise or brush them out. The footprints disappeared as they entered a rocky pass. Another dead-end, in a way, but another compass point. The area he was searching got smaller all the time.

A straight line from this point north would run slightly east of the hollow, past the caves and strike Round Mountain Road up near the Wilkerson farm.

But the casualties were mounting as well, although he suspected that this one was no great loss. If his suspicions were right, he now knew one thing. The escaped prisoners had come to the area and were staying somewhere not too far from here. Maybe in one of the caves? One of them was probably dead at the bottom of the hill. He wondered what had happened. A disagreement between the two escaped convicts? A meeting between the convicts and another group—Haneys he called them, although it might not be true.

He climbed down the cliff and picked the dead man up and slung him over his shoulder and carried him through the woods back to where he had left Traveler. After wrapping him in an old Army blanket, he lifted the dead man over Traveler's back and tied him on. His horse was skittish with this kind of burden but Clark talked to him and calmed him down. He dug into his satchel and gave him the last apple. He took Traveler by the reins and led him back through the trees to the Chattanooga Road. He had to get the man to the sheriff as soon as possible so that he could be identified.

He met several people on the Chattanooga Road. They were all curious as to who Clark had slung over his horse and what had happened to him. Clark volunteered that he had found the man dead and generally where he found him but not his suspicions about who he might be.

He went first to the general store. Sam joined a small group of other people outside when Clark rode up. "What happened Clark?" Clark jumped down off of his horse. "I don't know much. Just that I found this man dead off the Chattanooga Road at the base of Bald Bluff."

"Who is he?"

"I don't know. I don't think he's one of our people. I think he might be one of the escaped prisoners."

"Let's have a look at him," said one of the men. The ladies were leaving, taking their young children by the hand.

"Someone ought to fetch Deputy Pell," said Clark.

"I'll go after him," one of the men volunteered.

"I'll get them wanted posters," said another.

"Bring him around back and we'll lay 'im out there until we get word from the sheriff," said Sam. Clark walked Traveler around back and they took the man off of the horse and laid him out on the floor. They held the wanted posters up to his face. "Looks like Neddles," most of the men agreed.

"Hey, Clark, there's a reward for this feller. Looks like you'll be comin into some jingle." It hadn't occurred to him that there was any reward in it. He would figure out some worthy cause to give it to. He could think of a couple right off. If he wasn't able to get back to work soon, he might have to give some of it to the Clark Ammons relief fund, he thought darkly.

The men stood around talking—their errands forgotten in the new excitement. In a few minutes, a man came riding back with news that Charley Pell had just arrived home and was on his way to the store. Sure enough, within a few minutes, Deputy Pell arrived—still wearing his uniform. They brought him around back where he walked over to the body, stooped and looked carefully at him. "Looks like Neddles, all right. We'll get his measurements and compare them to the ones they took at the prison and we'll see for sure." He looked at Clark. "Where'd you find him?"

"Out east on the Chattanooga Road, at the base of Bald Bluff."

"At the base?"

Clark nodded. "As far as I could tell, this man and one other walked to the edge of the cliff and then this fellow (he pointed) either fell or was pushed off."

"How did you find him?'

"I was camping out in that area—looking for our famous hound and I saw some buzzards circling. I followed to where they were circling—expecting an animal—and found this fellow. The rigor mortis was gone so he must have been dead for several hours, but the animals hadn't really gotten to him yet—although the flies found him quick enough."

Charley nodded. "I should go out there and have a look. No sense in even trying this evening. We need to take the body down to the county seat. Will you do it in the morning? Sheriff'll want to know what you found."

"Sure."

"I'll send a fellow down to the county seat to tell the sheriff. They'll be expecting you in the morning and like I said, I'll go out there in the morning, not that you're likely to have missed anything," he added quickly.

Clark lowered his voice. "You need to take a man with you. I think it's dangerous back in there right now."

Charley nodded, keeping his own voice low. "I guess you're right. I'll get one or two fellers to come with me. Will you stay out at the place tonight? I hear you're not staying in yours."

"Not for a spell anyway." He thought about it. "I guess it'll be O.K. I want to go and see Sarah though, so I'll be a few minutes getting out there."

"We'll fix a plate for you. Come on when you get ready."

Charley rode off toward home and the men began to disperse. Sam walked up to Clark and said, "I'll put him on a block of ice overnight."

"I'll be here first thing in the morning to get him. Can I borrow a wagon to carry him?"

"O'course, I'll have it ready about sunup."

Clark thanked the man then walked Traveler across the street to Sarah's house. She was standing on the front porch waiting on him. "What happened?" she blurted. "Did he shoot at you?"

"No. There was no big gun battle. He was dead when I found him."

"Thank goodness! A group of my boys came by here a little while ago shouting something about Doc killing one of the convicts in a gunfight up at Bald Bluff." She paused. "I was going to come but I decided to wait." She paused again. "I knew you would come see me," she smiled and led him into the house and pulled him onto the sofa beside her.

"There was no question about that. Well you told me to pay attention to the convict angle and I brought one of 'em back in two days." He smiled. "Tell me to do something else." She leaned back and crossed her arms with her right hand raised to her face. She appeared to be seriously considering something, but then she smiled and said, "All right, then, kiss me."

Clark smiled, too, but he knew that he wasn't at his particular best. He was about to make some comment to that effect when Sarah took the matter completely out of his hands by pulling him almost on top of her and kissing him deeply. A few minutes later, Clark asked, "Any other suggestions?" Sarah just smiled.

A little while later, but not too much later, Clark arrived again at Deputy Pell's place. Millie Pell busied herself with putting together a heaping plate of leftovers for Clark along with some coffee. Charley joined him at the table. "What're you thinkin, Clark?"

"We know that those prisoners did come here. And I've gotten word that a woman resembling Annie Mae Cooper's description has been carrying what looks like food back into the hills—in the area of the caves. So they were probably hiding out back in there—one of them probably still is."

"I'll go out to Bald Bluff in the morning and see if there's anything else out there. What're you gonna do next?"

"After I take this body to the sheriff, I think I'll spend some time in the woods between the Cooper's place and the caves. If anyone sticks their head out there, I'll see it."

"What if nobody shows?"

"Then I'll think of something else."

Charley nodded. "I just ain't got that kind of patience."

Neither have I, thought Clark, I hope that Gray Eagle has found something. He finished his plate and took his dishes over to the washtub. He thanked Mrs. Pell for dinner and asked her if he could impose further to heat some water. "I've got a couple days of dirt caked on me and I'd like to get rid of it." She went and got him a clean washrag and a bar of soap while the water heated. He took an actual tub bath on a Wednesday night—kind of unheard of in those parts—and probably a story that would make the rounds.

# 16

**Wednesday Morning**

The next morning Clark and Charley headed out to the general store. Sam had already packed the body in some ice and covered it with a sheet for the trip to the county seat. As Clark prepared to leave, Sam motioned him off to the side. "What is it, Sam?" Clark asked in a low voice.

"I heard somethin this mornin that might interest you."

"Go on."

"Well, Seth Haney was in here fumin about his boys."

"What happened?"

"They was all het up about that missin girl. Seems someone, he didn't say who, made some wisecrack like askin 'em where they had her. Anyway, Seth said they packed up and left. Didn't want to be arrested again for somethin they didn't do."

"That is very interesting, Sam. When did they leave?"

"Reckon they must have left yesterday."

"Any idea where they went—friends? Relatives?"

"If Seth knew he wasn't sayin."

"I'm glad you told me, Sam. They're either really afraid of being falsely accused—or they've just gotten themselves a lot of freedom by disappearing." Sam nodded his agreement.

Clark took the wagon and set off down the mountain while Deputy Pell and a few more rode out to the spot at the foot of Bald Bluff. It took longer than normal for Clark to get down the hill to the county seat. He wasn't as good at handling the wagon as he was with his horse and with a wagon you went slower anyway. Several people passed him headed in the same direction including several of his neighbors. Many already had some version of what had happened—most of them wrong. In one version, the neighbor was astounded to see Clark because he had heard that he had been killed by the convict. Clark told the man wryly that rumors of his death were premature.

By the time he reached the long hill into town, news of the death had already arrived and a small group of people had gathered to see the body. Among them was Cyrus McLeod, the editor of the paper—*The Mountain Messenger*. McLeod was a short, squat man. His reddish sideburns bristled as he pushed his way through the crowd. "Mr. Ammons," said McLeod, "we'd like to get a photograph of this."

"I'd like to oblige, but I've got to see the sheriff first."

"I'm sure the sheriff wouldn't mind if we captured this historic moment, sir."

"He probably wouldn't but all the same, I think I'll report in to him first."

"Are you going to deny the people, sir?"

"For a little while, I guess I am," he paused, "Sir."

Clark jiggled the reins and the horse moved slowly up the hill, through the small knot of people who craned their necks for a look at the body. Clark suspected that quite a few of them would dash into the undertaker's for a quick look as soon as they could.

Clark wasn't expecting any packages and besides he was in a hurry to get rid of his burden so he tugged with his left hand at the top of the hill and the horse turned down the road toward the county prison leaving the train station behind. Along this road, too, several people had gathered but Clark just nodded pleasantly and kept the wagon moving on through town.

When he arrived at the prison, a more formal delegation was gathered to greet him. Sheriff Mosley was there, along with the coroner, Mendel Johnson, and, of course, the warden, Deke Sutton. "Brought us a package, did you?" asked Sheriff Mosley.

"One you won't want to keep," he said as he stepped down off the wagon and extended his hand to each of the men.

Deke gave him his ugly, charming grin, "He'll be less trouble than some of my guests."

Mendel Johnson took charge since the body was officially his. "Let's bring him inside. We'll lay him out in the barn and have a look."

Clark drove the wagon through the prison yard and into the barn. Sutton barked an order and two of the inmates went to the back of the wagon, unwrapped the dead man and carried the body over to a wooden bench. They left as quickly as they could, picking up their tools and heading back to their regular work of mucking out the stalls.

The other men stood back as the coroner carefully inspected the body. After a few minutes, he solemnly looked at them and pronounced, "Gentlemen, this man is definitely dead." All of them chuckled in appreciation of a routine that Johnson had repeated every time he did his duty. He had no medical training. His chief qualification was his uncle's ability to get votes for him. But he had spent some time with the Boonesville doctor and learned a few things so he had earned the respect of most people. "It was good that you packed him in ice. It helped preserve him."

He began by measuring the man's body and noting the measurements on a small pad that he carried with him. He was taking measurements for use in the Bertillion system that was used to do positive identifications on dead people (and some live ones that refused to give their names).

He carefully compared his notes with the description from the state prison. "This is Alton Neddles. His measurements match up as well as his physical description."

"Well, Mendel, what else do you know?"

He pointed to his head and neck. "His skull was fractured in the fall, but he definitely has a broken neck and that's probably what killed him." He rolled him over and pointed to his back. "He also had a bullet hole in his back. The bullet didn't come out so it was probably a small caliber of some sort. I'll dig around in there and see if I can find it." He looked at Clark. "It was easy to miss. As you know, he's messed up pretty bad." He paused. "My best guess is that he died within the last two days but I don't really know." He looked at the men.

Sheriff Mosley said, "Well, do your duty, Mendel. After you're through, I'll send him down to the undertaker. He'll do what he can, which probably isn't much and we'll send him on to Nashville." He turned to Clark. "Speakin of Nashville, I'll telegraph 'em about this bird. There's a hundred dollar reward for him—dead or alive. I reckon it's yours."

Clark nodded. "I've got a couple of things I want to do with it." He changed the subject. "Ran into Cyrus McLeod on my way in this morning. He wanted to photograph the body but I told him he couldn't until I saw you first." He grinned slyly at the sheriff. "I thought you might like to be in the picture."

Mosley clapped him on the back. "Right you are, boy," He turned to Deke. "Deacon, we'd put you in there, too, but it'd probably break the camera."

Deke chuckled. "Can't believe this face ain't good nuff for prosperity."

"Mendel, let me know when you find the bullet." He turned to the two men. "If this didn't put you off your feed, I thought we'd eat lunch. Had the boys cook us up a good one cause I knew you were comin." The men left the barn and walked back to the gray stone building that housed the mess hall. They walked to a table in the back and immediately one of the inmates began bringing food to the table. Fried steak smothered in gravy, fried pork chops, fried potatoes, turnip greens and black-eyed peas quickly appeared on the table. "Dig in, gentlemen."

After each had a full plate, Clark began, "I ran into Ziggy Neddles on Saturday."

"Ziggy Neddles?"

"Yep, you know I said I was going to try to ride around the boundary of the problem? Well, over in Eighteen Mile, some folks told me how to find the Neddles clan so I rode out there and talked to them."

"That was dangerous. What happened?"

"I told them that we were having some problems with a dog. Ziggy was wary, at first, but when I told him why I came, he was as nice as he could be—even told me he'd kill the dog for me if it came over his way."

"That's interesting."

"I thought so, too. The way he acted, there was no connection between them and the dog."

"Of course, he could have been covering up but it don't sound like it." Tom changed the subject. "We got to get the story out that he was dead when you found him, otherwise you'll have to watch your back from now on."

Clark nodded.

"How'd you find him?" Deke asked.

"Buzzards. I had found part of a trail near Hound's Tooth Ridge. There were some heavily-laden mules that were packing something out of that area. After the attack on my cabin on Sunday night, I decided to camp out in that area and search it more thoroughly. I was up there early yesterday and I was trying to pick up the trail. When I went back, they had brushed out their tracks, so I guess they saw me." He paused. "Anyway, I picked the direction I thought the trail must have led and I was walking a line in that direction when I came to a little hill, climbed it and from there I saw the buzzards."

"Mendel says he was shot. I wonder why?"

"My guess is that they ran into whoever is behind our original problem. I think that there's another group up there running a moonshine operation. I'm calling them Haneys, but I'm still not sure."

"That makes sense. Unless maybe Neddles had a row with his partner."

Clark looked doubtful. "Maybe. But that would leave the other fellow, Goss, alone up there—dependent on the Neddles to hide him and keep him fed. Of course, they might have had a fight over the girl, but it just doesn't make sense."

"Well, if you're right, there's still one of 'em up there."

"I think I know where he is, or was," said Clark. "Since I saw you last, I've been told about a girl taking food in the direction of the caves."

"Any chance that it's the missing Evatt girl?"

"Maybe, I'm planning to go up in there and see if I can find out where she was headed. If it was the Evatt girl and she was taking them food, I doubt if they kept her, though."

"What are you gonna do?"

"I've got the eyes of an eagle looking for her," he said mysteriously.

"Talkin about your Cherokee pal?" asked Deke.

"That's the one," answered Clark. "He saw a young woman up there, too. Said he's going to try and track her for me."

"I'd like to meet him some day," said Tom.

"He's an interesting fellow. I was working my ginseng patch a few months after I moved here when he just showed up. He said he's been living alone up there in the woods for the past thirty years. I've never seen where he lives, he just kind of shows up from time to time. He tells me stories about the history of the Cherokee and teaches me about woodcraft. It's a funny thing, though. I have no idea how to find him."

Tom changed the subject, "I haven't told Mrs. Mosley about the attack on your place. Charley sent word to me on Monday that it had happened. I told you before about what you're to do if you find one of those prisoners..."

"I heard. Don't worry about me. It's personal now, anyway. You couldn't call me off even if you tried." The men nodded again. They understood.

"If it's not the prisoners, who is behind it?" Deke asked.

Clark raised his hands. "I'm not sure. You know, I'm real curious about the Haney boys. They reappeared almost exactly when our troubles started. Now, as things have heated up, they've disappeared again. They have a history of attacking a girl, too, so..." He let it hang.

The coroner walked in and threw a slug onto the table. "Here she is, boys." Clark dug in his pocket and pulled another one out of his picket and threw it on the table, as well. "I dug this one out of my wall."

"They look the same," said the Sheriff. He turned to Mendel. "Care for some lunch?"

"Sure." He sat down and helped himself from the platter and bowls on the table.

"Clark had a good idea," said the Sheriff. "You're up for reelection this time aren't you?" Mendel was so occupied with the food that he just nodded. Mosley went on, "I think we'll invite Cyrus McLeod up here to take pictures of us with the convict. Might weasel our way into the story, as well."

"Good idea," Mendel said through a mouthful.

Tom turned to Deke. "Why don't you—"

"Send one of my boys up to the paper and invite Cyrus down here." Deke finished.

"You're a mind reader."

"Hell, I wouldn't even have to be a lip reader to get that." He called out to one of the warders that was finishing up his lunch, "Go on up to the paper and ask that McLeod fellow if he'd like to join us down here at the prison." The man nodded and left.

"Well, that'll take care of that." They settled back and had coffee while they waited on the editor.

"Now Clark, if you find that other prisoner, you come back here and get me, you understand?"

"Well, if I see him out walking, I might try to take him but if I can't get him easy, I'll come get you."

"You need to be careful. These boys are killers. We know that. That feller won't hesitate to kill again."

Clark nodded. "I've already been shot at. You can bet I'll be careful."

In a few minutes, the warder was back, followed by Cyrus McLeod. "I'm glad you're going to see reason, " he boomed, "and permit me to photograph this heinous villain."

"Me 'n Mendel are happy to oblige, Cyrus. But Clark did right bringin the body here first. After all, what if it wasn't the prisoner? You might have wasted a photograph."

"Well, where is the dead body?"

"Mendel just finished diggin a slug outta him. He's in the barn. We'll go out there and you can photograph him directly."

"That's fine. I'll want to do a story about the incident, as well."

After Mendel had finished his lunch, they went out to the barn where they spent the next hour posing for photographs. Clark was anxious to be on his way but Cyrus kept them for another hour asking questions about what happened. Clark was glad for the ability to set the record straight—at least about not being the shooter. It was mid-afternoon when he was finally able to head the wagon out of town. He went as fast as he could so that he could get back about sundown.

Sam was shutting up the store when Clark drove the wagon onto his yard. "Made it back, did you?" he asked.

"Yes sir. Thanks a lot for the loan of the horse and wagon."

"No trouble a'tall," he said. "I talked to my dear, sweet wife and we would be pleased to have you for supper, Clark. Stay over, too, if you like."

Clark considered. "I appreciate the offer, Sam and I'd love to have supper with you folks but then I really need to get back out into the woods." He didn't say that he was anxious to be where Gray Eagle could find him.

"Let me shut this place up and we'll head on over."

After supper, Clark rode east down the Chattanooga Road. It was very dark when he reached the spot he wanted to use as a camp. He decided he would risk a fire—for a little while, at least. As soon as he had put up his tent, he banked his fire and crawled inside, pulled the covers over his face and soon was asleep.

Clark was walking along the path retracing his steps from the day before. He was on the trail of the man with the cut in his boot heel. He was almost to the spot where he had found the dead man. For some reason, he smelled coffee and thought that he might be close to a campsite or something. Somewhere off to his left, Traveler made a noise in the woods. At almost the same time, a man appeared out of the shadows. At his side was a big black hound. The hound leapt at him—with great bounds he covered the distance between them. Clark reached for his gun but it wasn't there. He must have left it back at camp. He looked around for some sort of weapon—a rock—a stick. The hound was almost on him. As it prepared to spring at him, it gave a deep baying howl.

Clark sat up. It was still dark. He was in the middle of his tent. His rifle lay beside him—its cold steel feeling strangely comforting. Clark's heart was beating fast and hard in his chest. It was a nightmare. But had he really heard the hound? Was it near—maybe drawn by his scent? He listened intently but could hear nothing except the absolute stillness of the night.

# 17

## Thursday Morning

He woke well before dawn and fixed a hot breakfast, followed by a warm shave. By daylight he had extinguished his fire and packed up his camp. He searched the area but found no signs of either human or animal visitors. It was all a dream. But dreams often told you things if you would listen. He tried to remember the dream in detail but it didn't help. It was like trying to put your finger on a drop of mercury—whenever you push down, the mercury just slides away. Maybe this dream was caused by indigestion, he thought. The part about coffee was interesting but he wasn't sure what it meant.

Traveler waited patiently, tethered to a tree. Clark was not a patient waiter. He did not know if Gray Eagle would find him. He did not know if Gray Eagle had found anything. He did not know what he would do, exactly, if Gray Eagle did not show up. Maybe he would head toward the caves and see what he could find on his own. All in all, it was a frustrating situation. With a mental shrug, he walked over to Traveler and fished around in his saddlebags until he found a book then he walked over to a tree and sat down to wait.

He didn't wait long. Within a few minutes, he heard Gray Eagle's voice almost behind him. "You would think that you would save some food for an old man who has walked many miles through the woods in the dark."

Without looking up from his book, Clark handed the old man a fried egg sandwiched between two pieces of bread.

Gray Eagle took the offered food and grinned. "I had hoped to find you before you put out your fire but it took me a little longer than I thought it would. Of course, without the smell of your breakfast it would have taken even longer." He tore off a bit of the food and chewed it deliberately. Clark waited patiently while the old man ate. Clark handed over his canteen but Gray Eagle waved it away. When he had finished, he looked at Clark. "Your manners are much improved."

"I have learned that you will tell me what you know when you are ready."

"You were not here yesterday morning. Perhaps you should tell me what happened."

"On Tuesday, I went back to Hound's Tooth to see if I could find more of the trail that I first found on Sunday. The trail had been erased but while I was looking I saw some buzzards. They were circling a dead man. It was Alton Neddles, one of the escaped prisoners that I thought might be involved. I spent the evening with Deputy Pell and yesterday, I took the dead man to the county seat for identification. What about you?"

"You were curious about the girl. I spotted her on Tuesday, near the caves. I followed her for a time but lost her. My old bones would just not allow me to keep up with her as she moved through the steep rock passes that lead to the area of the caves." He looked at Clark. "This is a story that you need not remind me of."

"Only every chance I get."

"Among my people there is a saying that a lifetime of successful hunting can be ruined by one arrow in the chief's backside." He shook his head ruefully.

"Anything else?" Clark asked with a laugh.

"I returned to a spot where I knew I would be able to follow her return. When she came back down the trail, I was able to follow her back to her house. It was the Cooper woman."

"At least we know who she is. And because of that we know she was feeding the convicts."

Gray Eagle allowed himself a small smile. "We know more than that. Yesterday, I went back to the area where I lost her but this time I was concealed in a better location. Despite my ancient bones, I was able to follow her to her destination."

Clark broke into a wide grin. "So you found the other prisoner?"

"A good hunter does not give up after a single failure, my son. I watched him carefully yesterday. He came out to meet the girl. They had a conversation of some sort and the girl left apparently upset. The man came out of the cave only once after that. He did not ever go far from the cave mouth and he always carried a rifle."

"What time of day did the girl come?"

"On both days, she came in midday," he paused. "What do you want with this man? It does not appear that he is behind the hound problem you spoke of. Is he your problem? Should you leave him be?"

Clark considered for a moment. "He may know something about the other group in the woods. His friend was probably killed by them, after all. And I'm a sworn officer, now, so I can't just leave it."

"If it is about duty, then you will not leave it." Gray Eagle considered. "I cannot be part of this. This fight is not my fight. But I will help you capture him, if that is what you feel you must do."

"How long will it take us to get there? I want to try and get him out either before the girl comes or after. I don't want her to be there"

"We can be there in an hour if we move quickly."

"Have you finished your food?" Clark asked politely, but rising to his feet in anticipation.

Gray Eagle stood, as well. "And I just complimented you on your manners."

Clark led Traveler through the woods as they followed the loping gait of Gray Eagle who moved spryly for an old man. They covered several miles in a generally northerly direction, picking their way around the dense thickets. It was just about an hour later when Gray Eagle waved them to a stop. "You should leave your horse here. We are getting close to the caves."

Clark nodded. He tied Traveler to a tree and slipped a feedbag over his head. Clark looked around at his surroundings. He thought that he was about half a mile east of the first of the caves and about three miles as the crow flies from the Cooper farm out on Round Mountain.

Gray Eagle signaled that they should stay low. They both crawled to the edge of a rise and peered over. About a hundred and fifty yards ahead along a more southerly direction, they could see a cave opening.

They slid back down below the crest where the man could not see them if he came out. "That is the place," said Gray Eagle, in a low whisper. "I know this cave. The entrance is small but the cavern is large. You can build a fire in there and the smoke will rise above your head. It is a good cave—unless the bear wants it. Your friend," he gestured in the direction of the cave, "may be lucky that you found him before the bear did. Winter is approaching."

From his post, with a spyglass, Clark watched the cave closely. Within a few minutes, a man peered cautiously out of its mouth. Then he walked outside. As Gray Eagle had said, he was carrying a rifle and he never got more than thirty feet from the mouth of the cave. When an acorn fell off to his right, he swung around quickly. He was obviously very nervous. Clark handed the glass to Gray Eagle who watched a minute or two then whispered, "We'll have to be very careful."

Gray Eagle studied the area for a few more minutes then put the glass down and turned to Clark. "You see the approach off to the left?" He pointed, indicating a tree covered ridge. Clark nodded. "If you will approach in that direction, I will try to draw him away from the cave—over to the right. If you can get between him and the cave, you can capture him—perhaps without having to shoot him." Clark nodded again and began to move silently off to the left while Gray Eagle moved away to the right.

With great care, Clark moved to a spot that would provide him with a lot of cover but was only a few paces from the entrance to the cave. He was shielded by a large clump of mountain laurel. The man was only a few paces away. After another minute or two of waiting, a loud animal noise sounded off to the right. The noise repeated and the man's attention was drawn to it. Peering ahead, he moved further away from the cave lifting his rifle and cocking it. As soundlessly as he could, Clark left his concealed position and moved to a spot between the man and the cave mouth where he knelt behind a rock and waited. The animal noises had stopped and the man stood uncertainly for a minute before uncocking his rifle.

Just as the man was turning around, Clark fired a shot in the air, chambered another round and pointed his rifle at the man's chest.

The man stared wildly for a second—looking around frantically for the source of the shot. When he spotted Clark's rifle pointed squarely at him, he shouted, "I give up! Don't shoot!"

"Better put the gun down," said Clark. "The reward for you is dead or alive." The man lowered the gun gently to the ground.

Without leaving his concealed position, Clark called out, "Lay flat on the ground and put your hands behind you." The man did as he was told and Clark advanced slowly toward him—not lowering his rifle while he pulled a pistol out of his waistband and cocked it. He then leaned his rifle against a tree and advanced on the man. When he reached him, he knelt and put the barrel of the pistol against the man's head. "If you so much as sneeze, I'll shoot," he said quietly. The man said nothing but kept himself rigid while Clark used his free hand to bind the man's hands using a small coil of rope that he had carried with him. When his hands were tied, Clark stood up. It had been a very dangerous operation to get the man tied. Now that he was somewhat incapacitated, Clark felt a huge wave of relief. Anything could have happened if the man had fought him.

"Get up," he said. The man rose slowly to his feet. Pointing his pistol at the man's chest, Clark asked, "You, Johnny Goss?" The man nodded but said nothing.

"I'm going to take you to the sheriff."

Clark raised his hand and waved in the general area

where he thought Gray Eagle was. A low birdcall came in response.

"What you doin?" Goss asked.

"Just saying 'thanks' to a friend."

Before leaving the area, Clark took a quick look around but there was no sign of a dog and no sign that there ever had been one. There was also no sign of any moonshining operation. He had suspected it, but now he had proof.

He motioned to Goss, "Get moving." Within a few minutes, they reached the place where Traveler was tied. Without taking his eyes (or gun) off of Goss, Clark untied his horse and stowed the feedbag. He made Goss lie over the back of the horse where he trussed him securely before mounting Traveler himself. The three of them headed out through the woods. It was slow going through the trees and several times, branches whipped across Goss's head and face as they ploughed through heavy brush. Goss said nothing the entire time, not even when a large branch caught him squarely in the face. He's a tough bird, thought Clark.

When they reached the Chattanooga Road, the going was easier and they made better time. As he rode back into Hagood's Mill, it was early afternoon and several men gathered around him as he reached Butler's store. "What you got there, Doc?" One of the men asked.

"The other escaped prison, Johnny Goss."

"Where'd you find him?" asked another.

"At the caves." He addressed the group, "I want to take him down to the jail to see if we can get some truth out of him. Maybe we can hang a charge or two on him."

"I'd just like to hang him," one of the men said.

"If a court convicts him, he will hang. But we're not going to administer any frontier justice here." He paused. "I need a few of you men to come with me. He may have friends around here that might want him back. Any of you willing to go?'

Several of the men nodded and moved toward their horses. Another man brought up a spare horse and Goss was transferred from Traveler's back. Clark ended up with an escort of four men and the six riders set off down the hill toward the county seat at a fast pace. They would all feel safer when Goss was someone else's responsibility.

Hurrying as fast as they could, they arrived at the county jail by late afternoon. The sheriff wasn't at the prison farm but one of his men rode off to get him while one of the warders took the prisoner into a cell and chained him to a cot. The rest of the men stayed with Clark until the sheriff arrived. The sheriff gave each of them a voucher equal to one day's jury pay and sent them home with his thanks. Clark added his own thanks as the men headed back toward Hagood's Mill.

"Clark, I can see that you just ain't any good at takin advice," said Sheriff Mosely.

"What do you mean?"

"I thought that I asked you to come and get me or Charley if you found that bird."

"You did, but I had a chance to get him and I didn't want to wait. With Neddles dead, I was afraid that he might already have gone. I didn't think he would stay much longer."

The Sheriff agreed that was probably true. "Still," he added, "I wish that you hadn't taken such a risk." He changed the subject, "Well, let's get in there and see what he knows."

Clark accompanied the Sheriff into the prison and Clark said, "He admitted that he was Goss but he hasn't said much of anything else."

"We've got ways of opening 'em up in here."

The men went into the cell where Goss sat on his cot chained to the wall.

"You Johnny Goss?" The sheriff asked. The man nodded. Tom turned to Clark, "Good thing I brought a can opener." Without appearing to move from his spot, the sheriff lashed out with his fist and knocked Goss off the cot onto the floor. "When I speak to you, you answer, hear?"

The man looked at the sheriff then stood up shakily and sat back on the cot.

"Yeah."

The sheriff knocked him to the floor again. "Yes sir."

The man sat dazed on the floor.

The sheriff stood up and moved toward the man. He kicked him in the ribs. "Yes, sir," he repeated.

The man was doubled over in pain. He looked up and choked out a "yes sir" through heaving breaths.

"That's better." The sheriff looked at the man. (And Clark looked at the Sheriff. This was a side of Tom Mosely that he had never seen, or even suspected.)

The sheriff went on, "You were in prison for a killin. Your pals broke you loose and killed again. There's one of my folks dead. Your partner's dead. You got only one chance to make it through the night. You better start talkin."

The man rubbed his ribs where the sheriff had kicked him. "What you wanna know, sir?"

"I'll start with any easy one. Did you kill Neddles?"

"No, sir, I didn't. Me 'n him was pals. Alton said he'd found that we warnt the only uns out in the woods. There was others 'n he thought maybe we could take a bite out'n their chaw."

"What kind of chaw was it?"

"Some boys is makin shine, sir. Got 'em a cabin somewheres back in there. Got a still 'n they're totin it out 'n gettin good money for't."

"Where is the cabin?" Clark interrupted.

"I don't zackly know. Alton done found it. I didn't never leave the cave. Ain't my country." He paused. "He did say somethin bout a old loggin track, though."

"Any idea about who they are?" Clark followed up.

"He said they was local. He's pretty sure about that. Brothers, he said but I can't recollect their names. He might not've said. Said he didn't know 'em well."

"Did you kidnap a girl on Sunday evenin?" asked Tom.

"No, we didn't do nothin like that. We was hidin out.

Didn't want to cause no troubles here. Didn't want no one lookin fer us. We holed up in that cave 'n every day we got food. We was tryin to figger out what to do next. We figgered we'd lay out there and then when things quieted down, we'd light out and go somere's else. Like I said, we didn't want no trouble up here."

Clark nodded at the Sheriff. It made sense.

He turned to Clark. "Any sign of your hellhound?"

Clark shook his head, "No. No signs of one anywhere near the cave."

Goss spoke to Clark, "He warnt ours, Mister, but we heard him. That's one o' the reasons I didn't never go out."

"You knew Neddles was dead?"

"I knowed it. I was plannin on leavin, tonight, maybe. Maybe try and get back to my own people."

"Who brought you the food?" asked the sheriff.

Goss shook his head. "You can kill me but I ain't sayin nothin bout that."

Clark motioned the sheriff over to the side of the cell. "I know who it is. It's the Coopers. Annie Mae. She's a Neddles, by the way. The family must've gotten her to take food into him. Sarah told me that the Wilkerson boy had seen her or someone that looked like her."

"You sure?"

"Yep."

"Damn, the Coopers have been my strong supporters up there. If I arrest them, I'll lose a few more votes. Oh, well..." he trailed off philosophically. "I might have to forget you told me that." He walked back over to Goss. "All right, so what do you know about Neddles' death?"

"Not much. T'other afternoon, Monday it was, he left. Said maybe we'd be in a better place next evenin but he didn't never come back. Then I heard he was kilt." He stopped. He probably thought they were going to ask him how he knew. But since they already knew who told him, there was no point in it.

The sheriff turned to Clark, "Got any more questions for this bird?"

"None that I can think of."

The sheriff walked out of the cell with Clark. "What do you think?"

"I think he's told us what he knows except for who gave him the food and clothes."

"I agree. We'll let him stew overnight and I'll have another crack at him in the morning but there's probably not much else he can tell us. Let's go find the Deacon." They headed back to the sheriff's office and met Deke hurrying to meet them.

"Heard you brought me another guest," he said to Clark.

"That's right, Johnny Goss."

"Do tell."

"Deacon," said Mosley, "I don't expect any trouble tonight but when word gets out, his friends might try to spring him. We need to put extra guards on duty and don't let him out of his cell. And make sure the guards are good ones. I'll telegraph the state prison tonight and tell them to come get him—then he's their worry." Deke nodded.

As they walked toward their horses, Tom looked shrewdly at Clark. "Looks like you've got another reward coming. Deputy work is payin pretty well, despite the original salary."

Clark chuckled, "I plan to give most of it away but I might keep a bit."

"Good idea." Tom changed the subject. "If you don't have to get back, why don't you come back to my place for supper and stay over till the morning?"

"I'll have dinner with you, Tom, but then I'll head up to the hotel. I've imposed on your hospitality enough, lately."

"Don't feel like singin, eh? Well, come on to supper, anyway." The men left the prison and rode down to town. As they ate the supper that Lucy had warmed for them, Tom said, "It's a real relief to be rid of this problem." He looked at Clark. "But it doesn't really help us much, does it?"

"Not really, although I'm glad we got them. We've still got the same problem we had to begin with. I'm pretty sure that the men that killed Neddles are behind the rest of our problems. He tried to cut in on their operation so they killed him. It was interesting that Neddles found a cabin or something back there. That's probably where the girl is, if she's still alive."

"She might not want to be alive," said Tom. The men kept their own thoughts on that count. After dinner, Clark thanked Tom (and Lucy), left a note for Mrs. Mosley, and headed back up the street toward the hotel.

The Boonesville Finest Luxury Manor Guest House and Restaurant was probably the best place in town, which wasn't saying much. It had been the town's only such establishment until the railroad finally clawed its way into town in the 1880s. Then, its location. right across the street from the train station, added to its viability, if not its appeal. The name was enough to put Clark off it. The first time he saw it was when he stepped off the train in Boonesville when he first arrived several years ago. His intention was to take the train as far as it went then get off and ride until he had gone to as high a spot as he could go. When they got Traveler and all of his portable worldly possessions out of one of the baggage cars, Clark had looked around and sure enough, right there across the street was the Finest Luxury Manor Guest House. In Clark's travels, the grander the name, the worse the service. The BFLMGH was no exception to the rule.

The host of the establishment was a German, named Karl Schmidt. He ran the place with German precision and the accompanying Teutonic politeness. When Clark had walked in the place, Schmidt's greeting exuded a certain Old World charm, "Roomz arrre fifty cent und vater is extra," was his apparent standard greeting.

"Guten tag to you, too," Clark had returned. The man looked at him through his bushy eyebrows and said nothing else.

On his first visit, Clark had quietly slid him the four bits for the night, plus the extra for water, vowing to never spend another night there. Occasionally, he broke his vow, and he almost always regretted it.

When he entered the place on Saturday evening, he was greeted by the distaff half of the Schmidt family, Mathilde. Mathilde was Karl's equal in every way, including looks and friendliness. (The only major difference was that her beard was not quite as thick.)

"Ve only got one room und it's over the stables." She paused. "Und vater is extra."

With a private smile, so as not to give Mathilde the impression that she was worth smiling at, Clark had paid and gone out to his room.

After washing off the dirt, he pulled out his map and looked at it. He crossed out the marks that related to the girl taking food back in the woods. She was connected to the convicts but not to the rest of the trouble.

He started thinking about the dates and the coincidences. The convicts showed up. The Haneys showed up. The problems started. Something was working at the back of his consciousness. There was some other fact that might have a bearing, if he could only put his finger on it. He lay down in the comparative luxury of the bed—hoping that he didn't end up with too many fleas and continued thinking about it. People came. People went. Problems came. Problems went. He closed his eyes. What was it? Something was there if he could only see it. Maybe it would come to him. Something in his dream—something about Traveler, maybe. He fell asleep.

# 18
## Friday Morning

Breakfast at the BFLMGH was more like a riot than anything else. At 6:00 AM sharp, a series of platters would be placed on a long table in the dining room. At one end of the table was a stack of plates exactly equal to the number of hotel guests, along with the requisite number of forks, knives and cups. At the other end was Mrs. Schmidt. Her main role was to yell at the customers to keep moving and not take more than one of anything and heaven help you if you inadvertently tried to leave the room with your napkin tucked into your shirt. No one had been shot but there were some tense moments.

The trick, as Clark knew from previous visits, was to be in line early. The food at the top of the heap was generally pretty good but as you moved toward the bottom of the pile, the quality declined a mite. You might also find that if you were toward the back of the line, they would probably not have any of some of the dishes. The Schmidts knew exactly how much of a thing you needed and they weren't about to ruin your health by preparing more than was necessary. The seasoned travelers knew this, so despite arising earlier than usual, Clark was not the first in line.

With a plate of food in hand, the next trick was to find a place to sit. Someone had obviously told the Schmidts that using tables and chairs decreased their life expectancy so, as with everything else, they set out only the exact number of tables and chairs required. This created another free-for-all as the guests fought over the better seats.

By dint of some reckless walking and a carefully placed elbow, Clark was able to beat out another guest to a small wedge of bench between two traveling peddlers and across from some government nabob out of Nashville. The only good thing about breakfast was that the other breakfasters did not want to talk. The traveling men kept their faces in their newspapers and after a few weak attempts to start a conversation, the government man retreated inside his newspaper, as well.

The newspaper was, of course, *The Mountain Messenger*. Because nothing much happened in Boonesville, the paper was still full of stories about the dead prisoner. They had not gotten word of the capture of Johnny Goss and Clark hoped to get out of town before that episode made it to the beet-red ears of Cyrus McLeod. Before breakfast was through, all three of Clark's breakfast mates had cast speculative glances at him, so Clark knew that his picture had to be in the paper.

After breakfast, he went out back and saddled up Traveler. After he finished he walked around and looked at his horse. "You've been trying to tell me something. What is it?" he asked affectionately. "I know you would tell me if you could. What do you say we head back home?" At that, Traveler snorted and tossed his head. Clark rubbed his ears and swung onto his back.

His first wish of the day was granted when he cleared the little bridge at the foot of the hill and made it out of town without further contact. He would not have to answer any questions today, at least, he thought.

For the first few minutes, Clark tried not think about the events of the past few days but it was like telling yourself not think about pink elephants. The more he tried to not think about it, the more he thought about it. With an inward mental sigh, he gave himself permission to think. Maybe instead of trying to think about everything, I need to begin by eliminating the things that are not important, he thought.

All that stuff about the escaped convicts had been a diversion. The Neddles clan, the girl in the woods, the Wilkersons—all important but not really what he was concerned about. The death of Alton Neddles, though, was connected. He had stumbled onto something back in there... an old logging track...a cabin... a moonshine operation. That much was no surprise. Clark had been thinking moonshine for a while.

He turned his thoughts back to Traveler. Then he knew. Traveler had done more than warn him when his cabin had been attacked. He had told him who was out there. And with what Sam and Sarah had told him, he could put it all together. Now, he knew who he was after. And it all tied together so neatly. In this case, though, knowing "who" did not help much. He had to find them. And the girl. He spurred Traveler gently but his horse understood and picked up the pace. They cantered most of the way up the mountain.

Unlike other recent mornings, this morning Annie Mae Cooper could not wait to start her errand. Maybe he's finally gone, she thought. She had gone to the cave the day before and Goss had not been there. She had left the food inside the cave, just in case. Goss had been looking at her in a way that she really didn't like from the first time she had brought food up to the men. Now, with Alton dead, she was almost afraid to even go. But her kinfolk had laid a burden on her and she was honor bound to look after the friend of her kin. She had thought about asking her husband to come with her but he didn't know she was doing this and would've been furious at her if he found out. He hated her people and had little to do with them.

She had put a kitchen knife inside her cloak that morning, just in case, but she hoped that the food was still there and that the man was gone. On Wednesday, when she had last seen him, he was talking about leaving and she had done everything she could to get him to go. The only problem was that he wanted her to go with him. He had started talking that tripe a few days earlier when Alton had not been there and she had shown up with their food. Now, with Alton dead, it had gotten worse. Well, there was nothing for it but to convince him to leave and quickly.

She was deep in thought as she climbed through the rocks that led to the cave. When she approached the clearing, she was shocked to see an old Indian sitting in front of the cave. He was dressed in buckskin and wearing a ceremonial headdress. She had only seen Indians dressed like that in picture books and she was so surprised she dropped her basket.

Without getting up, the man spoke, "The man you seek is not here. He has been taken to jail. You should not come back here. This place is dangerous."

With a sigh of relief, the woman picked up her basket and began walking back down the trail. When she had gone a few paces she turned because she was going to ask the man when they had taken him. When she looked at the spot, however, no one was there. The place where the man sat was empty and the mouth of the cave was forbidding somehow.

A sudden wave of fear came over her and she walked quickly away from the area, casting anxious glances over her shoulder.

After a minute or two Gray Eagle emerged from the cave, happily munching on a piece of fried chicken the woman had left the day before. He had wanted to let her know what happened. If Clark was right, there were some dangerous men out in the woods and she needed to stay away. The opportunity to have a little fun was just too good to pass up. With a chuckle to himself, he headed back into the woods.

Despite the likelihood of coming into some jingle (reward money for both prisoners), Clark still had to work. He had several farms he had to visit to check on mending animals—and he really wanted to see Sarah.

It was mid-afternoon when he finished his rounds and school had just let out when Clark walked into the schoolroom. Sarah looked up from a stack of papers and smiled, "So the prodigal has returned... " She stood and walked over to him, kissing him lightly, but still kissing him. "What a hero you have become."

"It's my modesty that has made me great," said Clark.

"And a lack of good sense," Sarah added. "What you did was dangerous. But I am so proud of you." She hugged him. "Tell me what happened."

"There's a lot to tell." Clark told her about Gray Eagle's discovery and their capture of Johnny Goss. Then he told her his suspicions. "You and Traveler gave me the key clues," he said.

She looked at him with a serious expression, "You have to find that girl, Clark."

"I know it. Something Goss told me should help. Seems that his partner, Neddles, stumbled onto something back in the hills. He told Goss that he found a moonshining operation at a cabin on an old logging trail. If I can find the cabin, I'm pretty certain I can find the girl."

"What will you do next?"

"I plan to go back in there and search the area." He laid out his map. He had connected all the dots and had marked out an area of about thirty square miles. "The answer is somewhere in here."

"Why do you say that?"

"Everything that has happened was bounded by these spots. You have to assume that the people behind it are somewhere inside the boundary. I've already found a trail that seems to lead in this general direction." He pointed to a spot north and east of Squirrel Hollow. "I've spent time searching the area, already. I'll pick another area and search that next. It's not that big. Might take a few days, at most."

"I wish you would hurry. I don't like you being gone. I don't know where you are and I worry about you."

"I don't like being gone either." They looked at each other. The moment got too long without words. Clark kissed her gently and put his hat on. Sarah put her hand on his face. "I miss this face. Please don't do anything else brave." She sat down and began leafing through her papers.

Clark let himself out. He hoped that she was not upset. And he hoped she understood. He also knew that he was probably hopeless on both counts.

He rode out toward his place. He needed to check on his animals and pay Cal Hagood for taking care of them. He was also curious to know if anyone had been up there, checking it out.

The Hagood place was deserted, even Abigail and the children were out. He went into the barn and checked on his animals. They all looked to be in good shape. He took some money out of his saddlebags, wrote a note to the Hagoods and wrapped the money inside and then placed the note inside their door. Then he rode on up the hill to his cabin.

His place looked forlorn, all boarded up and with all the animals gone. Almost the way it had looked when he first saw it. He looked carefully around for any signs that someone was there. Everything appeared normal, but Clark was cautious.

He tied Traveler up in the thicket next to his home and began a careful inspection of the ground. He could see several sets of footprints around his cabin. Judging by what he could see, it was probably the Hagoods coming to see if everything was all right. There was one interesting set of prints, though. It appeared to come out of the woods and up to his cabin. The right boot had a cut in the heel—the same as the mark he had seen up at Squirrel Hollow. He had thought that the first print had been made by Seth Haney. Perhaps, Seth had been checking out his place, as well. That was still a puzzle, unless... After making sure that his cabin was secure, he headed back down the trail.

He decided to go back to Squirrel Hollow. It had all started there and maybe a search of the area around it would yield additional clues. He looked up at the sky. The morning sunshine had gradually been replaced by dark gray clouds and the wind blew from the southwest. There would probably be snow tonight. He had enough clothes to keep warm so he would be all right. He was in a hurry to start searching and he needed to find a good place to camp.

He headed further out the road, he knew that he could reach the hollow by turning north almost anywhere but he wanted to completely skirt the Haney farm. About a half mile down the road, he turned and rode back about a mile or so before the pine trees became too thick to ride anymore. He dismounted and walked Traveler back into the hills. He wanted to reach the hollow with some daylight left. He looked up at the sky. Already the dark gray clouds covered most of the sky. And it was no warmer.

When Clark reached the entrance to the hollow, it was almost dark. He decided to search the area north and east of the hollow. This, he felt, was the direction where they came from. In the remaining gray light, Clark methodically searched the ground. He scanned the area for trails or trash or any sign that a human had been there. He also turned over any small mounds of leaves that he ran across. The light was fading and he was really doubting the value of his search when he absently kicked over a small pile of leaves. His foot hit something soft and he thought it might be an animal for an instant but it flew through the air and landed a few feet away. Clark walked over and picked it up. It was a sugar sack and it was filled with cotton. It had obviously been there for several days. Clark looked around for other sacks but found none.

So that's how they did it, he thought. Now he knew how the hound made no tracks and he knew that it had come from that direction. He looked around but there was almost no light left. He would have to quit for the day. Besides, he hadn't made his camp yet.

He went back to the hollow and pitched his tent in the shelter of a bank that would protect him from the wind and some of the snow. Then he built a place for his fire just outside his tent and quickly made a screen of pine branches to shield the light. He was pretty certain that it was dark enough already to hide the smoke, so he built a fire using several pieces of tree limbs that had fallen. He broke them with his foot until they were small enough to fit inside the circle of rocks. The fire flared up just as the first snowflakes fell. They were big and wet. He quickly picked up enough wood to last him till morning and covered it with a tarp.

It's just barely cold enough to snow, he thought. Might not get much but he hoped it wouldn't turn to rain during the night. Snow would be a help to him.

He opened a can of beans and ladled it onto his frying pan. As they warmed, he scraped them over to the side of the pan and put a piece of salted ham to cook on the other side. The juice from the beans ran under the ham while it cooked. He poured the last of his canteen into his coffee pot and poured in some grounds to make coffee. He cut off a piece of bread and scooped a mixture of ham and beans onto the bread and ate it quickly with some of the beans spilling onto the ground. He was hungry and he wished he had cooked two pieces of ham. He cut another slice of bread and used it to wedge the beans onto his fork. When the pan was empty, he used the bread to soak up the rest of the ham juice and ate it—drinking down his last few sips of coffee. All in all, a good meal and a good day. He only wished that he could read.

Instead, he banked his fire and pulled his pine screen over it into a sort of lean-to. He would want coffee in the morning and the fire would keep him warm. He walked through the woods, even more silent now because of the light carpet of snow, down to a small stream at the bottom of the hill. He filled both canteens in the cold water and brought them back up the hill. He had taken all his blankets off of Traveler except one, which he draped over his horse. He had tethered him in a thicket that would keep most of the snow off of him. He took off his coat and crawled inside his bedroll. Then he put his coat over the outside of the bedroll. He waited while the heat gradually built inside the tent.

He felt warm inside his tent in the bedroll under the jacket, breathing the clean cold air from outside. His rifle lay within easy reach. He tried to go to sleep but he was excited. He thought he knew who was behind it. He had found out how they did it. He had more proof that the answer lay in the area he was searching. With a little luck, tomorrow might just be the day. A little luck and a little help from the weather.

# 19

**Saturday Morning**

It was still and dark when Clark woke up. He turned over and pushed open the flap of his tent and peered outside. The snow reflected what little light there was and he could just make out his fire still smoldering away under the lean-to. Reluctantly, he sat up, reached for his boots and began lacing them on. He put on his jacket and hat and crawled out of the tent. He started up his fire by adding some dry twigs and blowing on it. Once it was going good, he put on some coffee and got out what he needed to make pancakes. After breakfast, he put out his fire and sniffed the air. It still smelled like snow but he thought it was a little warmer than last night. When the sun came up, it might start melting the thin layer of snow, just enough to help him.

He sat there as the first light came over the forest. He could hear some animals stirring. Birds and squirrels were already up and in the distance, he heard the sounds of several deer moving through a thicket. He walked over to where Traveler was tethered and gave him a feedbag and talked to him for a minute. After he had eaten, he led him down to the stream, refilled his canteen and then let Traveler drink his fill before returning him to the thicket. The sun was up now and it was starting to warm things. Already, a few drops of water were falling from the treetops where the sun hit them.

Clark started walking toward the area where he had found the sack. He had to assume that there was a trail. If there was something going on back in there, they would have come through there. If they came that way often enough, they might have made a trail. Funny thing about trails, they always melted first, even if no one walked on them. By nine o'clock, the sun was shining brightly and the southern face of the hill was a dazzling, noisy, display of melting snow. Clark hurriedly crisscrossed the area walking in northerly and easterly directions. About fifty paces almost due east of where he found the sack, he found a trace of a trail. The snow had melted in a fairly straight line through the trees. It was patchy, but worth checking out.

Clark followed the general direction the trail led, keeping to the side. The melting snow left the ground soggy and he would make clear boot prints on the path. He didn't want to give away the fact that he had found the trail. He kept walking for several hundred paces in a generally northeastern direction. It was hard going because he had to keep in sight of the quickly disappearing trail while dodging along through the trees. The last bits of the trail had pretty much disappeared when he came to the old logging road. He had not even suspected it was there.

Of course the woods were crisscrossed by logging roads. The lumberjacks had to get the logs out so they built roads to haul them out. Clark's place was at the end of one. He wondered where this one ended. Clark thought about what Goss had said about the cabin. Neddles must have found this old road and followed it. Somewhere back in there was probably an old cabin, like his. And at the cabin...

He scouted along the edge of the road. There were definite signs of traffic. Several sets of boot prints were visible along with mule tracks and even some horse tracks, running from northwest to southeast. Clark reckoned the road ran roughly from Round Mountain Road down to the Chattanooga Road or close to each with various forks off of it to get to the timber. From where he stood, Clark figured that he was about a mile and a half from Squirrel Hollow and maybe three miles from the caves where the convicts had been hiding out. The tracks on the road led in both directions and they were not recent but Clark decided that he would follow it in the southeasterly direction first. Now, though, he would have to be extremely careful. They used this road—probably at night but maybe in the day, too. At least it would be easier to follow than the path had been. He set off along the southern side of the road, picking his way carefully through the trees—always keeping the logging road in sight.

He followed for almost three miles—sometimes seeing more signs of activity, sometimes seeing almost none at all. He had to stop and look every time to make sure that there was not some other trail branching off but always there was activity on the logging road. By about eleven o'clock, he had come to a place where the road snaked its way between two hills. He couldn't easily walk on either side of the road and he suspected that there might be something on the other side.

The only thing to do was to climb one of the hills and see what was there before going ahead. He decided to climb the one on the right side of the road. He studied it for a minute or two—picking out his best approach. He slung his rifle over his shoulder and began climbing. He made most of the trip on all fours, scrambling up the hill using small trees as handholds when he could get them and tufts of dried grass and roots when he couldn't, all the while being as quiet as he could be. It took Clark about ten minutes to reach the top. It was an area about twenty-yards square and there were still hardwoods on top. The loggers must have decided they weren't worth the effort.

Clark crawled to the edge, using the trees as a screen as much as possible. When he reached the crest, he peered cautiously over. There, below him, was an old logging cabin. There were no signs of activity and its run down condition suggested that it just might be abandoned. The illusion was shattered when a young woman came outside dragging a length of chain that was attached to her ankle.

It had to be the girl, Laney Sue, down there. He thought that he could probably get the chain off of her but first he had to know if there was anyone else down there. He settled down to watch and sure enough a man came out on the porch and called something to the woman. He was too far away for Clark to positively identify him but he knew who he was. The girl picked up a small axe and headed out to the woodpile that lay some forty feet or so from the cabin. The man went back inside and Clark had an idea. The woodpile was next to a few nearby pine trees. They would provide him with enough cover to at least get close to the girl. Then Clark thought of something else—the hound. It had to be down there somewhere.

Clark checked the breeze. What little there was came from the northeast and blew across his face. He would not give his scent away from the spot next to the girl. He cautiously backed away from the crest of the hill as he heard some timid chopping sounds. As quickly as he could he went down the hill. At the bottom, he moved cautiously around the right side of the hill keeping to the tree line— and straining both his eyes and his ears. As he neared the pine trees, he was pleased to hear the sounds of chopping; the girl was still there. It took him another five minutes to reach the screen of pine trees.

Clark could now plainly see the girl's face. She had a blank expression like someone in a trance. He made a low bird call and the girl stopped chopping and looked in his direction. He called to her, softly, "Start chopping again and don't look up." She gave a sharp gasp, but immediately did as she had been told. A little louder, Clark said, "My name is Clark Ammons and I'm here to get you out." Tears streamed down the girl's face but she continued chopping. "I'm going to ask you some questions. Just nod or shake your head a little."

The girl nodded.

"Are you Laney Sue Evatt?"

She nodded.

"Are there two men?"
She shook her head.
"Three?"
She nodded.
"Does the third one stay here?"
She shook her head.
"Do they have guns?"
She nodded.
"Do they leave at night?"
She nodded.
"Stop chopping, then chop the number of times when they normally leave."
The girl stopped. Then chopped eight times, then paused and chopped one more time.
"Between eight and nine?"
She nodded.
"Do they go out during the day?"
She shook her head.
"Do you know of any reason why they would stay here tonight?"
The girl shook her head.
"I can't get you out by myself but I will be back tonight. Hang on."
She nodded.
"Don't act any differently. I'll be back."
The girl nodded and Clark silently backed out of the pines.

He hated to leave her. He had a pretty good idea of what her life had been like but the best time to come back would be at night when they were gone. Then they could get the girl safely. He figured that they chained her so they could sleep during the day and do what they did at night. If he had tried to free her then, there would have been a gun battle with at least two of them and one of him. If he had been killed, there would be no one that knew where she was. He looked at the sun. It was about noon. It would take at least two hours to get to town. Another two hours or so to round up enough men to do the job and then at least two more hours to get back. That would work. He had time more than enough time to arrange everything. He wanted to be there by 9:00 with enough men to finish it. Of course, there was a good chance that they wouldn't be able to catch the men at night but that was a separate problem. He had to rescue the girl.

# 20

## Saturday Afternoon

Now that he knew where he was and where he was going, he could move a lot faster. Within an hour, he had reached Traveler and was leading him out of the woods at the entrance of the hollow. Then he was riding hard down the track where it all started. He cast a sidelong glance at the cutoff to the Haney place. Tonight, we'll see, boys, he thought.

He decided to go through the Wheeler place. He would get Ezra to go back with him on the way. As he rode through the back of his farm, Ezra hailed him, "Clark! What's all the fuss?"

He reined up. "I found the girl, Ezra and the hound, too, I think. We've got to get her out tonight. Can we meet here?"

"O'course. I'll go with you."

"Thanks, Ezra."

Clark started off again and rode through Ezra's field. He waved at some little Wheelers out in the yard but didn't stop. He galloped down the road now, explaining the situation to the men he met along the way and asking them to meet at the Wheelers by six.

One of the men said he thought that Charley Pell was at home so Clark went there. Charley came out onto the porch as Clark clattered up and jumped off his horse. "I found them, Charley. They're up in a logging cabin a few miles back of Squirrel Hollow. I've already got a few men meeting at Ezra Wheeler's tonight."

"I'll get a couple more and round up the sheriff. We need to wait til he gets here, but I'm sure I can find him by suppertime." Clark relaxed a little.

"I'll ride up to Sam's and see if I can get some more men."

"Do that, Doc. I'll meet you at the Wheelers."

Clark jumped back on Traveler and they trotted the rest of the way. There were several men gathered at the store and Clark explained to them what was happening. All of the men left quickly to get their guns before gathering at the Wheelers after an early supper.

Clark's next stop was at Black Smith's. Black was in his normal position, hunched over his anvil, smashing his huge hammer on a piece of molten iron. He stopped and looked up when Clark walked up. "Afternoon, Doc. Need some shoes?"

"Not right now, Black. But I do need you." He quickly explained about finding the missing girl and her chained condition.

"I'll get my tools and meet you down at the Wheelers," he offered.

Clark thanked him and headed to his last stop. He walked Traveler across the road and down to Sarah's house. She had been in the back and didn't hear him coming so he knocked. In a moment, she came from the kitchen, her hair still up, but with one exposed wisp falling across her face.

She smiled. "Mr. Ammons, you look, and smell, disheveled."

He kissed her gently, then stepped back. "I found the girl, Sarah. She's in an old logging cabin back in the woods chained at the ankle."

"The poor girl."

"We're rounding up the men and going back to get her tonight when I think they will be out working."

Sarah nodded. Then she walked back into the kitchen and began dishing food on to plates for each of them. When they finished eating, she began covering pots and putting lids on her stove.

"Sarah?" he asked. "What are you doing?"

She came out of the kitchen and put on her cloak. "I'm going with you." Clark stared at her. "You need at least one woman with you to take care of the girl. You're not thinking."

"I guess you're right," he nodded. "You'll be safe enough, but I want you to keep to the back. I expect some shooting."

"I can stay with the girl and some of the men can take us back. I don't want any part of the rest of it." She stopped.

He stepped to her and held her tightly. "Well, come on, if you're going," he said gruffly, to cover his real feelings at the moment. She finished fixing her hat and gloves, extinguished the lantern and went out with Clark.

"You can ride with me as far as we ride." He lifted her up onto the horse and she sat across his legs with her left arm hooked around his waist. They rode slowly past the church and some other men also heading for the Wheeler farm. Several groups were ahead of them. Clark heard more than one set of anxious words from people left behind and fervently hoped that no more tears would be needed.

When Clark and Sarah arrived at the Wheelers about thirty people were already there.

If this had been a simple still-busting operation, no one would have been there, including local law enforcement. That chore would have been up to the hated revenooers. But this was different. The attacks on the boys and Bobby Dunstan, along with the kidnapping of the girl had created a different situation. Whatever was going on back there was a threat to the community. The men were willing to risk their lives to defend their neighbors.

Hattie Wheeler was giving coffee to the men and there were several other women there, as well. It was about six when the sheriff rode into the yard followed by several other men and a pack of hounds. He waved to Clark and motioned him to join him off to one side. "You found the girl?"

"Sure did." Clark described her location and the situation.

"You think she'll be alone?"

"I don't know. They wouldn't chain her unless they left her alone. They probably sleep during the day and work at night when their fire wouldn't be visible and come back in the early hours of the morning." He paused. "They might leave the dog to guard her as well."

"Hadn't thought of that." Tom turned to Sarah. "We'll have her back soon."

"I'm going with you."

Tom looked at Clark.

"It's her decision to make. She's right, though, we need to take a woman with us."

Tom looked like he was going to argue, but he nodded. "You're right. I can see why that would be a good idea." He walked over to the porch and talked to the group, "Clark found the girl a few miles from here in a cabin on a logging road. We've got two men, maybe three, back in there, too. We've got two jobs to do: the first is to rescue the girl. We think that she's in the cabin alone although the hound may be guarding her.

Our second job is to arrest those men. We've probably got a moonshine operation back in there. We know they're armed. They shot up Clark's cabin and killed one of the escaped convicts, although that wasn't any great loss. And they killed Bobby Dunstan with their hound. If we can get to the cabin without raising a ruckus, we can wait there for them and grab them when they return."

"What if we can't?" one of the men asked.

"Then, it's a manhunt. I've brought my bloodhounds and we'll keep them back a little, just in case. I've already sent word to post watches on both the Chattanooga Road and Round Mountain Road in both directions, though if they get that far..." He let it trail off. "Okay, we'll need a sureshot team forward—Charley, Ben, and Philip will do and I'll lead. We can ride our horses as far as Squirrel Hollow, then we'll have to walk the rest of the way. According to Clark, they use the old logging trail to move their liquor, but I wouldn't think they'd move any until later. They wouldn't want to attract attention by having any rendezvous before midnight so if we're at the cabin by nine, we should be safe on the road. Our aim is to capture these men, not to kill them but if you're attacked, get low and return the fire."

He looked at Sarah. "Miss Sarah is going with us as far as the cabin. I want you to stay back and to the inside, Miss Sarah." She nodded. "After we get the girl, I'll need a couple of men to take her and Miss Sarah back. We'll need an extra horse or two to carry the ladies back down the hill." One of the men said he had brought extra horses.

"Hattie. Hattie!"

"Yes, Sheriff."

"All right if we bring the girl back here?"

"O'course."

"Okay, any questions?" There weren't any. They had done this kind of thing before over the years—although nothing had been quite this dangerous.

It was completely dark, with no moon, when the men rode out the backside of the Wheelers' taking the same path that Clark had used several times. As they passed by the Haneys, Clark wondered if there was someone watching, maybe trying to warn the boys. There was nothing they could do about it, anyway.

He was riding toward the back so that Sarah would not be among the first attacked if there was trouble but he was chaffing to get to the front. Sarah noted his impatience. "When we get to the hollow, you'll be needed to help lead so I'll stay back here by myself."

"You're sure?"

"Yes, I can manage but you have to promise me to be very careful." She said this all quietly.

In a few minutes, they reached the hollow and tied their horses. A couple of the younger boys were asked to stay and guard the horses. They were very disappointed not to be in on the real action but agreed to do what was required. The group walked on through the woods with Clark taking the lead and Sarah now in the rear. They made a fair amount of noise and Clark didn't like it but it couldn't be helped. Several men had lanterns and a few had old miner's helmets with lamps. The evening was cold and their breaths fogged. When they reached the logging road, the going was easier but the danger was greater. They did not care about making prints. It would end tonight—one way or the other. They had gone almost three miles when Clark whispered to the sheriff to halt the group.

Tom hoarsely whispered for the group to stop and they did, forming a loose semicircle around him and Clark. "We're about a quarter mile or so from the cabin." Clark checked the wind. It came from the south. That meant that the wind was somewhat behind them and could possibly alert the dog. "The road goes between two steep hills. One group needs to stay on the road. With your permission, Sheriff, I'd like to take another group around the far side of the hill on the right. With a little luck we can be at the cabin before anyone spots us. If there's anyone there, they'll probably be watching the road. We should also put all the lights out. One more thing, the wind is behind us so the risk of the hound getting our scent is strong. If it attacks, he's likely to be a scary sight. But don't let the paint fool you—just shoot it, it'll die." He paused. "But it would be a lot better if we don't have to shoot."

He turned to Tom. "If you hear the hound, move quickly to the cabin, we have to get to the girl before the men come back to check. If you hear shots be careful, we might have been spotted. I'd like to take two men with me. Bobby, you take my right side. Sam, you take my left. Only fire at something in front of you or beside you on the outside. Don't shoot inside or behind you or we're likely to shoot each other. Everybody understand?"

"We got 'er, Doc."

"Sheriff, if we get inside without any problem, I'll give this birdcall." He made a low sound. "Otherwise, be careful of anyone coming along the trail. We won't come out that way."

Sheriff Mosley organized his men in three lines with the first to go forward to the foot of the two hills, still out of sight of the cabin. The second line was in the middle and Sarah with them. The third line was in the rear, guarding back in that direction, just in case the men were somehow behind them on the trail.

As the sheriff's men moved into position, Clark led his group around the base of the hill—retracing his steps from earlier in the day. The going was slow because they wanted to be in position without giving themselves away. Clark flinched at each twig that snapped. They could not see where they were going. Every twenty paces, Clark would say his name in a hoarse whisper and each man would do the same so that the men would know where each was and so that they could stay on course. After about fifteen minutes or so of walking, Clark could just barely make out the cabin. There was at least one lantern burning somewhere inside and the smell of wood smoke hung over the area.

Suddenly, a low growl sounded somewhere off to their right. The men strained to see what had caused the noise. Then with a rush a black shadow capped by a fiery face sprang out of the blackness.

Despite the fact that Clark had expected it, he was frozen for a second at the sight of it. Its face was hideous and it emitted a mournful howl as it launched itself into the air.

Then all three men fired, with Clark's shot just a fraction of a second before the other two and the beast tumbled in a heap almost at their feet.

For a second they all stood still then Clark poked at it with his rifle. It emitted a hoarse growl but didn't move. At least one of them had hit the mark well.

"Damn, what a beast!" Sam said.

"I guess they know we're here," said Clark. "Let's get to the cabin as quickly as we can." They moved much faster, running through the trees. In a moment they broke into the clearing, Clark leading the way and the others following. When they got to within about fifty feet of the cabin, Clark called a halt and told them to get low to the ground. "There may be someone in there with her. We can't just go up to the door. Bobby, you move over to the right and cover that area over there. There's a trail up there that someone might come down. Sam, stay on my left side and come with me." Clark crawled towards the cabin, while the other two men flanked out to cover the sides of the cabin. He could hear the sounds of the sheriff's men as they were moving toward the cabin, as well.

When Clark was near the door, he peered inside. He could see the girl sitting inside. She was tied to her chair and gagged. She was peering outside anxiously. Clark spoke, "Laney Sue. It's me, Clark Ammons." She whimpered and he entered the cabin cautiously. The other men came inside the cabin, as the sheriff's men arrived. Clark untied her gag. She was crying. Clark said, "You're free or you will be when we get this chain off of you. We brought a blacksmith and we'll get him in here and he can take care of you." He paused. "There's a lady with us, too, Sarah McGee. She came to see after you, as well."

The sheriff walked inside the cabin. "We were worried about you when we heard the gunshots but we figured that it was only the dog. What happened?"

"The dog was out there and he jumped us. We shot at him and I think we killed him. He's over in the woods." Clark gestured.

Sarah had entered the cabin and the men made way for her respectfully as she came to the girl's side. Black Smith was already working at freeing Laney Sue from the chain.

"Clark, you're all right?" Sarah asked.

"Just barely."

Sarah hugged Laney Sue. The girl was crying, almost hysterically now. She didn't even notice the blacksmith as he freed her from the long chain.

Clark waited a few minutes before talking to her again. "Laney Sue. Do you know who they are?"

She shook her head.

"Are they up at the still?" he asked.

She choked out, through her sobs, "They were."

"How far is it from here?"

"Not too far. Up the hill." She waved her hand. "I was there twice. They took me up there."

Sarah looked up at Clark—a meaningful look that said the girl had had enough.

Clark nodded and walked over to the sheriff. "What now?"

"They probably rabbitted. That's why I brought the dogs. You never know when you'll have to chase people down. There'll be enough stuff here to give 'em a scent."

He picked up some old clothes and went outside.

One of the older men and two of the teen-aged boys were asked to take Sarah and Laney Sue back to the Wheelers. They would take her there and then send someone after her kin. Sarah left Laney Sue alone for a minute and walked over to Clark.

"Is she all right?" Clark asked, in a low voice.

Sarah shrugged her shoulders. "Physically, she appears to be fine, but I don't know. Look at how her eyes are darting around. She's afraid of these men and they just rescued her. She's going to have a hard time, I'm afraid."

Clark nodded. "Well, do what you can. We've still got the hard part ahead of us."

Sarah looked at Clark. "I'm going. You remember what I said about being careful."

Clark looked around to see if anyone was really looking, then gave Sarah a kiss before she gathered her charge and shepherded the group out the door.

Some of the men had found some coffee and were now stoking up the stove to make a pot. Others had lit torches and brought in some wood to make a bonfire. It reminded Clark of some command posts he had seen.

The sheriff raised his hand to get their attention. "Men, we've got to get after them." The Sheriff looked around at the circle of men—their faces visible in the flickering torchlight. "Most of us are needed to track these people but a few of you, " he paused, "are needed to stay here, smash up that still up yonder and wait here overnight—just in case they circle back." He paused again. "Who wants to stay here?"

Several hands went up quickly.

"All right, you stay. The rest of you, let's get going." The dogs and their handlers pushed to the front of the group and with a yelp the dogs set off after the men. For a few minutes, they went in a fairly straight directionthrough the woods toward the Chattanooga Road. After a few more minutes, Clark made his way to the Sheriff. "Tom, it's pretty obvious that the men are headed for the Chattanooga Road."

"Yep, I figured as much, I have men on the lookout for them—I posted them east and west both on the Chattanooga Road and on Round Mountain. When they reach the road, they'll be caught between us and them," he brought his hands together with a smack, "and we'll have them."

"I'm not so sure, Tom. I think they'll jump into a creek before long—they've used them to cover their tracks several times up here—and then the dogs'll lose their scent. Besides, I think I know where they're headed." Quietly he told Tom his suspicions—and his plan.

Tom grunted. "I'm not happy about it, Clark. "

"Why not?"

"Because, ultimately, these men are my responsibilities. They've killed before. If you find 'em, they'll be desperate."

"Tom, if you don't find them, they'll get away, but I'm pretty sure I know where they're headed. If I go now, I can beat them there. Besides, I am a sworn officer. And if it'll make you feel any better I'll take Charley with me."

"Can't do that. I need Charley with the dogs."

"Then I'll take Bobby and Sam. We're wasting time, Tom. I need to go."

"All right, but you know my standing orders. Surround them, hold them till we get there—if they're there." He paused. "You know that if you're wrong, you've made enemies for life?"

"I know it. I hope I'm wrong."

Clark executed a brisk salute which was barely visible in the flickering light and began rounding up Bobby and

Sam—the same team he had chosen earlier. The men moved out from the group and stood with Clark while the rest of the group continued to push through the woods chasing the dogs who were chasing the men.

Clark pulled his group together, "I think I know who we're chasing and where they're headed. I want to try and get there before they do." He quickly told them where they were headed. "Any questions?"

"Any idee what we do once we get there?"

"Not really, I guess we just play it by ear."

"Just like Miss Owens," Bobby offered.

"Better than that, I hope," Clark added. The men chuckled and began retracing their steps. When they passed near the cabin, the sounds of the still destruction up the hill sounded a lot like drunken revelry but they didn't stop to find out. Clark did stop into the cabin long enough to grab a little of the glowing paint and a brush he had noticed earlier before they continued.

They jogged down the trail that led back toward Squirrel Hollow where they paused for a few minutes to allow Sam (the oldest member of their party) to catch his breath. When they reached the back cutoff to the Haney place, they men crossed the old split rail fence and followed roughly the same path the boys had taken when they raided Old Man Haney's apples. It was approaching midnight when the men neared the Haney house. The place was dark. Either Seth was asleep or the worst had happened and the whole group was gone.

There was only one thing to do—wait. The men got as close to the house as they could and settled down. For the first few minutes, Clark was agitated. What if he had guessed wrong? Not only would the criminals have gotten away clean but he would have slandered a neighbor. Yet, in a way, he hoped he was wrong. He didn't want anyone in their community to be involved. He quickly reviewed his facts and conclusions. He was pretty certain that he was right.

He was thinking about this when Sam touched his arm and pointed in the direction of the barn. Two men were moving out of its shadow stealthily toward the Haney home. Without knocking, they entered the house.

"What do we do now?" whispered Sam.

"Let's get closer—maybe we can hear something. The men spread out in a loose semi-circle around the front of the house. In a minute or so, a lamp was lit in the kitchen and the smell of wood smoke filled the still night air as a fire was stoked inside.

Old Man Haney's voice came through the window. "You boys shouldn't've come here."

"We couldn't think o' nowhere else," a younger voice answered. "Figgered maybe you'd hide us out."

"You can't stay here. I gotta get you out. What happened?"

"Don't rightly know. We thought everything was fine. We was up at the still makin a batch. We had the mules all ready to go when the dog set up a ruckus then there was shots from down to the cabin. Reckon someone shot him. Then there was sounds o' commotion down at the cabin."

"I crept down there 'n saw a whole passel o' men swarmin around."

"A whole passel you say?" asked Seth.

"Must've been twenty or more," said another voice.

"Someone done found out about our still and I know damn well who twas."

"Doc."

"That's the one. That damn busybody. You shoulda kilt him."

"We tried. Han't a been for them Hagoods we'd a done it too."

"I'm not so sure, but we'll let it be for now. We gotta get you out. Can't stay here."

Clark motioned with his hand and they all pulled back to about thirty yards of the house. "What now?" one of them asked.

"We wait," Clark answered in a whisper. "We've got them surrounded. Maybe we can get them out in the open one at a time. Otherwise, we'll just wait here until the Sheriff turns up." Clark gave the men spots to move to so that the entire house was surrounded.

Once again, the men settled down to wait. In a few minutes, Seth came outside by himself and headed to the barn. When he was inside, Clark crawled over to Sam. "I'm going to go in and get Seth. If anyone tries to leave the house, fire a shot to warn me. Pass it on." Sam slipped off into the darkness to relay Clark's instructions.

Clark slipped quietly into the barn. Seth's animals knew him so he wasn't worried that they might fret. Seth had lit a lamp and was over in a corner of the barn hitching a horse to a wagon. He was muttering under his breath but he was making good progress. He probably doesn't know about the roadblocks, thought Clark. Clark had concealed himself in a dark spot near the door. When Seth finished hitching his horse he headed back toward the door. As Seth walked past Clark, Clark put his rifle barrel against Seth's chest. The man stopped dead in his tracks as Clark stepped out into the circle of light created by Seth's lamp.

"Clark," asked Seth. "Have you taken leave of your senses?"

"No, Seth, you know why I'm here," he said quietly.

"Honest Clark, I have no idee."

"The two men in your house Seth. I want them. Alive, preferably, but either way."

"I still don't know what you're on about Clark." He forced a grin. "Hell, come on in and take a look for yourself."

"So they can kill me this time. It's no use Seth. I've got other men with me and besides, I know they're there. You need to put that lantern down slowly and lie face down and I'm going to tie you up." Without another word, Seth did as he was told. It wasn't hard to tie and gag him. Then Clark went to one of the barn doors and painted with the paint he had taken from the cabin. Then he made his way back out into the yard.

Once again he found Sam and told him in a whisper, "I've got Seth tied up in the barn. In a few minutes, they'll come out looking for him, we'll get them then. Pass it on."

Sam moved off into the night and the men resumed their watchful waiting.

In about ten minutes or so, two shadowy figures emerged from the house and made their way toward the barn. "Seth!" one of them hissed. "Seth!" he called again. With a shrug that could be seen in the pale light, the two men walked to the barn.

They opened the big barn door and then stood in shocked silence as they read the message painted there in glowing letters:

"Haskells. You're surrounded." And it was signed "Doc."

In the silence, it was easy for the men to hear the sounds of rifles being cocked. Without moving, they raised their hands as the men advanced on them, threw them to ground and bound their hands and feet.

The men took the Haskells inside while Doc retrieved Seth from the barn. He was tied into a chair along with his nephews and when the gag was removed, he spat out one sentence, "I tol you you shouldn't 've come here." He said nothing else and neither did the boys. The men made some coffee and waited on the sheriff.

# 21

**Very Early Sunday Morning**

It had been another hour or so before the Sheriff and the rest of the men had arrived. The dogs had done a good job of following the men for a while, until they reached a creek. A pretty easy way to get away from tracking dogs is to go into a creek and then pull yourself out using a tree branch. The dogs might be able to eventually get back on the scent but in this case, they hadn't and after a while, the sheriff had given up and headed in the direction of the Haney farm.

They had approached silently, expecting either nothing or a standoff. Instead, they found Clark and the rest of the men calmly drinking their second pot of coffee with Seth Haney and his nephews tied up in the kitchen.

After turning over the men to the sheriff, Clark and his team had walked across the backside of the Haney place to retrieve their horses. The rest of the men rode away and Clark picked his way through the dark night toward his cabin. When he reached his cabin, he was surprised to find that the place was unboarded and all lit up and he could smell smoke from his fireplace. Maybe Abby Hagood came and opened the place up, he thought.

When he opened the door, he was shocked to find Gray Eagle sitting in his chair. He looked so out of place that Clark just stood there with his mouth open as Gray Eagle, with wire spectacles Clark had never seen before, looked up from reading *The Hound of the Baskervilles*.

"Conan Doyle writes a good story," he said, to Clark's further astonishment.

When Clark finally found his voice, he said, "Gray Eagle, you're welcome here and thanks for opening up my house, but what's going on?"

Gray Eagle smiled, "I came here to tell you that I had found the cabin where the girl was being held. When you were not here, I went looking for you. I was wandering around the woods when I stumbled onto your army so I knew that you had already found the cabin and were going to rescue her so I decided to trail along and watch the fun."

"So you were there all along?"

Gray Eagle nodded, "I wanted to see how you did. I almost killed the hound for you. I had an arrow knocked but you finally woke from your trance and shot it," he grinned.

"So, how did I do?" asked Clark.

Gray Eagle seemed thoughtful. "You did well, my son. I could hear the other two men as they moved through the woods but you were almost totally silent." It was the first such praise that Clark had ever received from the old man.

"Thank you for the kind words. I know that I still have much to learn and I hope you live to be a hundred so that you can teach me well."

"Who says I am not already older than that?" He paused. "But I enjoy teaching you. For a round eye, you are a good student."

Clark grinned. At that moment, the mournful baying of a hound cut through his cabin. It sounded as if it came from the general direction of the barn. Clark turned quickly and took several steps toward his back door, then quickly turned back toward where Gray Eagle was... But he was gone. The book was sitting on the table, the place marked by a gray eagle feather.

"That's one thing I positively have to learn from you, old man," he said aloud.

## Sunday Morning

He woke up later than normal but early enough to clean up and change into his Sunday best. The Hagood family had not yet left for church so things were back to normal.

When he reached Sarah's, she was ready and pacing on her front porch. She was all smiles when he hopped off his horse. "Mr. Ammons," she said, "It's good to have the real you back." He took off his hat as he approached her—because it was polite and also because her arms were circling his neck, pulling him close. When they had properly greeted each other, she asked, "Did everything work out?"

"We got them all at the Haney place. Old man Haney and the Haskells. They ran there after they left their still. We actually got there before the Haskell boys." He paused. "Did you get Laney Sue back to her parents?"

She nodded. "We sent someone after her folks last night and about midnight they came and got her. They were really grateful to you for finding her."

Clark shrugged. "I just wish I could have found her sooner." He pulled out his pocket watch. "I guess we should head on over." Sarah smiled and slipped her arm through his for the short walk. "Now, remember Clark, you won. No need to rub it in."

Clark grunted and said nothing but he smiled broadly as they walked toward the church.

When they reached the church there were small groups of people gathered around the door. At the middle of each was at least one of the men that had taken part in the events of the previous evening. More than one group broke off at Clark's arrival to call him over to validate at least part of the story they were telling. By the time all the stories were told, each of them men would probably have captured the group-single-handed, but it didn't really matter. An observer would also notice that attendance was down a little and that most of the men who were not there had been part of the still-destroying outfit from last night. Obviously, still destroying kept you out too late to make it to church.

The ringing of the church bell and the agonized pounding on the piano signaled the end of the conversations and the beginning of the service.

Clark stayed awake during the sermon—paying attention, more or less, to Preacher Elrod's very appropriate anti-drinking sermon. Pity, he thought, that most of the men who needed to hear it were home in bed this morning, nursing hangovers. The preacher made no mention of the hound incident and of course, failed to acknowledge his role in stoking the community's fears. After the service, Clark and Sarah waited in line to shake the preacher's hand as they left. Clark raised one eyebrow, signaling that there was more that he could say, but he left his comments for another day.

As Clark and Sarah were preparing to walk back to her house, Charley Pell elbowed his way through the small knot of people surrounding them. "Glad I caught you, Doc. You, too, ma'am," he looked at Sarah.

"What's going on Charley?"

"Sheriff sent word that he would like you to come to his house for lunch tomorrow," said Charley.

"I'll be down."

Charley looked uncomfortable, "He'd like Miss McGee to come, too." He looked at her. "In fact, Mrs. Mosley is positively interested in your attendance."

Clark and Sarah looked at each other. "It's a school day, Mr. Pell," she said.

"Sheriff knows but he said he'd really appreciate your coming and that he knew the kids would love a day off." He looked from one to the other of them. "What do you say?"

Sarah looked at Clark and nodded. "I guess you're right. The children would appreciate a day off. Tell the sheriff, we'll both be there."

Charley looked relieved as he thanked them and went to catch up with his wife and children who were waiting somewhat impatiently to get to their lunch.

"Thank you," said Clark. "I don't know what's up but I appreciate your coming."

"Oh, I'm going for very selfish reasons. I want to meet Mrs. Mosley. I have to decide how much competition she truly is."

Clark grinned in response.

After eating a quick lunch with Sarah, Clark set off for Boo's house. Clark did not own a carriage and he didn't want Sarah to have to ride in the open for the long trip to the county seat. Boo had the best carriage in the area (in fact, on reflection, he probably had the only carriage in the area) and Clark thought he would lend it to him.

Boo greeted him warmly, offering him lunch leftovers (which he declined) and a glass of sherry (which he accepted). "Mr. Ammons, it's always a pleasure to see you. In fact, I had hoped that you would pay a call. I understand you solved the hound mystery."

"Yes sir. We've gotten to the truth."

"So it was Seth Haney and his nephews." He nodded to himself. "Seth was always a taciturn one—never really fit into the community. Of course as long as Lucinda was alive he toed the line. And those nephews of his didn't fall far from the tree either. Ah well," he added philosophically. "I hope that my information was helpful."

"Your information was very helpful."

"How so?"

"You told me that the last sighting of the hound was by a Haney boy. Sarah connected the Haneys and the Haskells for me. When I finally put two and two together I had my answer."

"I see. Well, I am always glad to be of service. In fact, I may just make a speech about this at the next meeting of the Jackson County Historical Society. So thank you for including me." He changed the subject. "You must have come for a reason, Doc. You're not the type to make social calls. What can I do for you?"

"Sheriff Mosley has invited Miss Sarah and me to lunch tomorrow—" he began.

"And you'd like to use my carriage," Boo finished.

"You're a quick study Boo. That's about the size of it."

"I'd be delighted. We have no plans to go anywhere tomorrow. Say, I have an idea. Grant!" He bellowed. "Grant!"

Grant poked his head around the door. "Yes, sir?" He nodded at Doc. "And how are you?"

"Fine, Grant. Thanks for asking."

Boo addressed Grant. "Didn't you say that you needed to go to Boonesville?"

"Yes, sir, I did. I need to go to the drug store to pick up some fainting medicine for Miz Olivier."

"Clark here needs to borrow our carriage to take Miss Sarah to the county seat. Would you mind driving them?"

"Oh, no, that's not necessary," said Clark quickly.

"I'd be honored. No trouble atall."

"I don't want to impose... "

"Yes, sir. Like Boo say, I need to go anyway. And besides, getting away from the old man does my heart good," he grinned.

They agreed that Grant would pick them up a little before ten in the morning at Miss Sarah's.

Clark collected his animals from the Hagoods, thanked them for their kindness, paid Cal for his troubles and spent the rest of the afternoon getting his home back into shape. He even had time for his pipe and bit of fiddlin' around. It was good to be home.

## Monday Morning

In the morning, the three of them went "down the hill" in Boo's carriage. Grant had washed and polished the black buggy to a high shine and it was a pleasant trip with the sun warming them inside the comfortable carriage as they recounted the events of the past few weeks.

When they reached the Mosley's, everyone in the household was lined up outside to greet them. After exchanging pleasantries, they were led into the dining room, which was obviously set for "company." China, crystal and silver were present in abundance.

"I'm not complaining, you understand, but it never looks like this when I come alone," Clark said.

"That's the important part of what you said, Clark—alone. Today, we have a charming visitor with us," said Tom with a grin.

"Clark has told me about your lovely singing voice, Mrs. Mosley," said Sarah. Mrs. Mosley blushed, "Clark, you must be part Irish to lay that blarney on this girl." She turned to Sarah. "It's Clark that has the voice, but thank you and please call me Belinda."

After they sat down, Lucy came in with food. After everyone was served, Tom began,

"Clark, I don't want to talk business but we never would have solved this thing without your help. You told me who had done it—even before you set out after them. How did you know?"

"I had a lot of help, Tom. Boo started me in the right direction, Sarah pushed me further; even Mr. Sam Butler gave me a good clue. And, of course, Gray Eagle really solved the escaped prisoner problem. I just mopped up."

"Begin at the beginning, please."

Clark smiled. "It began with my belief that we were dealing with humans—not a satanic hound. Things generally happen for a reason. Why would someone fix up a dog to scare people, I wondered? They wanted people to stay away, obviously. So the question was, from what? I figured it was something criminal. Tom, you told me that there was an upswing of drunk and disorderly conduct and that pointed to a local supply of hooch."

Tom nodded.

"Then, I had a whole bunch of clues. The problem was that they related to two different problems—the hound on one hand and the prisoners on the other."

"So what were the clues?" asked Mrs. Mosley.

Clark considered. "All right, let me see... First, we had the fact that the Haskell boys had disappeared. Sam gave me that. I just didn't recognize it as a clue, at first. And one of them had fallen and hurt himself. That suggested a limp but for a while I didn't notice. Sam also told me that a lot of sugar had disappeared while the Haskells worked there. Another important clue that I just put off to the side. Then we had the fact that the last hound sighting was by a Haney. Boo gave me that. Then Sarah told me that the Haskells and Haneys were related so Seth Haney was their uncle. That's when things got interesting."

"How so?" asked Tom.

"Two things diverted me. The Haney boys came back and they had a history that suggested they might be involved—especially when the girl disappeared. Then we had some escaped prisoners that came to the area as well. This led to some very interesting points that muddied the water." He paused. "Are you sure you want to hear all this?"

"Of course."

"All right." Clark went on. "There were footprints that led from Haneys to the spot where the boys originally spotted the hound. I thought they might be Seth's but he denied he knew anything about it. When I spoke with him, he pointed out to me that his boys never had an alibi when anything happened. But that also meant that he never had one either. He even sent his boys to buy a lot of sugar, which was suggestive. Of course, since they were innocent, they were in no real danger but it was strange that he pointed a finger at them unless he was trying to divert suspicion from someone else. I even had a dream about him, at least I think it was him." Clark paused again, thinking about his last statement.

He went on. "Then we had the escaped prisoners. There was the clue of the girl in the woods." He looked at Sarah. "Sarah investigated that one at great risk, I might add. Other than that, the convicts were not relevant except that Alton Neddles got himself killed by the Haskells for trying to muzzle into their moonshining."

"That was a lot of area to search Clark. I figure about two hundred square miles and no roads to speak of. How did you find them so quickly?"

"I made a map. And I circled the problem."

"Circled the problem?" asked Mrs. Mosley.

"Yes, ma'am. Boo had told me that the legend was local so I went out the Chattanooga-Murphy Road to Eighteen Mile and I came back on Round Mountain looking for people that knew about it. That gave me the eastern boundaries. And I plotted everything that happened. I found a trail that pointed in a general direction and I found a sugar sack in Squirrel Hollow and another one on the eastern side of the Hollow, this time stuffed with cotton. That let me know I was on the right track."

"What was the purpose of that?"

"They put cotton in sacks and tied them to the dog's paws so it made no prints."

"Ingenious."

"I thought so. Mark Haskell was good with animals. I used him on my place at one point. Traveler warned me he was out there the night they shop up my cabin. He must have trained the hound. But it was really Jimmy's injury that allowed me to put it all together. I found a trail in the woods and one of the men had a limp. Then they erased the trail even though it could not be followed to their still. That was very suggestive. That meant that there was something about the tracks, themselves that they did not want me to see. It had to be the limp and when I connected it up, I knew who they were because they had disappeared."

"You know when you explain it, it all sounds so simple," said Tom.

"Most things are I guess. People do things for a reason. The hard part is simply recognizing the real clues from information that sends you in the wrong direction."

"That reminds me," said Tom. "What did the Haney boys do with all that sugar?"

"Applesauce. Seth had a pantry full of it."

"Which reminds me, Mr. Ammons," said Mrs. Mosley, "I take it on good authority that you like apple pies. Lucy made up some today in your honor."

They spent the next few hours getting better acquainted—and not talking about crime. About four o'clock, Clark looked meaningfully at his watch and suggested that they needed to head home.

They walked out on the porch to say their good-byes. As they stood there, Tom took Clark by the arm. "One more thing, Clark."

"Yes?"

"You're fired."

"Fired?"

"Yep, you're no longer a deputy."

"I'll try to get over it."

"Don't you want to know why?"

"If you want to tell me," Clark grinned.

"Gross insubordination." Tom grinned in return. "Of course, I intend to overlook it the next time I need your help. Oh, and one more thing," he reached into his coat pocket and pulled out an envelope. "There's two hundred dollars in there, reward money for the prisoners." He looked at Sarah. "I just wanted you to know that Clark is a man with solid financial prospects." He turned back to Clark, "Not bad pay for a job without a salary."

He turned back to Sarah, "He's all yours, ma'am."

Sarah smiled and linked her arm through Clark's. "He always is."

Mrs. Mosley pecked Sarah on the cheek and then kissed Clark's cheek, as well. "She's a wonderful girl, Mr. Ammons," she said in a conspiratorial whisper meant to be overheard. "Better do something about it soon," she added with emphasis.

They both smiled at her. Lucy was standing quietly with them and as they started to leave, she addressed Sarah. "I feel better knowin he's taken care of but I reckon I still got to feed him sometimes till he smartens up," she said as she handed some food to Clark.

"He's told me how nice you are to him, Lucy. Thank you."

As they walked to the carriage, Grant had a word for them, as well. "You know, Doc, I'm about as deef as old Boo and it hurts my neck to be turnin round so ifn you don't mind, I'll just let you folks alone for the ride back..." He let it hang.

Clark and Sarah had a pleasant return trip up the mountain but this time neither of them really noticed the crisp, clean air or the beautiful scenery or the glorious colors of the late autumn sunset.